Mary Elizabeth Phillips

A handbook of German literature

Mary Elizabeth Phillips

A handbook of German literature

ISBN/EAN: 9783337204921

Printed in Europe, USA, Canada, Australia, Japan

Cover: Foto ©Andreas Hilbeck / pixelio.de

More available books at **www.hansebooks.com**

A HANDBOOK

OF

GERMAN LITERATURE

BY

MARY E. PHILLIPS, L.L.A.

REVISED, WITH AN INTRODUCTION, BY

A. WEISS, Ph.D.

PROFESSOR OF GERMAN AT THE ROYAL MILITARY
ACADEMY, WOOLWICH.

LONDON
GEORGE BELL AND SONS
1895

PREFACE.

THE object of this little work is to supply a want, which the writer believes to be felt by many teachers and learners of German in our schools, by placing in the hands of the pupil a text-book which may form the basis of lessons, and furnish a useful introduction to the study of German Literature.

In treating a subject of such scope within the narrow limits which the writer has permitted herself, it has been found obligatory to allot a few words only to many authors, who may, with advantage, be studied at greater length at a later period. No attempt has been made to deal with many of the less important modern writers, and the effort throughout has been to bring the *greatest* into greatest prominence, as the most fruitful and effective beginning of all study. This is the reason of the space—large in so small a book—allotted to Goethe and Schiller and their immortal works.

A synopsis of great works has in all cases been given, and criticism not wholly disregarded, so that a bald list of names and dates alone may not be placed before the learner.

The Author cannot let this opportunity pass without acknowledging her great obligation to Dr. A. Weiss, Professor of German at the Royal Military Academy, Woolwich, who, in addition to many valuable suggestions, has with vast pains and ability corrected and *proved* the whole of her work by untiring reference to originals and recognized authorities, and has also furnished the list of books which is placed at the end.

It is hoped that this little book may be useful in the preparation of candidates for the Army, and the University Local Examinations, and for the Examinations for the Junior and Senior Leaving Certificates.

M. E. P.

CONTENTS.

INTRODUCTION.

FREDERICK THE GREAT, although not very fond of the German language, made the following prophecy in his " Littérature Allemande ": "We shall have our classical authors; our neighbours will learn German; and it may happen that our language, polished and brought to perfection, will be extended, in favour of our good authors, from one end of Europe to the other." This, no doubt, has been fulfilled, especially since the Franco-German War; and on the twenty-fifth anniversary now legitimately celebrated by all faithful to the Fatherland, I have the honour of writing these lines as a short introduction to a book on German literature, which, I fairly trust, will contribute in no small degree to the further realisation of the Great Frederick's hope.

Literature, in any case that literature with which we shall have to deal, and the language in which it is produced, have nothing to do with political controversy; they do not speak to one nation alone, but to all, whatever their nationality, who strive after true happiness by improving and enlarging their minds.

It is, therefore, easy to understand that, even in France, the study of German has been greatly increased, and made a significant part of liberal education.

The High Schools in Italy now devote a part of their curriculum to German, in addition to French and English, whilst a still greater development has taken place in this country.

Whereas, some thirty years ago, Italian was required or preferred, it is now superseded by German as a branch of English education. The Civil Service Commissioners have made this language an optional, and in some cases an obligatory subject.

Since July 1892, Papers on German literature have been set at the examinations for Army candidates. For girls and women this subject occupies an equally conspicuous position in the local and other examinations.

Out of the host of books on German literature, a select list has been added to this new publication, which list, it is hoped, will be a guide to the advanced student in his further and independent reading, but not one of them could be recommended as a school-book. Those written in German, however excellent they may be, are out of the question, for the scanty time allotted to German in even the best English schools is so much absorbed by the learning of the language itself, that, to save time, the literature must be studied in English.

I entertain all respect for the works of F. Metcalfe and I. T. Lublin, based on Vilmar and Kluge respectively, but, in these books, sufficient justice has not been done to the early and most modern periods. In the latter an index is wanting altogether; and, besides, the original works were written for educational purposes of the Fatherland, and they, therefore, show too many German tendencies. There is a book beyond praise, Mrs. F. C. Conybeare's translation of the " Geschichte der deutschen Litteratur " by Wilhelm Scherer, one of the greatest authorities on the subject, and that this translation is edited by Professor Max Müller, is a sufficient guarantee of its excellence. But, forming two volumes of 826 pages together, it would not do as a school-book. The lives of Lessing, Heine,

Schiller, and Goethe could not be better read than in the "German Classics," edited by Professor C. A. Buchheim, Ph.D., the "doyen" of German Masters in England, who, perhaps, has done more than anybody else for the propagation of German in the United Kingdom.

The private tutor, who is frequently but unjustly called "crammer," always ready to provide for the most urgent needs, has quickly compiled a few pamphlets on German literature. They are, however, only lists of names and dates, and unfit for real educational culture.

A book was needed corresponding to all the requirements of our days, and I have no hesitation in declaring that Miss Phillips has provided one that was a distinct "desideratum."

If the Cambridge student reading for the modern languages tripos, or the teacher lecturing on the life of the author just set for the Oxford and Cambridge Local Examinations, should not find this course sufficient, it may at least, in each of these cases, be useful as a preliminary to further study of the subject. The candidate who is compelled to commit to memory, just for the hard day of his examination, only a table of names and dates, will do better by a cursory reading of a work of moderate size, underlining or extracting what seems desirable.

The young scholar, who, by his own choice—and I am sure he (or she) is not a *rara avis*—or by the regulations of his scholastic authorities, is bound to study German literature thoroughly, has not hitherto been provided with a book which he might steadily work through, as with his Cornwell in Geography, or Morris in History.

At the request of the publishers, I have had the pleasure of looking over the proof-sheets of this volume, and of letting the author have any sugestions that might occur to me. It would, of course, have been impossible to carry out this task satisfactorily without taking great care and pains, and, but for the inexhaustible resources of the British Museum at my disposal, I should scarcely have undertaken the work.

" Prove all things; hold fast that which is good." With this thought my work was commenced, but the further I got in the proof-sheets, the more pleasure they gave me. Having had much experience in teaching the German language and literature to English students, I became with every page more and more convinced that this was the book required. My efforts would be useful, and, therefore, the hunt after a correct title, date, quotation, or note, was joyfully pursued. I wanted to assure myself that there was nothing which I could not endorse, and to be able to declare the book reliable in every respect.

Miss Phillips has very kindly accepted most of my suggestions for her book, which treats of the German Literature as far back as it can be traced at all, and down to the most modern poets and even novelists. A long and studious residence in Germany has enabled the author to characterise the Germans correctly, and to put forth some new ideas about their literature.

In certain controversial cases, of course, those who do not profess to be specialists, have to take a side. Thus, concerning the famous Lachmann-Zarncke controversy about the Nibelungenlied, our author refers to and adopts the opinion of Wilhelm Scherer, whose book could not be left unread by any writer on German literature.

The reader of this book will find it an advantage that it is not divided into chapters classified under the headings, for instance, of novel or philosophy, prose or poetry. The whole plan is chronological, and will form in the student's mind a clear picture of the development which he can easily attach to his history learned before.

Last, not least, it has to be mentioned that the book is written without visible religious or political bias. Its device, as that of a handbook of literature ought to be, is " Truth," that idea of truth expressed in the three words in commemoration of Herder as the aim he had successfully striven after :

" Licht, Liebe, Leben."

It is a book that may be put in the hands of a student of any age, creed, or aspiration.

ALOYS WEISS.

Royal Military Academy, Woolwich,
    September 2nd, 1895.

A HANDBOOK OF GERMAN LITERATURE.

CHAPTER I.

THE ORIGIN OF GERMAN LITERATURE.

It was the Roman historian, Tacitus, who first fully described the ancient Germanic tribes, or Teutons. His book, "Germánia," written A.D. 98, if somewhat idealistic in tone, is still substantially true to nature.

The Germans, he tells us, know no riches but their flocks and herds, are simply clothed, and imperfectly armed, hospitable in the extreme, and hold their women in high honour. After telling the story of that barbarian who, having lost his whole possessions at dice, set his freedom on the last throw, lost, and voluntarily allowed himself to be sold as a slave, Tacitus adds: "So great, even in a bad cause, is the Germanic obstinacy; they themselves call it *constancy*," and this has remained the Teutonic boast to our own day.

More than three centuries earlier, Pytheas, a learned navigator, sailing from Marseilles on a voyage of discovery, had come upon the Teutons at the mouth of the Rhine. Cæsar fought with them, and wrote of their freedom from all control, their lawlessness, and love of plunder. These barbarians were the people who in the pride of their strength were to crush out the effete civilization of the Roman Empire, who were to form mighty armies, mighty nations, and who already possessed in themselves the germ of that poetic power out of which a great literature has grown. For young nations bear in themselves the "epische Stoff"— they *live* the heroic poems which later generations *write*.

Mythology.—In the earliest times all the Aryan or Indo-Germanic tribes worshipped one god, the Aryan Dyaus (Greek—Zeus); later, different tribes preferred different gods. The Goths and Vandals, for instance, worshipped two divine brothers (resembling Castor and Pollux); the people inhabiting the shores of the North Sea—the ancestors of the invaders of Britain—adored a goddess, Nerthus; round the Rhine, Wodan held supreme sway, and he, at last, became the chief of all the gods of the northern mythology, the husband of Freya, the sunny, joy-bringing spirit of the spring.

Sagas.—Five cycles of legends grew up during the migration of the Germanic tribes, the "Völkerwanderung," viz.:

1. That of the Ostrogoths (Ostgotische Sage), treating firstly of Ermanrich (died 375 A.D.), and later of Dietrich von Bern, known in history as Theodoric the Great.

2. That of the Franks, or people of the Lower Rhine, whose hero was Siegfried.

3. The Burgundian Saga of the brothers King Gunther, Gernot and Giselberr, with their sister Kriemhilde, the tough old hero Volker, and the traitor Hagen.

4. The Saga of the Huns, whose hero is King Etzel—Attila, "the Scourge of God, the Destroyer of nations" (died 453).

5. The Longobardische Sage, treating of King Rother, King Ortnit, Hugdietrich and Wolfdietrich.

These sagas, handed down as traditions from a time when the Germanic tribes were yet barbarians, furnished material for poetic treatment at a later period when the German epic was in its full glory.

Translation of the Bible by Ulfilas.—Christianity was preached among the Teutons at a time when Arianism was rife in the Church. In the fourth century, the Arian Bishop of the Western Goths, Vulfila or Ulfilas (died 381), made his translation of the Bible. This is a most valuable work for the study of the Gothic language. The manuscript now preserved at Upsala is written in silver characters on purple parchment, and may once have been in the possession of some king of the Goths.

Wessobrunner Gebet.—The oldest fragment of German poetic literature is the so-called " Wessobrunner Gebet," a Saxon poem, written in Bavaria in the beginning of the ninth century. It opens with a description of chaos before the creation of the world, and ends in a prayer. Hence its name.

Characteristics of earliest Poetry and Language.—Alliteration was an essential element of old Germanic poetry, it gave not melody but strength. The search for forcible expression is especially visible. Unaccented syllables are discarded as the language grows, the Old High German " mannisko " becomes German " Mensch," and the same process is everywhere noticeable. The melodious softness of the Gothic tongue stiffens into the rough strength of the German. The German language is rich in consonants, not in vowels.

The Hildebrandslied.—In the monastery of Fulda (Hesse-Cassel) was discovered the " Hildebrandslied," a fragment of a poem written in the beginning of the ninth century by an unknown monk. The subject is the combat of Hildebrand, the armour-bearer of Dietrich von Bern, (*i.e.* Theodoric of Verona) who has been many years in exile among the Huns, with his son Hadubrand. The father asks Hadubrand's parentage, and learning it, seeks pretexts to avoid the combat; the son, believing Hildebrand long dead, insists upon the fight. They fight accordingly, and the poem breaks off leaving the issue unknown.

The "Hildebrandslied" shows wonderful dramatic power, is alliterative, and belongs to the Saga of the Ostrogoths.

Muspilli.—Another early fragment by an unknown author, apparently a layman, is "Muspilli," the "World-Fire," a description of the destruction of the world set on fire by the blood dropping from Elijah, who conquers Antichrist in fight, but is wounded by him. The poem describes the pains of hell and the joys of heaven.

The Heliand *and* Krist.—Two early sacred epics are to be noticed in the ninth century, "Der Heliand," of unknown authorship, written about 830, picturing the Redeemer as a warlike hero whose kingdom was emphatically "of this world," and the "Krist" or "Evangelien-harmonie," written about 870 by Otfried, a monk of Weissen-burg. The former marks a transition when heathenism, only half conquered, left its stamp on Christianity; the latter is wholly Christian, and is the first work which bears no trace of the old paganism. Otfried wrote in rhyme, traces of which appear in the ninth century, and expressed his belief that the angels help pious poets in their work.

The Ludwigslied, written probably by the monk Hucbald, celebrated the victory of King Ludwig III. over the Normans.

Sacred Literature in the Tenth Century.—The monastery of St. Gallen was the centre of monkish learning; sacred poems in Latin were numerous. The two most famous of the monks of St. Gallen were Ekkehard, who died in 973 (known to us in modern times through Scheffel's masterly novel, though in fictitious environment), and Notker Labeo or "the Thick-lipped," who died in 1022. Ekkehard wrote, in the beginning of the tenth century, "Walther von Aqui-tanien, or Walther mit der starken Hand," in Latin hexameters indeed, but containing some of the most moving scenes ever produced by German poet. Notker translated from the Latin, and his translations belong to the transition from Old High German to Middle High German, the former lasting, according to Jakob Grimm, until the beginning of the eleventh century.

The first German Poetess was the nun, **Hroswitha von Gandersheim** (920-968), who wrote six comedies in Latin prose on the model of Terence, several **Legends**, and a **Eulogy of Kaiser Otto I.** Hroswitha is remarkable as having been the first dramatist after the Romans. She treated her subjects with some of the boldness of the modern realist, but her pictures of vice aim at the teaching of virtue.

Rudlieb.—In the eleventh century was written, in Latin hexameters, the first " Ritterroman "—romance of chivalry —the world had seen, one of the beginnings of fiction, entitled " Rudlieb " or " Ruodlieb." Only a fragment has been preserved, showing on the part of the author, a Bavarian monk, considerable skill in the arrangement of his adventures, but, as is to be expected, little power of character-drawing. The analysis of character, apart from religious self-examination, is a modern product ; earlier generations would have said with Carlyle: " Know,"—not thyself, but—" what thou canst *do*."

CHAPTER II.

THE great authority on German literature, Wilhelm Scherer, considers that, in addition to the two most fertile epochs— *i.e.*, from 1150 to 1300 and the Golden Age of Goethe and his contemporaries—another Blütezeit, or Golden Age, should be reckoned, namely, that earlier period when the cycles of legends—the matter which was to be used in what is usually called the "erste Blütezeit"—were growing up among the people. Poems there were undoubtedly, and their loss does not destroy their influence. Charlemagne collected the legends, but the century after him let them sink into oblivion again. Still, an echo of them remained, and, in what we may term the first *articulate* Golden Age of German Literature, they made themselves heard once more.

The causes leading to the especial brilliancy of the hundred and fifty years from 1150-1300 have been considered fourfold.

1. The impetus given to an enthusiasm partly religious, but thoroughly poetical, by the Crusades.

2. The patronage extended to poetry by the Hohenstaufen dynasty.

3. The spirit of chivalry in its full vigour.

4. The introduction of models from France.

We may divide the poetry of the period into three classes: 1. That of the Court. 2. That of the People.

3. That of the Church. The style was either epic or lyric. The epic poem, at home in a heroic age, was thoroughly objective. The lyric poem, purely subjective, took its place after it. To these may be added didactic poetry, partaking, as it always does, of the nature of both, partly objective, partly subjective, and far behind the epic and lyric in artistic value. The language was *Middle High German*. ·

The Transition Period, or beginning of the Golden Age is marked by the following poems :

Annolied, a eulogy of the saintliness of Anno, Archbishop of Köln, written about 1180.

Rolandslied, by "Pfaffe" Konrad, 1173-1177, and *Alexanderlied*, by Pfaffe Lamprecht, towards the end of the twelfth century.

These two Pfaffen, or priests, are harbingers of the poetry of chivalry which was soon to flourish. Their tendency is to combat the old heathen sagas, and to bring French influence to the front. Neither is strongly subjective in the treatment of his theme.

Konrad imitated the "Chanson de Roland," and emphasized especially Roland's glory, as the Christian hero fighting against the Moor. Religious enthusiasm was his inspiration.

Lamprecht gave a rendering of the "Alexandre" of Aubrey de Besançon, revelled in oriental description, and was less essentially an ecclesiastic in the treatment of his subject.

Spielmannsgedichte, or Songs of the Wandering Minstrels. *König Rother* is founded on the "Heldensage," and anecdotes of the crusades are introduced into it. History and mythology, home and foreign affairs are intermingled, with little regard to probability and chronology.

Herzog Ernst is a banished knight, son of Otto the Great, and Duke of Suabia. The poem is full of fabulous adventures.

König Orendel, the Ulysses of German literature, after un-
heard of vicissitudes, returns to find his wife faithful to him.
The satiric fable **Reinhart Fuchs** ("Reynard the Fox"),
by Heinrich der Glicheser, shows unprecedented German
humour.

These early poems mark the beginning of that wave of
poetic thought which culminated in the
Blütezeit des Volksepos. The great national epos of the
German people, powerful as their language, richly imaginative
as their thought, is the epic, or series of epics, known as the
Nibelungenlied.—The authorship is a disputed question. Karl Lachmann, who has separated from it much that
detracted from the worth of the whole, and divided it into
twenty "Lieder," holds that it is the work of many hands
probably during the twenty years from 1190-1210. This
is the most credible hypothesis. The theory of *one* Nibelungen poet is rendered almost untenable by the inequality of
the poem. Some passages of Homeric grandeur contrast
with the worse than mediocrity of others.

The poem divides itself naturally into two parts, the
centre-point of the first being the death by treachery of
Siegfried, the hero. The centre-point of the second part is
the vengeance of his wife, Kriemhilde.

In form it is composed of a stanza of four lines, rhyming
in pairs and marked by the cesura:

> "Ez troumde Kriemhilte | in tugenden der sie pflac
> wie sie einen valkan wilden | züge manegen tac
> den ir zwên arn erkrummen | daz sie daz muoste sehen:
> ir enkunde in dirre werlde | nimmer leider sîn geschehen."
> (Lachmann, 1841.)

This first verse gives the keynote to the whole story of
the first part.

/ "Kriemhilde dreamt in her girlhood that she tamed a
falcon many a day. But two eagles tore it to pieces before
her eyes. Never had she felt so great a sorrow." The

falcon was Siegfried, the eagles Gunther and Hagen. The fulfilment of the omen it is the work of the poem to unfold.

Siegfried, a dauntless hero, strong and beautiful, invulnerable because he has bathed in the blood of a dragon which he has overcome, hears of the beauty and pride of Kriemhilde, sister of the Burgundian King, Gunther. He goes, therefore, to Worms on the Rhine, helps King Gunther against the Saxons, conquers them, and promises Gunther further help in his wooing of Brunhild, provided he shall receive as a reward the hand of his sister, Kriemhilde. 'This Brunhild, a queen in a distant land beyond the sea, will give her love only to the suitor who overcomes her in combat. Siegfried, by the help of his " Tarnkappe," which renders him invisible, fights with and overcomes the warlike queen; Brunhild all the time believing that Gunther conquers by his own strength. They return to Worms, and the bridal feast takes place for both pairs, Gunther and Brunhild; Kriemhilde and Siegfried. However, the Amazonian queen refuses obedience to her husband; Siegfried, at Gunther's request, overcomes her a second time— again made invisible by his Tarnkappe—and taking her girdle and ring, gives them to his own wife. This is the fatal turning-point of the story. Then Siegfried takes his queen home to the Netherlands, where he rules over the Nibelungen, and possesses the greatest treasure ever won by hero. After a lapse of time, how long we are not told, Siegfried, accompanied by his old father, Siegmund, as well as by his wife, comes back to Worms at Gunther's invitation. One evening the two queens quarrel over the heroic deeds of their respective husbands. Brunhild treats Kriemhilde disdainfully, and the latter in revenge boasts that it was Siegfried, not Gunther, who overcame Brunhild in fight. As confirmation she shows Brunhild's ring and girdle.

From this moment Siegfried's fate is sealed. Brunhild wins over her husband to side with her against Siegfried, and finds a ready helper in Gunther's warrior, Hagen, who has cast greedy eyes on the Nibelungen treasure. They affect to require Siegfried's help in a new Saxon war, and Kriemhilde, in order that the treacherous Hagen may, as she thinks, shield her husband in fight, shows him the one vulnerable spot between Siegfried's shoulders, where a linden leaf, blown by the wind, kept the dragon's blood from touching him. She marks the spot with a silken cross. The scheme to discover the secret from Kriemhilde having succeeded, overtures of peace are sent to the Saxons, and the heroes go hunting. At the end of the day Siegfried is thirsty, Gunther, Hagen and he run a race to a spring. Siegfried far outruns the others, but waits until they come up with him, in order that King Gunther may drink first. Gunther drinks; then Siegfried stoops, and the treacherous Hagen drives a spear into his back, where the too unsuspecting Kriemhilde has marked the silken cross. Siegfried falls and dies—"the flowers are all beflecked with his blood." The picture of Kriemhilde's despair finishes the first part.

Nibelungenlied. Second Part.—The character of Kriemhilde as an avenger now develops. Hagen has brought the Nibelungen treasure to Worms, and sunk it in the Rhine. She knows her brother's treachery and her own present helplessness, but she bides her time, and her time comes. King Etzel (Attila) seeks her hand in marriage. She favours his wooing, goes with him to the Huns, and causes the Burgundians to be invited to visit them, with the determination to compass their ruin. Mermaids of the Danube prophesy to Hagen on the way that they shall "return no more to the Burgunderland." The prophecy was fulfilled. Except the chaplain, no one returned.

The heroes are entertained by the Markgraf Rüdiger, a generous, open-hearted warrior, who is wrecked, too, at last in the universal ruin, and they find Dietrich von Bern and Hildebrand, his armour-bearer, in the land of the Huns.

When the "Nibelungen," as the Burgundians are called for the first time in this part of the epos, arrive at Etzel's court, Kriemhilde loses no time in stirring up animosity between the Huns and her brothers' people. They fight with terrible loss on both sides. The Burgundians are all imprisoned in one building; the Huns surround it and set fire to it. The Burgundians, in the frightful heat, drink blood to quench their thirst. Not a man comes out alive except Gunther and Hagen. Hagen is brought before Etzel and Kriemhilde, with whom is Dietrich, lamenting his fallen men, for only Hildebrand survives. Kriemhilde asks Hagen where he has hidden the Nibelungen treasure, and, as he will not reveal the secret while one of his king's race still lives, she has the head of her brother Gunther brought to him. "Now," cries Hagen, "where the treasure lies is known to God and me alone. From thee, fiendish woman, it shall remain hidden for ever."

> "Den schatz weiz nu nieman wan got unde mîn,
> Der soll dich vâlentine immer gar verholn sîn!"

At this Kriemhilde, seizing Siegfried's sword, strikes Hagen dead at her feet. Hildebrand, maddened by her action, rushes on her and kills her with one blow. Etzel and Dietrich remain weeping—"as ever joy is turned at last to sorrow"—and in this sweeping tragedy the Nibelungenlied is ended.

Gudrun.—The *Volksepos* second in importance is Gudrun. This, unlike the Nibelungenlied, is the work of one poet, probably an Austrian (about 1190). The "Gudrunstrophe" has the third and fourth lines ending in an unaccented syllable.

> "Dô kom an einem âbende daz in sô gelanc
> Daz von Tenemarke der küene degen sanc
> Mit sô hêrlîcher stimme, daz ez wol gevallen
> Muose al den liuten : dâ von gesweic der vogelîne schallen."
>   (Gûdrûnlieder. L. Ettmüller, Zürich, 1841.)

" Es war an einem Abend, dafs ihnen das gelang,
Dafs vom Dänenlande der kühne Degen sang,
Mit so herrlicher Stimme, dafses wohlgefallen
Mufste allen Leuten ; auch hörte auf der Vögel Lied zu schallen."
(Transl. of A. Keller, Stuttgart, 1840.)

The story of Hilde, which forms the first part of the poem, serves as a prologue to the longer and more interesting second "Lied," the story of Gudrun, Hilde's daughter.

Hilde.—Hagen, King of Ireland, puts to death every suitor who dares to woo his daughter Hilde. Notwithstanding the danger, Hettel, King of the Hegelingen (Friesland), ventures, with the help of his three faithful "Mannen," Wate, Frute, and Horand, to seek the love of the princess. He wins her to his side, and subsequently, after showing his prowess in arms, succeeds in appeasing the wrath of King Hagen, and marries Hilde.

Gudrun.—The story of Gudrun is much longer, and contains more of the tragic element. Hettel and Hilde have a daughter, Gudrun, to woo whom Hartmut of Normandy crosses over the sea. The king refuses him Gudrun's hand on account of old enmity between the two royal houses. Then Herwig of Zealand comes as a suitor, and, being rejected also, has recourse to his sword to win his bride. His valour wins Gudrun's heart, and the betrothal takes place. But, while Hettel and Herwig together are engaged in repelling an attack of the Moors, Ludwig of Normandy and his son, the rejected Hartmut, carry off Gudrun. Father and lover rush in pursuit, but are worsted in the battle; Hettel falls, and the Normans put to sea with Gudrun and her maidens, under cover of the darkness. So many of the fighting men are slain, that Herwig is compelled to wait thirteen years, till the boys have grown to manhood, before going to rescue Gudrun from her captors. During this time, the heroine undergoes cruel humiliation at the hands of Hartmut's mother because she remains

constant in her rejection of Hartmut's suit.   The crowning
insult is that she, a king's daughter, is compelled to wash
clothes upon the strand.

The supernatural element is introduced only once in the
poem, when a speaking sea-bird, in answer to Gudrun's
questions as she stands on the shore, announces that
Herwig is coming to her rescue across the sea.   He and
the same old heroes who fought for Hettel, Wate, Frute,
and Horand, arrive at last, together with Ortwin, Gudrun's
brother; a wild and sanguinary contest ends in victory
for Herwig, and Gudrun is restored to her lover and her
people.

The unknown author of Gudrun has told his tale with
the clear simplicity of a simple age.   He does not wholly
disdain to touch the chord of sentiment, to picture something of the inner workings of his heroes' minds and feelings, but he never dwells on them, he goes straight on
with the action of his tale.   Most touching are the verses
which treat of Gudrun's hard captivity, and of her unalterable faithfulness to her betrothed.   Such nobleness of
soul is the dearest theme of German song.

Minor popular Epics of the Blütezeit.—The
abundance of sagas provided the singers of this fertile time
with a rich variety of subject.   There appeared now a
number of less important poems, all founded on the real or
fabulous adventures of the hero, Dietrich von Bern—the
poetical and legendary representative of the great King of
the Ostrogoths, Theodoric—of which only a list of the
chief names need be given here.   These are :

1. Der grosse Rosengarten.
2. Der kleine Rosengarten.
3. Ecken Ausfahrt.
4. Die Rabenschlacht.
5. Sigenot.

6. Alphart.
7. Dietrichs Flucht zu den Hunnen.

From the Longobardische Sage are taken :

1. Ortnit.
2. Hugdietrich.
3. Wolfdietrich.

Fidelity and constancy, the perpetually recurring theme of the commemorators of the German heroes, are eulogized again in the last. Wolfdietrich is the illegitimate son of Hugdietrich, who, to favour his other sons, commissions the boy's tutor, Berchtung, to kill him. But the latter first saves Wolfdietrich's life, and then suffers every vicissitude, rather than fail in his faith to him. He follows and serves his master in adversity in something the same manner as Hildebrand serves Dietrich von Bern.

The four different existing texts of this work attest the popularity of the subject.

CHAPTER III.

"ERSTE BLÜTEZEIT" (CONTINUED). THE EPICS OF THE
COURT, OR "HÖFISCHES EPOS."

WE have seen how the sagas of the Völkerwanderung
formed the groundwork of the Volksepos. For the poetry
of the Court foreign material was utilized—those cycles of
legends which form a lesser or greater part of nearly all
the literatures of Europe. A brief enumeration of the
subjects will lead most easily to the consideration of the
poets.

1. The British or Arthurian Legend; heroes, King Arthur
and his knights.

2. The Spanish Legend of the Quest of the Holy Grail.

3. The Classical Legends of the Trojan War, and the
deeds of Alexander the Great.

4. French legendary treatment of the history of Charlemagne.

Unlike the poets of the Volksepos, nameless and hidden
from posterity, the poets of the Höfisches Epos are known
to us by name as well as by their works. The most important are the four following:

Heinrich von Veldeke, a native of Mastricht, who
may have been at Court when, in 1184, the Kaiser Friedrich
Barbarossa knighted his two eldest sons, and celebrated the
event by the most magnificent festivities. The patronage of
poets and poetry was now general among the nobles, and
in many of the courts of German princes. Hermann,

Landgrave of Thuringia especially, a little later, made himself famous in this respect.

Veldeke enjoyed his full share of fame. The work which first made him celebrated among his contemporaries was his translation of the "Æneid," in which he drew not from Virgil himself, but from a French translator, Benoit de Saint-More, in whose "Roman d'Enéas," the spirit of antiquity had been replaced by the romance of the Middle Ages.

Hartmann von Aue, a Suabian who took part in the Crusades of 1189 and 1197.

In addition to his lyrical "Büchlein," in which his own love-stories are told with charming simplicity, Hartmann's epic poems are four in number. The two first belong to the Arthurian Legend.

1. *Ereck und Enite* (the story called in Tennyson's "Idylls" "Geraint and Enid") tells how the knight, too much occupied by his lady's love, is in danger of "verliegen," *i.e.*, giving way to cowardly sloth, or what in the age of chivalry was called such—is roused by her grief at his unworthy conduct to resume his knightly deeds, but subjects her in revenge to a series of petty tyrannies, until they are finally reconciled.

2. *Iwein oder der Ritter mit dem Löwen.*—In this poem the knight himself is in fear of "verliegen." He leaves his beautiful wife to "ride abroad redressing human wrong," fails to keep tryst with her, and so loses her love. After having been a prey to madness from which he is miraculously healed, he frees a lion, and at last, hiding his real name under the pseudonym of Knight with the Lion, he wins his lady's love again.

3. *Gregorius auf dem Stein* is founded on a French legend. Gregorius, like Œdipus of old, has unknowingly married his mother. When this is discovered he condemns himself to the hardest penance. Chained on a rock in a lake, he

lives miraculously for seventeen years on water alone. Then his repentance is accepted; he becomes pope and is canonized.

4. *Der Arme Heinrich*, an old Suabian tradition, is known to readers of Longfellow as the "Golden Legend," and was freely adapted by Hartmann from the Latin. The Suabian knight, Heinrich, banished from men as a leper, can only be healed by the heart-blood of a maiden, voluntarily given to save him. The daughter of a peasant is ready to sacrifice herself for him, but at the moment when she is to die, his soul, shaking off the bonds of selfishness, refuses to allow her to suffer, and resigns itself to the Will of God. This resignation brings about his miraculous cure, and the maiden becomes his wife.

These four poems form Hartmann's best known work.

Wolfram von Eschenbach.—The greatest poet of the Höfisches Epos is unquestionably the Bavarian knight, Wolfram von Eschenbach, both in his representation of the unvarying truth of nature and in his untrammelled breadth of view, for Hartmann and the other poets saw no further than the canon of chivalry, and must be judged from the standpoint of their own time.

Wolfram died about 1220, and may have been sixty years of age. It is remarkable that he could neither read nor write, and boasted of his inability as being a knight, not a clerk. His chief works are:

Parzival, which, belonging at once to the Arthurian legend and to the Spanish legend of the "Holy Grail," united as they have frequently been, shows deep religious feeling, toleration of the heathen, and impatience of the cramping details of a knight's lessons in chivalry, where they might interfere with the broader claims of humanity.

Wolfram tells in the poem how Parzival passes through sin—unwittingly incurred—to holiness, and wins his way to the castle of the Grail at last. His mother, fearing to lose her son, had brought him up in ignorance of arms and chivalry. The chance sight of a band of Arthur's knights arouses the spirit of adventure latent in him. He follows them, and his mother falls dead when he passes from her sight. This is Parzival's first unconscious sin. Then he slays a kinsman and robs the body of its sword, thus erring again, this time in the hasty ignorance of youth. At Arthur's court he learns the rules of chivalry and etiquette, one item—important in its consequences—being, not to ask unnecessary questions,—frees and marries the Queen Condwiramurs, and goes again to seek adventures. His wanderings bring him to the castle where the Holy Grail—according to sacred legend the vessel in which Christ dispensed the Last Supper, afterwards used by St. Joseph of Arimathæa to receive His Blood from the Cross—can be found only by one who *asks* its whereabouts. He finds the "Grailking" Amfortas sick, but refrains from questioning. Had he not done so he would have healed the king, and found the Grail. When Parzival discovers this he cries out against the injustice of God, and swears henceforth to trust only in his lady's love, no longer in God's help.

At last he is shown by a pilgrim the vanity and sin of his self-sufficiency, through repentance becomes worthy to find the Grail, and is called to be "Gralkönig."

"Parzival" is after the French of Chrestien de Troyes, but the German poet has developed and idealized a far more prosaic original.

Titurel.—In the series of songs left in a fragmentary state to which the name "Titurel" has been given, Wolfram von Eschenbach re-introduces at greater length some of the minor characters in "Parzival," and paints them throughout with the stroke of a master hand. Titurel is the first "Gralkönig," the great-grandfather of Parzival.

Willehalm is apparently Wolfram's last work, the end

not having been reached. The hero is St. William, Count of Aquitaine, who fought against the Saracens in the year 793, and, in the poem, carried off a Moorish lady, who became a Christian. She is baptized by the name Giburg, and is a beautiful poetic creation.

"Willehalm" is not written with the vigour and freedom of "Parzival," and perhaps shows signs of failing power.

The fourth poet remaining to be classed with Heinrich von Veldeke, Hartmann von Aue, and Wolfram von Eschenbach is

Gottfried von Strassburg (died at the beginning of the thirteenth century). In ideals and high conception he remains far behind Wolfram, and appears not to have been of noble birth. He makes social conflicts his favourite subject. While possessing undoubted poetical genius, Gottfried seems to have been carried away by his own proficiency in word-painting, by love of conceits, and, in short, by the substitution of artificiality for nature. His poem,

Tristan und Isolde, is adapted from a French rendering of the tale of Arthur's knight, a subject treated in Tennyson's Idyll, "The Last Tournament."

Tristan and Isolde have been overmastered by a love-philtre prepared for Isolde and Marke, her affianced husband and Tristan's uncle, when Tristan is conducting the "blonde Isolde" from Ireland to Cornwall. Gottfried finds no word of upbraiding for Tristan's guilty love for Marke's wife, no blame of his treachery to his uncle. The poem was never entirely finished.

Other poets of the "Höfisches Epos" are:

Eilhard von Oberge, author of another "Tristan und Isolde," anterior to that of Gottfried von Strassburg.

Konrad Fleck wrote "Flore und Blancheflur," the well-known story of the two child-lovers—typical, perhaps, of the loves of flowers, lily and rose—adapted from the

French, which had already appeared in the dialect of the Lower Rhine about 1170.

Rudolf von Ems, died in 1254, followed Gottfried von Strassburg in manner, but adopted graver, less worldly matter. His works are: "Der gute Gerhard," who ransoms Christian captives from the heathen, and refuses the crown of England;

Barlaam und Josaphat, the latter an Indian prince, converted by the former to be a Christian hermit. (This is founded on a legend in the life of Buddha.)

Wilhelm von Orlens, half historical.

Alexander, another rendering of the deeds of Alexander the Great.

Weltchronik, brought down only to the time of Solomon.

Frequently classed with Rudolf von Ems is

Konrad von Würzburg, who died in 1287, at Basle, apparently of an epidemic, since his wife and daughters died at the same time. His works, of mediocre value, are: "Trojanerkrieg" (with the continuation by a later poet about 60,000 lines), one of the longest Middle High German poems.

Frau Welt, a legend from the French, tending to show the deceitfulness of worldly glory.

Otto mit dem Barte, an old German saga.

Die goldene Schmiede, in praise of the Blessed Virgin Mary. The popular story of the

"*Schwanritter,*" "Swan-knight," known to us in the modern "Lohengrin."

Konrad's poems, flowing from a too prolific pen, are full of violations of taste, and wanting in true poetic feeling. He believed in his own merit, however, and wrote a "Klage der Kunst" in which he lamented the too cold reception of poetry by an unappreciative world.

The consideration of these minor poets brings us to the satirical writers of the period, the chief of whom are:

Stricker, an Austrian, author of "Pfaffe Amis," who ranks also as a minor epic poet of the time, having written "Daniel von Blumenthal" and a rendering of the "Rolandslied." His satires, however, which were numerous, form his chief title to remembrance. He is didactic in tone, holds to a strongly expressed moral, and is in the main a strict churchman. This does not prevent him from introducing a fraudulent priest into his best remembered satire.

Pfaffe Amis deceives first his bishop, then all with whom he is brought into contact, plays tricks of all sorts, harmless and the reverse, and deals largely in false relics and sham miracles. His tricks are, at a later period, attributed to the German favourite, "Tyll Eulenspiegel."

After Stricker, the writer of the story of a discontented peasant, who set his heart on shining at court, has to be noticed. This is

Wernher der Gartener, who wrote "Meier Helmbrecht."

Meier Helmbrecht was the son of a peasant, spoilt by his mother, vain, fond of dress and foolishly ambitious. As his father will not permit him to go on his travels, he defies him and joins a robber-band. After having returned home and told his adventures, supposed to be courtly, but really only of drinking and wild revels, he goes back to his robber companions, followed by his sister. She is on the point of being married to one of the robbers, when the officers of justice swoop down upon them; Helmbrecht is blinded as a punishment, and afterwards driven away and finally hanged by the peasants. The satire is written as a warning against the rising discontent of the times.

CHAPTER IV.

SIDE by side with the epic or narrative poem, lyricism, practised by princes, even emperors, was in its mediæval glory.

Minnesingers: *Heinrich von Veldeke*, already mentioned among the epic poets as the author of an Æneid, did essential service to poetry in general by the introduction of purer rhyme, by which the mere assonance of an earlier period was now entirely superseded. Veldeke's lyric poetry is gay and lively, extensive in volume and excellent in kind. He was one of the founders of "Minne-poesie" (Love-poetry), and seems to have been of especially susceptible and lively temperament. His graceful songs bear witness to this: "the song of birds and the trees in bud" can console him, even in parting from his lady. As a rule the lyric poets "Minnesinger"—sons of the troubadours as they are, having inherited the mantle of the old "Spielmann" and added to it the courtly grace of a chivalrous age—are witty, bright and lively, whatever shortcomings may fall to their share.

Minnegesang was not wholly devoted to songs of love, though that was its primary object. We may divide the subjects into three classes:

1. Love-songs, celebrating the service of woman.
2. Religious songs, celebrating the service of God.
3. Political songs, celebrating the service of feudal lords.

According to the style of the troubadours introduced from France, Minnepoesie was, in general, destined to be sung. There were three principal forms:

1. Das Lied, the strophe of which contained two equal parts called "Stollen," and one unequal part called "Abgesang."

2. Der Leich, having metrical changes.

3. Der Spruch, which contained a religious or political doctrine.

There are three valuable collections of the lyrics of this time:

1. The *Pariser Handschrift* (so called because the MS. is preserved in Paris), or Manessische Handschrift, as it is also styled, containing the poems of 140 German singers, the most valuable of the Middle High German lyrics.

2. The *Weingartner Handschrift*.

3. The *Heidelberger Handschrift*, now in Stuttgart.

The principal poets whose names are preserved are the following:

1. *Spervogel*, who wrote on the subject of worldly wisdom.

2. *Ritter von Kürenberg* wrote in the popular, as distinguished from the courtly style, and used the Nibelungenstrophe.

3. *Dietmar von Aist* also wrote in the popular manner, and used for his songs short lines rhyming in pairs.

4. *Heinrich von Morungen*, a Thuringian and a follower of Veldeke, wrote bright and fanciful lyrics which often show the influence of the French troubadours.

5. *Friedrich von Hausen*, a knight from the Palatinate who was in high favour with Frederick Barbarossa, died while on the Crusade, in 1190, shortly before the death of the Emperor. In his love-songs he laments the necessity of leaving his lady for the holy war, and is fond of representing conflicting emotions.

6. *Reinmar von Hagenau* gives utterance to interminable lamentations of unrequited love. His style is flowing and full of melody, but a certain artificiality shows itself in his verse; fashion rather than feeling is his motive power.

7. Walther von der Vogelweide, born about 1160, probably in Austria (Tyrol), was in 1204 one of the poets in the "Wartburgkrieg," died in 1227. His name is the greatest among the writers of Minnepoesie. It was his to show the wide-reaching influence of song, and as with the modern French *chansonnier*, politics played an important part in his widely-sung lyrics. But love, religion, his own poverty, everything furnished Walther with subject-matter for poetic utterance. He composed political songs for several princes, songs which ran like wild-fire through the land; yet, though he passed from court to court, he seems to have experienced the proverbial ingratitude of princes, for he possessed nothing of his own until late in life, when the Emperor Frederick II. granted him a small freehold, which happy event caused him, as usual, to break forth into song—

"I have a fief! Hearken all the world, I have a fief!"

Walther has been called the greatest German lyric poet before Goethe. His fresh and striking pictures impress themselves at once on the imagination. That wearisomeness of detail, that artificial piling of figure upon figure, the one destroying the other, which marks the poet made, not born, is nowhere to be found in Walther. If he is describing a maiden, some happy characteristic, dashed in with one touch, brings her before the mind's eye at once. One telling line in the opening of a lyric takes the place of whole verses of details. Again, in his political songs and "Sprüche" he never fails to hit the mark he aims at. Often the whole gist of his subject is contained in one line alone, as in a "Spruch" favouring the election of Philipp von Schwaben, one line sums up the entire poem in the command—

"Set the crown on Philip's head !"

That chafing under the Papal claims which prepared the German states for the repudiation of the Pope's authority long before the time of Luther, also finds expression in Walther von der Vogelweide with dramatic picturesqueness, for his many-sided genius applied itself to all the burning questions of the times. Walther von der Vogelweide is the greatest of all the Minnesingers, and Minnegesang, having in him reached its culminating excellence, begins after him to decline. The degeneration of "Minne" had already begun before the death of its greatest representative in 1227.

Decline of Minnegesang.—The ever-recurring plaint of the Minor Minnesingers is the degeneracy of the times, and the avarice of men who should be the patrons of poets. A few names only can be mentioned here :

Heinrich von Meissen, died 1318, called "Frauenlob" from the subject of one of his poems. There had been a discussion as to the relative value of the two words, "Weib" and "Frau." Walther had declared himself in favour of "Weib," Heinrich von Meissen preferred "Frau," hence his sobriquet. His "praise of women" reaches its climax in his laudation of the Blessed Virgin.

Ulrich von Lichtenstein wrote his own memoirs from 1222-1255, entitled "Frauendienst." He was one of those men who prepared the way for Cervantes' ridicule of knight-errantry. Although a married man with a family —a circumstance which appeared to him an insignificant detail—he served two ladies, and for them performed the wildest and most extravagant feats. On one occasion he struck off his own finger, and sent it to his lady, because she expressed anger that the finger had only been wounded, not lost, in her service. At another time he had an operation performed on his mouth because she expressed herself dis-satisfied with the shape.

Ulrich von Lichtenstein's lyrics, which are interspersed in "Frauendienst," deserve to be classed after those of Walther von der Vogelweide.

One of the writers of this period, whose songs show the enmity existing betweed the rich peasants and the poor nobility in Austria and Bavaria, was

Neidhart von Reuenthal (died about 1240), whose special claim to popularity consisted in charmingly witty and grace-ful dancing-songs, partly to be sung in the open air in the summer dances, partly for winter dancing under cover. He mingled village poetry with the courtly style, and was often sarcastic as well as humorous.

During the decline of Minnegesang the *Streitgedicht*, re-lating the minstrel-war in the Wartburg, was written by an unknown poet about 1260.

Landgrave Hermann of Thuringia was an enthusiastic patron of minstrels, and so freely hospitable that Walther von der Vogelweide warned those who were "Ohrenkrank" not to come to that assemblage of "Böse und Gute." The three principal minstrels who, in the poem, take part in the "Sängerkrieg" are : Heinrich von Ofterdingen, a poet only mentioned here, Wolfram von Eschenbach and Walther von der Vogelweide. Heinrich von Ofterdingen sings the praises of the Archduke of Austria, Wolfram and Walther urge the superiority of Hermann of Thuringia. The poem is in reality a kind of apotheosis of Wolfram von Eschenbach, who is made to overcome an enchanter by the power of his universal knowledge, and unconquerable eloquence.

When, however, this poem was written, the glory of Minnegesang had passed away, and the years of scarcity which, in all literatures, seem to follow the years of fatness, had begun.

Didactic Poetry. Fables.—As early as the twelfth century didactic poetry had begun to be in vogue. In the beginning of the thirteenth a Herr von Windsbach, called " Winsbeke," earned himself the honour of being the only nobleman of the Middle High German period who wrote a didactic poem, the

Winsbeke, counsels of a knight to his son.

The *Winsbekin*, advice of a mother to her daughter, is a pendant to the " Winsbeke," written by an unknown author.

Thomasin von Zirclaria, an Italian ecclesiastic, who seems to have adopted German as his own language, wrote a long work entitled *Der welsche Gast*, 1215-1216. He gives, among other things, systematic teaching in etiquette : not to speak while eating; not to move one's hands while speaking, etc. ; and he holds with King Lear that a voice " soft, gentle and low " is an " excellent thing in woman." " Beharrlichkeit," by which he understands steadfastness in well-doing, is the chief aim of his teaching.

Freidank, who accompanied Friedrich Barbarossa to the Crusade in 1228, wrote a more popular work than that of Zirclaria, which he named " Bescheidenheit." The word was not used at all in its modern signification—modesty— but appears to have meant worldly wisdom.

Freidank was a warm supporter of the Emperor. He allows three classes only a place in the social system— Peasants, Nobles, Clergy. Traders he considers the outcome of evil.

Hugo von Trimberg wrote, about 1300, a satirical poem called the " Renner " against the deceit and flattery of chivalry.

Fables and " Beispiele," i.e. parables, were also numerous. Stricker, who has been referred to as the author of " Pfaffe Amis," wrote largely in those styles.

Ulrich Bonar, a preaching monk, was the author of a

hundred fables, called collectively the "Edelstein." This was the first German book printed.

Latin remained the language of science during the Middle High German period, but it is to be noticed that two friars, Brother David von Augsberg and Brother Berthold von Regensburg—both died in 1272—preached in German.

CHAPTER V.

A VARIETY of causes contributed to the literary dearth of the two centuries, 1300-1500. The German Empire was in itself too much distracted for literature to flourish. The Emperors, far from extending encouragement to letters, had their hands full enough in the attempt to maintain their own power. The clergy had degenerated; prosperity had spoilt them, and they were in need of that persecution which acts as the refiner's fire. The people, left to their own devices, were wild and lawless, and quickly lost the power of appreciation of poetic ideals which had distinguished them in the first Blütezeit. What writers there were, at this time, were of such inferior order that their mediocrity scarcely merits casual mention in what is only intended to be an introduction to the study of German Literature. This period will, therefore, be treated as cursorily as possible.

The " **Mystiker** " (Mystics), the first philosophers in the German language, of whom the chief was

Meister Eckart, died in 1327, at Cologne, were the sole opponents of the universal lawlessness. They taught that everything earthly is vanity, and that the one worthy aim of life is the striving after perfect union of the soul with God. Their influence was probably felt chiefly, though not solely, in monasteries.

Dissatisfaction with the clergy was growing among the people. The begging friars who had professed and practised poverty, still professed but practised it no longer.

Rulman Merswin, 1308-1382, a layman, wrote bitterly against the Church in faulty, tedious prose.

The Plague, "Black Death," which ravaged Germany from 1348-1350, was another hindrance to development of all kinds, but at last the Drama seemed to be awakening in this unfruitful time.

The Rise of the Drama in Germany has much in common with its rise in other European countries. First came the sacred plays, one of the earliest of which is

Von den klugen und thörichten Jungfrauen, played at Eisenach in 1322, and

Mysteries, Moralities, Carnival-plays succeeded each other with the scenic shortcomings of early dramatic art in England.

As time went on, the comic element developed in season and out of season. The modern hatred of the Jewish usurer is foreshadowed in the representation of Judas as testing the thirty pieces of silver, to see if they are good coin.

Scholars attempted to popularize Latin plays.

Reuchlin composed in Latin "Henno," which was acted in 1497, and contains the same story as the French "Maître Pathelin," and from time to time Latin plays were reproduced.

The Epic of the Period is represented by the

Tierepos, illustrating the cunning of the fox and his tricks played on the other animals. It had already been introduced from France at an earlier epoch, and made its second appearance in Germany at the end of the fifteenth century. Goethe's "Reineke Fuchs" is after the Low German version of the Tierepos "Reinke der Vos."

The Emperor Maximilian I., "der letzte Ritter," wrote

the last words of the epic of chivalry in his autobiography—

Theuerdank, which appeared in 1517.

Lyric Poetry found its expression in early popular ballads (Volkslieder), of which Germany possesses so many treasures.

The **Meistersänger** were attempting to continue the work of the Minnesänger, in a studied and systematic manner. Minnegesang was still heard only in faint echoes, the " Spielmann " was a thing of the past, but in the towns poetic guilds were beginning.

Before becoming " Meister," the aspirant had to pass through four preliminary grades in the " Meisterschule." He was firstly Schüler, secondly Schulfreund, thirdly Sänger, fourthly Dichter, fifthly and lastly Meister.

During the time of the eclipse of poetry, learning revived. *Humanismus*, study of the humanities, began. The universities were at work. Erfurt, soon to feel the shock of the Reformation, had in 1519 eight humanist professors.

The Didactic School found a representative in *Sebastian Brant*, who died in 1521. He translated Cato's Moral Maxims (a mediæval Latin poem), revised Freidank's " Bescheidenheit," and was the author of a long satirical poem—

Das Narrenschiff. More than one hundred fools are assembled on Brant's ship; the Fashionable Fool, the Bookworm Fool, the Miser Fool, etc. Woodcuts are given in the book, which appeared in 1494, and its popularity was great. A Latin translation made the " Narrenschiff " known in all Europe.

A satirical writer of great power, whose work resembles that of Sebastian Brant, was the adversary of Luther, *Thomas Murner*, a Franciscan monk, who died in 1536. His *Narrenbeschwörung* (1512) was another assemblage of fools, described in better verse than Brant's. 'Murner also wrote the satirical-controversial "Von dem grossen lutherischen Narren, wie ihn Dr. Murner beschworen," and "Schelmenzunft," and "Gäuchmatte." These works belong to the Reformation Period.

Martin Luther, born 1483, died 1546, in addition to his origination of the great religious upheaval of the time, which need not be considered here, performed the greatest possible work for language and literature by providing a standard of speech in his

Translation of the Bible.—In England, Chaucer's "Canterbury Tales" had produced an analogous effect; in Germany, hitherto, though High German was struggling to the front, the dialects still maintained a certain footing. A standard was wanting, and that standard Luther's Bible became. He determined, in 1521, to attempt the great work; in March, 1522, he left his retirement in the Wartburg, having finished the New Testament. The whole Bible first appeared in six divisions in 1534, and revised editions were afterwards published.

Luther mainly employed the language of the Saxon chancery. At first dialect hampered him, but clearness came with his rapid writing, and the language stood a thorough and solid foundation for the Modern German of to-day. The invention of printing, as in other countries, fixed the forms of the language, and aided in establishing uniformity.

The translation of the Bible is Luther's greatest, but not his only literary work. His pamphlets belong chiefly to religious controversy rather than to literature, but they possessed a forcible style, varied to the varying occasion, and unfailing fertility in figure. As a hymn-writer, of such hymns as "Ein feste Burg ist unser Gott," his claim to admiration is undoubted; indeed he is not only the founder of the German Protestant hymn, but, until the most modern times, he remains unsurpassed in it.

Disciples and opponents swarmed round Luther. Of the latter the principal, Thomas Murner, has already been named. Of the former we may mention the humanist knight

Ulrich von Hutten (1488-1523), who wrote Epigrams, "Lamentations," Dialogues, etc., against the Papal power, chiefly in Latin, but in the year 1520—three years before his death—he began to write in German.

A satirical writer, whose facile pen was also employed against Rome, was

Johann Fischart (died 1589). He possessed wonderful command of language, and is one of the greatest writers of the period. Satire, comedy, jokes of all kinds, are heaped together in his unwieldy poems, but the stamp of genius is on the unruly mass, and redeems its disorder. He drew inspiration from Rabelais, not only in his version of "Gargantua," entitled

Geschichtsklitterung, where he has largely added to the work of the French satirist, but also in "Aller Praktik Grofsmutter," a satire on "Praktik," or prophecies for the year, and in his "Bücherverzeichnis" (Catalogue of Books).

Fischart wrote most scathingly against the Jesuits (Jesuiter—Jesu*wider* as he styled them). Such writings are

Nachtrab' oder Nebelkräh' and *Das vierhörnige Jesuiterhütlein.* His best known work is

Das glückhafte Schiff von Zürich, which appeared in 1576, and describes how the ship brought "Hirsebrei" (millet-pap) still warm to Strasburg. Fischart may be considered one of the greatest German masters of diction in the sixteenth century.

The **Drama.**—The influence of Luther and his followers did not work against dramatic representation except when sacred events were treated with levity. Luther disapproved of the Passion Play on the ground of the unfitness of the sentimental treatment of our Lord's sufferings as those of a mere man, and the reformers abolished all plays from the legends of the saints. On the other hand, themes from the Old Testament were freely used. Nürnberg was the town in which the drama chiefly flourished. It had already been celebrated for its carnival plays in the fifteenth century, and was at the height of its fame in the time of

Hans Sachs (1494-1576).—As an instance of almost unparalleled versatility and fertility, Hans Sachs stands out, not in his own age alone, but in all ages. He wrote in all styles, from 1513 to 1567, and, according to his own calculation, finished more than six thousand works. It is unfortunate that the greater number of his writings are, in form, little better than the doggerel in which he himself has been described:

> "Hans Sachs war ein Schuh-
> Macher und Poet dazu!"

His prose was good, and had he not preferred a rhyming couplet, quite unsuitable to many of his subjects, it is probable that much greater literary value might have attached to his works. His description is vivid—he *sees* what he describes, which is in itself a mark of high poetic possibilities.

Sachs' many works are divided into "Meistergesänge" (4,276 in number), 208 Plays, besides numerous Fables, Farces, Allegories, Psalms, Dialogues, etc.

Some of his works are: "St. Peter mit der Geifs" (St. Peter with the Goat), "St. Peter mit den Landsknechten" (St. Peter and the Pike-men), "Schlaraffenland" (Lubberland), and "Die ungleichen Kinder Evä," the last a fable naïvely told, how God examined the children of Eve in religious knowledge, and some failed. Sachs dramatized this story twice, and, in one of the plays, places the end of an act right in the middle of the examination. Clumsy divisions of this kind are usual with him ; he divides his plays into acts and scenes, but sometimes in most unexpected places.

The influence of the English stage, with its earlier development, made itself felt, for English comedians were at this time travelling about in Germany, and a writer who drew ideas from it was

Jacob Ayrer, who died in 1605, and was, like Sachs, a native of Nürnberg.   He is far behind Hans Sachs in talent.   His sixty-nine plays, written in rough couplets, are divided into tragedies, comedies, carnival-plays, and—what causes him to be remembered—" Singspiele," the parent of the opera, which he first introduced in rudimentary form into Germany.

CHAPTER VI.

AT the period immediately preceding the Thirty Years' War, literature, as well as science, was steadily developing in Germany. Not that it was a time productive of master-pieces, but rather one of quiet growth. The highest triumphs of art are not reached at a single leap, and it is wrong to undervalue the silent years which are ripening precious fruit, or that imitation which brings after it the capability of original production.

In 1617 the so-called *Fruchtbringende Gesellschaft*, or *Palmenorden*, was founded at Weimar, having as its object the purifying of the language from foreign words, the establishment of grammatical rules, and a metrical system calculated to abolish at least some of the roughnesses of the preceding years. These Sprachgesellschaften—for others were afterwards formed—were copied in the first place from Italian Academies such as the Florentine "della Crusca." They were pedantic enough, no doubt, but the German language was in need of pruning, and a number of the principles they laid down have helped in some measure towards the solid basis of modern literature.

Philipp von Zesen wrote " Lieder " as well as novels, such as " Die adriatische Rosamund," where the problem of mixed marriages partly furnished the subject. He worked diligently, if blindly, to purify the language. Even classical names offended his patriotic ear—he would have named Jupiter "Erzgott," Minerva " Kluginne," etc. The Sprach-gesellschaften owed much to his diligence. He founded, in 1643, the "Deutsch-gesinnte Gesellschaft" (German-minded society), a name thoroughly characteristic of his work.

Martin Opitz (1597-1639) did good work for literature by the publication, in 1624, of his "Büchlein von der deutschen Poeterei," almost the first art of poetry produced in Germany. He was born at Bunzlau in Silesia, and was himself a poet, but it is his "Büchlein" that constitutes his best claim to remembrance at the present day. Posterity has not confirmed the renown he won among his own contempo-raries by his strained and artificial poems. The "Trostge-dichte in Widerwärtigkeiten des Krieges" (Songs of Com-fort in the Miseries of War) describe the horrors of the Thirty Years' War. Opitz also wrote some hymns, and a prose work, "Hercynia," or the "Sheepfold of the Nymph Hercynia," a work which transplanted the Pastoral Romance into German soil.

Paul Fleming (1609-1640), a follower of Opitz, wrote some secular poems and many hymns, such as "In allen meinen Thaten."

Friedrich von Logau (1604-1655) wrote epigrams.

Simon Dach (1605-1659) wrote "Lied von der Freund-shaft," and the well known Volkslied :

> "Ännchen von Tharau ist's, die mir gefällt,
> Sie ist mein Leben, mein Gut und mein Geld."
> (Herder's Translation, 1778.)

This was originally in Plattdeutsch "Anke von Tharow."

We may class together as hymn-writers *Friedrich von Spree* (died 1635), whose sacred songs are called "Trutz Nachtigall," *Johann Scheffler*, who wrote "Heilige Seelen-

lust " and " Der cherubinische Wandersmann" (collections
of hymns), *Paul Gerhardt* (1607-1676), who wrote some
beautiful hymns, such as "Nun ruhen alle Wälder," *Johann
Franck*, author of "Du schönes Weltgebäude" (died
1677), *Joachim Neander* (died 1680), and *Luise Henriette*,
wife of the Great Elector of Brandenburg; she died in 1667.

Opitz and those who followed in his steps are called
the **First Silesian School of Poetry.** Their characteristics are, the striving after purity of diction and simplicity of subject, and the avoidance of the strained and
extraordinary. In these respects the poets of the so-called
Second Silesian School of Poetry compare unfavour-
ably with them. They are bombastic and inflated in style,
and often extravagant in subject. Between the two schools,
forming a kind of transition from one to the other, stands

Andreas Gryphius (1616-1664), in whom the influence
of Shakespeare—only a shadow, indeed, still a perceptible
shadow—may be seen, although the Thirty Years' War had
not dealt kindly with the representation of the great English
dramatist in Germany, any more than with literature in
general. Gryphius, in his lyric poetry follows Opitz in
form, but in his dramas he may be classed with the Second
Silesian School. He was a man of considerable intellectual
attainments, and apparently of gloomy temperament, a fact
for which long acquaintance with the horrors of war may
be responsible. His lyrical work was fairly voluminous, but
it is as a dramatist that he is chiefly notable. Gryphius'
first tragedy is

Leo der Armenier, the story of a conspiracy in Constantinople, full of invective against tyrannical power.

Karl Stuart von England was written immediately after
the execution of that unfortunate monarch, and treats him
as a martyr.

Another tragedy is

Cardenio und Celinde, a love story, in which the supernatural element is introduced with that love of the horrible which distinguishes Gryphius. It contains, nevertheless, some excellent scenes. The dramatist, towards the end of his career, turned his attention to comedy, and wrote

Peter Squenz, adapted from the workmen's comedy in Shakespeare's "Midsummer Night's Dream." The adventures of Bottom and his companions had been brought to Germany by English actors, and Gryphius turns the satire against the Volkssänger (popular poets), and their ignorant treatment of mythological subjects.

Horribilicribrifax is a comedy where several pairs of lovers are represented, and the comic situations are brought about by the introduction into the dialogue of French, Italian, Latin, Greek, and Hebrew words, causing misunderstandings. Gryphius' public was not educated up to this linguistic proficiency, and "Horribilicribrifax" fell flat, although the military ostentation of the times is cleverly satirized in it.

The most natural of Gryphius' plays is a peasant comedy in the Silesian dialect,

Die geliebte Dornrose (the Beloved Wild-Rose).—The hero and heroine are a sort of village Romeo and Juliet, but the feud between their families is healed, and the play ends happily. In addition to lyrics, mostly of mournful import, Andreas Gryphius wrote "Singspiele," which were very bright and successful.

Das verliebte Gespenst (the Ghost in Love), a comic Singspiel, is especially so.

Andreas Gryphius, in spite of all his faults, his stilted style, and his revelling in horrors, is one of the greatest German dramatists before Goethe. He rarely succeeded in "holding the mirror up to nature," but it is much that he did occasionally succeed.

The seventeenth century saw innumerable foreign models introduced into Germany, and followed with more or less success, the tendency being, in all cases, to artificiality and exaggeration.

The Life and Death of Dr. Faustus was old in Germany, but Marlowe's tragedy brought it again into fashion, and it lived on to become a great poetic triumph in a later age.

The Pastoral fashion in lyrics had its day in Germany as in other countries. One of Martin Opitz's refrains runs:

> "Ein jeder lobe seinen Sinn,
> Ich liebe meine Schäferin,"

and all lyric poets posed as shepherds. In prose, Sir Philip Sydney's "Arcadia" was not without its imitators, and shepherds and shepherdesses also appeared in the drama. Belonging to the **Second Silesian School of Poetry** and marked by its defects, are Hoffmann von Hoffmannswaldau and Kaspar von Lohenstein. The former,

Hoffmann von Hoffmannswaldau (1618-1679) wrote "Erotische Lieder," greatly admired by his contemporaries, but really sentimental and frivolous, though possessing a certain effeminate prettiness. Another work is "Heldenbriefe."

Kaspar von Lohenstein (1635-1683) wrote bombastic "Lieder" and plays and novels in the false taste of his school. His best work is the "Heldenroman" "Arminius," a romance from old German history in his exaggerated and artificial style. The full title is "Liebes- und Lebensgeschichte des heldenmütigen Arminius und seiner durchlauchtigen Thusnelda."

It was inevitable that Lohenstein and similar writers should meet opponents in men of truer taste.

Christian Weise (1642-1708) worked for natural mode of expression in direct contrast to the inflated style of Lohenstein. His early poems are bright and witty, but his later works strained and lacking in inspiration. Weise wrote the satire:

Die drei ärgsten Erznarren in der ganzen Welt (the Three most arrant Fools in the whole World).

Johann Lauremberg (1590-1658), of Rostock, wrote the most delightfully humorous verse in Plattdeutsch. He was a worthy predecessor of his countryman Fritz Reuter, whose novels are to-day as worthy of praise as any in German literature. Lauremberg wrote :

Veer olde beröhmede Schertzgedichte. Nothing was farther from his thoughts than the attempt at elevated style, which was the dearest aim of his contemporaries ; but he was, nevertheless, a man of great learning, and his satirical writings, abounding in humorous images, turn the doctrine of the transmigration of souls into a satire on all classes of society.

Ludwig von Canitz wrote " Satires " after the manner of Boileau. He died in 1699.

Johann Christian Günther (1695-1723) was a man of great poetic capability, but of wild and dissipated life. His songs refer to his own loves, sorrows, faults, and repentance, and are marked by candour and truth to life, but marred by coarseness. He died when only twenty-eight. It was of Günther that Goethe wrote : " Er wufste sich nicht zu zähmen, und so zerrann ihm sein Leben wie sein Dichten. "

Christian Wernicke (1665-1725) was greatly influenced by the French and English classical schools. Imitating the style of Boileau, he wrote " Epigrams " against French fashions, and the absurdities of Lohenstein and his followers.

Heinrich Brockes (1680-1747) fell wholly under English influence, translated Thomson's " Seasons," and wrote " Irdisches Vergnügen in Gott " (" Earthly Joy in God "). Both Wernicke and Brockes belonged to Hamburg.

Novels and Romances of those times, if not remarkable for originality, were numerous enough. Those written by Zesen and Lohenstein have already been mentioned.

It became the fashion to adorn ancient German history with fictitious characters and imaginary events, drawn from the most diverse sources.

Anton Ulrich, Duke of Brunswick (1633-1714) wrote two interminable novels, entitled " Aramena " and " Octavia," in the former of which he introduces a prince of the ancient Germans, who is married to a queen of Nineveh by the high priest Melchisedek.

A more successful novel, in the early romantic style, was " Die asiatische Banise," by *Anselm von Ziegler und Klipphausen*, containing all the necessary points of interest, where a princess, captive to a bloodthirsty tyrant, is released by her bold and heroic lover.

There are, however, two novelists of this period whose works possess lasting interest, the first of whom, in date, is

Hans Michael Moscherosch (1601-1669). He was influenced by Spanish models, and in his satirical " Wunderliche und wahrhafte Gesichte Philanders von Sittenwald ", where he imitated in part Quevedo's " Dreams " (Sueños y Discursos), he turned them to good account. The second and greater is :

Christoph von Grimmelshausen (1625-1676), who wrote the novel " Simplicissimus " on the Spanish plan.

This book gives a realistic picture of the state of Germany during the Thirty Years' War. The hero, brought up in absolute ignorance of the world, and thrown unprepared into the wild soldier-life of the period, falls into all kinds of error from sheer inability to distinguish right from wrong; at last, disgusted with the world, he becomes a hermit.

Grimmelhausen's mode of procedure is good. He writes firm and well-ordered prose. To say that he depicts horrors, barbarity, the life of savages rather than of civilized men, is to say that he writes of the Thirty Years' War. It is possible that he sometimes falls into the error of the times, and yields to the temptation of exhibiting his learning where a pure literary taste would recognize its inopportunity, still "Simplicissimus" may be regarded as a masterpiece of its time.

Defoe had not failed to find disciples in Germany, and *Robinsonaden*, as they were called, found their place among the cosmopolitan imitations. The best of these was the

Insel Felsenburg by *Johann Gottfried Schnabel*, written about 1731, and resembling "Simplicissimus" in plan. The happy island of the book was first inhabited by a German Crusoe alone, but afterwards colonists flocked to it. Vice and unhappiness were left behind, and in this new Utopia, the inhabitants tell the stories of their own lives, which contain many allusions to the general history and social events of the times.

As a conclusion to the period of the Thirty Years' War, we may name here

Pater Abraham a Santa Clara, died 1709, of whose eloquence—jocular when necessary—Schiller made use in his sermon in Wallenstein's Lager, where part of a "Turk Sermon" of Santa Clara's is almost literally reproduced. He wrote "Judas der Erzschelm" ("Judas the Arch-rogue").

CHAPTER VII.

LEIPZIG. ZÜRICH. HALLER AND HAGEDORN. PRUSSIA. KLOPSTOCK. WIELAND.

A MAN whose name is of constant recurrence in the history of eighteenth-century literature in Germany, a man of wide-reaching, if only temporary influence, and of unbounded belief in his own genius and literary infallibility was the Leipzig critic and dramatist,

Johann Christoph Gottsched (1700-1766).—Had Gottsched's pretensions been more modest, it is probable that the valuable work he really accomplished would have met with more lasting appreciation. As it was, his overweening belief in his own opinions alone, his intolerance of contradiction, and his really narrow view of slavish adherence to the plans laid down by the French classic authors, caused his downfall during his own lifetime, and Goethe, who in his youth visited Gottsched at Leipzig, says in "Wahrheit und Dichtung," "Ganz Leipzig verachtet ihn, niemand geht mit ihm um"—All Leipzig despises him; no one associates with him.

Yet Gottsched was an energetic and able worker, though he fell short of genius, and some of the ideas he strove hard to carry out are praiseworthy in the extreme. As a Professor at the University of Leipzig, it was his aim to make that town a literary centre for all Germany. He inaugurated periodicals on the model of the "Tatler" and "Spectator," edited them himself, and wrote many of the articles.

He compiled a grammar, badly needed, and sufficiently scientific, for Gottsched was the best German philologian prior to Jakob Grimm. His

Kritische Dichtkunst, or "Critical Art of Poetry," carried on the work of Opitz, and sought to lay down hard and fast rules for the drama, as well as for poetry in general. Where he erred was in too strict adherence to the opinion of French critics, by which real genius is bound down to rules too small, too unimportant to be invariably enforced. He was afraid of allowing scope to the imagination, afraid of a return to the extravagance of Lohenstein, and his critical faculty was not sufficiently keen to distinguish true poetry from false. He did all in his power to attract the best actors to Leipzig, and adapted plays for the stage, a work in which he was largely aided by his wife, who undertook the comedies.

Gottsched's original poetical works were a total failure. He copied from Addison's "Cato"—itself a failure—

Der Sterbende Cato, which was possibly the best of his many attempts.

He translated "Racine," attained great celebrity, then attempted to assume the censorship of all publications, and thereupon plunging into literary quarrels, suffered in many circles ridicule as great as the admiration he had formerly received. The chief dispute initiated by Gottsched is the

Streit der Leipziger und der Schweizer, or the *Gottsched-Bodmer Controversy*, the great opponent of Gottsched being

Johann Jacob Bodmer, born 1698, at Zürich, died 1783. He, together with his friend,

Breitinger (1701-1776), also a native of Zürich, followed the English school rather than the French, not Addison or Pope, or any of the so-called Augustan poets, but chiefly Milton, of whose "Paradise Lost" Bodmer made a prose translation.

Neither Bodmer nor Breitinger possessed great original genius; the former especially was ambitious of literary fame, and both opposed Gottsched strenuously.

Bodmer had some appreciation of Shakespeare, and expressed a fastidious horror of rhyme, copied probably from Milton's opinion in the apology to "Paradise Lost." The chief critical and æsthetic writings of the two Swiss authors were Breitinger's

Kritische Dichtkunst, and Bodmer's

Vom Wunderbare in der Poesie ("On the Marvellous in Poetry"), and *Diskurse der Maler*.

Another Professor of the University of Leipzig at the same time as Gottsched, like him summoned to appear before Frederick the Great—who, during the Seven Years' War often visited Leipzig—was

Christian Fürchtegott Gellert (1715-1769). Gellert was originally intended for a clergyman; he remained all his life a strict moralist and a thoroughly religious man. His work was varied, but perhaps the worthiest of all he accomplished was the moral influence exercised over those who came in contact with him. His

Fabeln are excellent, possibly called forth by Lafontaine —though Gellert answered Frederick the Great as to his having imitated the French poet, "Nein, Ihro Majestät, ich bin ein Original"—but written melodiously and gracefully, until then a rare thing in the German since the Minnesinger. Gellert tried many styles, and gained more than deserved popularity in all. He wrote serio-comedies and a sentimental novel in the style of Richardson,

Das Leben der schwedischen Gräfin G., but his fables and *Erzählungen* are decidedly the best of his works. Some of his hymns are very melodious and sweet.

Rabener and *Zachariä*, two of the most talented writers of Leipzig, contributed for some time, together with Gellert, to Gottsched and Schwabe's periodical, "Belustigungen des Verstandes und Witzes," but left it and began the publication of the "Bremer Beiträge," in order to be independent of Gottsched—one of the many fallings off of partisans which the latter experienced.

A poet of independent standpoint may be mentioned here, **Albrecht von Haller**, of Bern, born in 1708, died 1777. He wrote "Oden ;" his

Ode an Doris is celebrated as a passionate love-poem, for the fire of which he thought fit to excuse himself in his old age;

Die Alpen, his masterpiece, showing his love for his native land, and

Über die Ewigkeit. The influence of the late Roman period and of the English poets is to be seen in his work, especially in his didactic poems and satires. Haller's language is not thoroughly correct in his first editions—as German-Swiss this was probably unavoidable—but he has high thoughts, and expresses them with appropriate earnestness.

Friedrich von Hagedorn, of Hamburg, also independent of Gottsched and the "Leipziger," was born in the same year as Haller, and died in 1754. He is remarkable for the thorough correctness and flowing elegance of his diction, and was the first to introduce the anacreontic style into German verse. As Haller followed English, Hagedorn followed French models. Some of his Lieder are: "An die Freude," "Der Wein," "Der Mai." His "Fabeln" are written with great elegance. The "Erzählung," or Tale,

Johann, der muntere Seifensieder, is still very popular in Germany.

A group of poets who also wrote Anacreonics, and were known as the

Hallische or Preussische Dichterverein may be placed here. The influence of Horace, and sometimes of Petrarch, is visible in them.

Wilhelm Ludwig Gleim (1719-1803), called "Vater Gleim" on account of his benevolent interest in rising poets, wrote Anacreontics and the

Preussische Kriegslieder eines Grenadiers, which bear witness to the charm exercised by Frederick the Great over his contemporaries. He wrote also "Petrarkische Lieder," "Fabeln," "Erzählungen," and "Halladat oder das rothe Buch."

Ewald Christian von Kleist, born 1715, fell at Kunersdorf, 1759, was a major in the Prussian army who sang of king and country, and, happier than the later unfortunate poet of his name,[1] died for them in battle. His great literary success, hailed with enthusiasm at the time but less prized by posterity, is the long descriptive poem:

Der Frühling, in the style of Thomson's "Seasons." Kleist wrote excellent Idylls, such as "Irin," and a short heroic poem, "Cissides and Paches."

Johann Peter Uz (1720-1796) may be classed with the "deutsch anakreontische" poets. In later life, however, he adopted a graver style and wrote the Odes: "Das bedrängte Deutschland" and "Theodicee."

Karl Ramler (1725-1798) wrote Odes imitated from Horace.

At this period, a poetess known as the "German Sappho," in the exaggerated phraseology of the time,

Anna Luise Karsch (1722-1791) was in great renown among her contemporaries, but posterity has forgotten her once celebrated "Gelegenheitsgedichte."

About 1744, when Gottsched was attempting to impose his universal censorship on German literature—tabooing, among other things, the opera as false art—a group of his followers who were members of the "Leipziger Dichterverein" freed themselves from his influence, and founded

---

[1] *Vide* Heinrich von Kleist, page 122.

the new periodical before referred to, the "Bremer Beiträge," with *Gärtner* (died 1791) as editor. These Leipzigers copied Richardson and Young. Chief among them were :

Friedrich Wilhelm Zachariä (1726-1777), who has already been named with Gellert. He wrote the

Renommist, Das Schnupftuch, Phaeton, and *Murner in der Hölle,* in the style of Pope.

Gottlieb Wilhelm Rabener (1714-1771), wrote satires in many forms, influenced by Swift and Cervantes. He satirized especially the German middle-class of the period, and his writings are now out of date, as the state of things parodied has in great measure passed away.

Johann Elias Schlegel, died 1749, wrote a tragedy, "Canut," and "Triumph der guten Frauen."

Johann Adolf Schlegel, died 1793—the father of the two "Romantiker" Schlegel—wrote "Fabeln," "Erzählungen," and sacred poems.

Johann Andreas Cramer, died 1788, wrote *Odes,* sacred poems, and a biography of Gellert.

Gellert himself belonged to this circle of poets, and was greatly admired by them. The sentimentality which has ceased to please in our time pleased in his, and Gellert charmed his readers as Richardson in England delighted his public.

A man whose best work comes very near the first rank of genius, who in a way achieved a great and admirable success, and who yet, judged from the highest standpoint, may be considered to have missed his own grand ideal, was

Friedrich Gottlieb Klopstock, born at Quedlinburg, 1724, died 1803.

The Swiss poet Bodmer's enthusiasm for Milton had not been confined to a limited circle. It was felt that a sacred epic was needed in German literature, that he would be a great and happy man who should be inspired to climb the sublime heights which the English epic poet had

E

reached; and when Klopstock, at the age of twenty-four, published the three first cantos of his

Messias, he had achieved greatness at a single stroke. Through all the interminable length of what is, rightly judged, a grand and lasting literary monument, Klopstock never surpassed, if he equalled the first Gesänge which he had finished when he was little more than a boy. A long life was granted him, but the immortality of Milton will not justly be his. He was capable of grandeur, capable of noble emotion, able to clothe his thought in the majesty of a grand hexameter; the consciousness of the dignity of his high theme was upon him, the realization of its pathos; and his own exuberance of sympathy was his fatal stumbling-block. Klopstock was born for a lyric poet; the power of representation necessary to an epic was beyond his grasp. He dares not describe our Lord's sufferings, they are "unspeakable." He feels, but he does not present to our imagination; his own emotion comes between the reader and the picture he should see, and the effect is that the majestic roll of the hexameter carries only a confused murmur, and is nothing but sound. Lessing's words apply only too well:

> "Wer wird nicht einen Klopstock loben?
> Doch wird ihn jeder lesen? Nein!"

Klopstock learnt from Milton, but he did not learn enough. The English poet knew that human interest is indispensable to human beings; Klopstock floats away into the ethereal, and his creations are bodiless, mere abstractions, which the mind cannot grasp. As Schiller says: "Klopstock zieht allem, was er behandelt, den Körper aus, um es zu Geist zu machen." That is the reason the "Messias," in its entirety, is very rarely read in our own day, even by students of literature.

Yet it is impossible to over-estimate the importance of the work Klopstock did for German versification and language by his perfection of the hexameter, and by his pure and lofty diction. "Loftiness of thought" is his too, and a sort of dim appreciation of infinity. The following lines may serve as an example:

> "Ich bin
> Ewig! und schwöre dir, Sohn: Ich will die Sünde vergeben;
> Also sprach er und schwieg. Indem die Ewigen sprachen,
> Ging durch die ganze Natur ein ehrfurchtvolles Erbeben.
> Seelen, die jetzo wurden, noch nicht zu denken begannen,
> Zitterten und empfanden zuerst."

"Empfinden," that is Klopstock's ever-recurring motive, and therefore it would have been better had his "Messias" been in lyrical form, where the feelings of the poet might have had full scope.

The manifold attempts made to interest Frederick the Great in German literature had failed in every case. He shewed some appreciation of Gellert—"le plus raisonnable de tous les savants allemands" as he called him—but remained cold enough in reality to the whole movement. The "Messias" was the last thing to kindle enthusiasm in a man nourished on the French of Voltaire. "Ich habe in meinem Leben kein deutsches Buch gelesen," he said, "et je parle comme un cocher." Klopstock, finding the hope of patronage from Frederick vain, turned his attention to the history of the ancient Germans, and wrote the three historical dramas in prose—*Bardiete*, or plays of the bards, as he was pleased to call them:

1. "Hermannsschlacht.
2. "Hermann und die Fürsten," and
3. "Hermanns Tod."

The first contains some really fine passages, but all are totally unfit for scenic representation. The same may be said of the three scriptural dramas: "Der Tod Adams," "Salomo," "David." Klopstock's

Odes contain some of his best work. The Ode "Hermann und Thusnelda" is one of his finest efforts.

The poet's later life was passed in great part at Copenhagen, where he was provided for by the King of Denmark, and so enabled to live without the sordid care of breadwinning. In the days of his early fame, the old puritanical Bodmer had urgently invited him to Zurich, and Klopstock acceded to his request. However, the old admirer of Milton and the inspired youth who was to write the new immortal epic were sadly disappointed in each other. Klopstock drank wine, smoked, and preferred the society of the young and frivolous to that of the grave and respectable associates of Bodmer. He had left Zurich greatly out of favour with his host.

Klopstock died in 1803, having lived to be nearly eighty years of age. His life was almost contemporaneous with that of

Immanuel Kant, the great metaphysician, who was born the same year as Klopstock, and died one year later. His work in versification, too, may be compared to that of Kant in philosophy—a thorough re-construction and remodelling of all that had gone before.

The poet of the " Messias " had remained faithful to the serious in literature ; he had not, in his works at least, been swept from one standpoint to another under the influence of the conflicting doctrines of the times. But it was otherwise with the poet who takes higher rank than he, as the producer of a great epic poem,

Christoph Martin Wieland (1733-1813).—The son of a Suabian clergyman, he was strictly and piously brought up, probably in that narrow and puritanical way which, as a rule, produces sooner or later the opposite effect to that desired. Wieland's first literary efforts, however, were in perfect harmony with his upbringing and education. He began to write strongly religious poetry, and found in Bodmer and his friends at Zürich as warm admiration as had, a few years earlier, been lavished by them on Klopstock. During the first period of his intellectual activity, Wieland wrote lyrical, didactic, and narrative poems, all with strong religious tendency. Such are: "Von der Natur der Dinge oder der vollkommensten Welt," "Lobgesang auf den Frühling," in which he prefigured the eternal spring-time of Heaven, "Moralische Briefe," "Anti-Ovid," where the praises of love and wine were hardly dealt with; a Biblical epic after Bodmer's own heart, "Der geprüfte Abraham;" "Sympathieen, Empfindungen des Christen," and songs in which he idealized his cousin, Sophie Gutermann, whom he treated as the personification of all angelic qualities in woman. Her marriage with a Monsieur de la Roche was at first a shock to the young poet, but he consoled himself with the reflection that his love for her was from soul to soul, and need not be troubled in its platonic serenity by her marriage.

The sentimental piety of the poet, however, which was purely artificial and in nowise connected with true religious faith, began to make way for the charm of antiquity—the Greeks replaced Abraham and the Biblical heroes. As was to be expected, Wieland exchanged from one extreme to the other before he recovered his mental balance, and attained the fulness of his poetic development.

The second phase through which he passed was that of sensuousness and materialism, under the influence of Shaftesbury, Sterne, Rousseau, Voltaire, and Diderot. During this period of his life Wieland wrote "Nadine," "Don Sylvio von Rosalva," and

Agathon, which was the story of his own life set in a framework of Greek cities, modern in colouring though classic in design. As a rule, Wieland's Greek descriptions are marred by the intermixture of modern sentimentality and an affectation of culture, wholly alien to the noble simplicity of antiquity. In "Agathon" he paints clearly his own mental and moral development; he shows the

workings of a human heart, the admixture of good and evil
existent in us all, and has cast away the fallacy of a perfect
hero in which the truth to nature—the one necessity in
all art—is violated. Wieland was growing to a higher
development than Klopstock ever attained. In 1768
appeared

Musarion, a delightfully fresh, graceful tale in verse,
where a misanthropical philosopher is converted to the
doctrine of Epicurus—that pleasure is the highest good—
that is to say, the doctrine of Epicurus himself, whose
definition of " pleasure " was absence of pain, not the
coarse enjoyment understood by his later followers. Wieland intended to teach a philosophy of the Beautiful in
" Musarion."

The third phase of Wieland's life is the time of graver
views and sounder judgment. He had arrived at the
capability of doing his best. Shakespeare attracted him,
and he made a prose translation of a number of his plays,
not of great intrinsic merit, but very remarkable in the
effect it produced. The great English dramatist was at
this time hardly known in Germany, and the influence of
Wieland's translation of Shakespeare may be considered
one of the principal causes of the great development of the
German drama which was soon to appear in full brilliance.
The

Abderiten, satirical sketches, or rather a satirical novel
against " Spiessbürgertum " (Philistinism), published in
Wieland's periodical,

Der Deutsche Merkur (beginning in 1773), represents
German life and manners clothed in a Greek garb, and
satirized with wonderful power in the most graceful and
polished style. The novel " Die Abderiten " ranks among
the poet's best works.

In 1780, Wieland's masterpiece, the epic poem,

Oberon, was published amid a burst of applause.

Goethe—who, after having ridiculed Wieland in one of the comic effusions of his youth, entitled "Götter, Helden und Wieland," had come to a juster appreciation of the elder poet, and was among the contributors to the " Merkur "— Goethe expressed his admiration in enthusiastic terms : " So lange Poesie Poesie, Gold Gold und Krystall Krystall bleibt, wird 'Oberon' als ein Meisterstück poetischer Kunst geliebt und geehrt werden."

Wieland had studied fairy-lore and chivalrous adventure as a preparation—to use his own words—for " den Ritt ins alte romantische Land." Shakespeare in the " Midsummer Night's Dream," Chaucer and the French romance of " The Adventures of the Knight Huon of Bordeaux," furnished him with material for his exquisitely finished poem. The interest is throughout well sustained, and the treatment not too subjective for an epic : the poet keeps himself in the background, and avoids the exaggeration of his earlier style. A quarrel and final reconciliation between Oberon, the king of the fairies, and his wife Titania are interwoven with the adventures of Huon and his love, who first failing in a solemn promise are as a punishment shipwrecked, undergo hardships and privations innumerable, but at last being purged from their fault by suffering, enjoy the perfection of happiness.

After Oberon, Wieland's epic attempts were inconsiderable. " Clelia und Sinibald " is one, but is in every way far behind his masterpiece. Towards the end of his literary career he made excellent translations of Horace's " Satires and Epistles," the whole of Lucian, Cicero's " Letters," and some plays of Aristophanes and Euripides. One of the most striking characteristics of Wieland's genius is its inexhaustible productiveness.

A few imitators of Wieland may be merely named here ; such are

Musäus (1735-1787) wrote "Grandison der Zweite,"

" Physiognomische Reisen," and " Volksmärchen der Deutschen," his chief work.

Von Thümmel, died 1817 ; " Reise in die mittäglichen Provinzen Frankreichs."

Wilhelm Heinse (1749-1803) ; "Ardinghello oder die glückseligen Inseln."

Hermes, died 1821 ; " Sophiens Reise von Memel nach Sachsen."

Sophie de la Roche, Wieland's first love before referred to, wrote " Geschichte des Fräuleins von Sternheim."

CHAPTER VIII.

In the year 1772, a society of young men in Göttingen, mainly students at the university, a number of whom mistook exuberant vitality and the excitability of youth for poetic inspiration, founded what they called the
Göttinger Dichterbund or the " Hain."
These young men had contributed lyrics to the "Musenalmanach of Göttingen;" they had clearly defined views on literary matters, and condemned with wholesale condemnation, or praised with indiscriminating praise—the inevitable defect of immature judgment. They reverenced Homer, and after him Shakespeare and the English ballad—Bishop Percy's "Reliques" were received with enthusiasm in Germany—and, as German idol, they adored Klopstock. This superabundant love of Klopstock was only equalled by their unmitigated abhorrence of Wieland, whom they styled "Sittenverderber," and, as a protest against his dangerous teaching, they once burnt his works. France and French literature shared with them the fate of Wieland, but amid all this bluster of abuse and prejudice, glimpses of genius were not absent. The greatest among them in originality and strength is the well-known ballad writer,
Gottfried August Bürger (1747-1794). He was a man of dissipated life, and his talents were in great measure wasted. Still, for fire and headlong irresistible force in the representation of the weird and unearthly, Bürger has rarely been equalled. His ballad,

Lenore, is perfect of its kind. The girl, carried away by her ghostly lover—or Death himself in the form of her lover—in a frantic race through the moonlit night, the grim triumph of the refrain, "Hurrah ! Hurrah ! the dead can ride," as Scott translates it—all form a striking example of the life and force of Bürger's style.

Der wilde Jäger (also translated by Scott) is founded on a well-known German legend, and can be classed with "Lenore." The third most deservedly popular ballad is "*Das Lied vom braven Mann.*"

Many of Bürger's *Lieder*, such as " Ich rühme mir mein Dörfchen hier ! " are well known, but the tenderness and delicacy of feeling necessary to love-songs was not natural to Bürger—his "Liebeslieder" and " Sonette," though full of passion are inferior to his ballads.

"*Münchhausens Abenteuer zu Land und zu Wasser* " is the title of his translation from the original English text (written by R. E. Raspe, a German).

Frau Schnips and *Der Kaiser und der Abt* are lively comic ballads, and if his life had been less torn and wasted by his own unbridled passions it is probable that Bürger would stand higher than he does among the writers of his age and nation.

The man who was really the life and soul of the Göttinger Dichterbund was

Johann Heinrich Voss, 1751-1826, a most diligent and clever translator. His is the merit of having really translated Homer, not according to the letter alone but according to the spirit, with a real echo of the Homeric grandeur and full comprehension of the Greek genius.

Unfortunately he wished to be too true to the original, and so, in part, spoilt his work. Voss translated also from many classic authors, including Virgil, Ovid, and Horace, wrote "Der siebzigste Geburtstag," the best of all his original poems, and

Idyllen, of which *Luise* had long more than its share of popularity, also *Lieder* and *Oden*. Prominent members of the Hain in the matter of noisy enthusiasm and hero-worship, were the two brothers

Christian, Graf zu Stolberg, 1748-1821, and

Friedrich Leopold, Graf zu Stolberg, 1750-1819, the younger being the better poet of the two. He translated the "Iliad," Æschylus, and Ossian, or Macpherson. The brothers published their works together. Their youthful search after ideals was marked by considerable eccentricity, but they ended quietly enough; Graf Friedrich-Leopold joined the Church of Rome and forgot his revolutionary tendencies. Schiller wrote of them in the "Xenien":

"Als Centauren gingen sie einst durch poetische Wälder;
Aber das wilde Geschlecht hat sich geschwinde bekehrt."

Ludwig Hölty, born 1748, died of consumption in 1776, wrote harmonious verse and tender descriptions of nature. He wrote Lieder, such as "Wer wollte sich mit Grillen plagen," "Elegien," and the idyll, "Das Feuer im Walde."

Martin Miller (1750-1814) began his connection with the "Hain," as a lyric poet, and wrote the song "Zufriedenheit." Later, however, he turned his attention to prose, and published a highly romantic and sentimental novel: "Siegwart, eine Klostergeschichte," representative of that German "Schwärmerei" (sentimental reverie) which Wieland had affected in his youth, but permanently abandoned in "Agathon."

Friedrich von Matthisson (1761-1831) followed Hölty in style and subject, and was admired by Schiller. His chief poems are: "Elegie in den Ruinen eines alten Bergschlosses geschrieben," where, from the starting-point of a description of the life of the knights of old, he falls into reflections on the past; "Genfersee" and "Abendlandschaft." One of Matthisson's friends,

Gaudenz von Salis (1762-1834), was the author of "Lied eines Landmanns in der Fremde."

A poet of child-like open-heartedness and really lovable character was

Matthius Claudius (1740-1815). Herder called him: "Den Knaben der Unschuld voll Mondlicht und Lilienduft der Unsterblichkeit in seiner Seele." He edited a periodical called "Der Wandsbecker Bote," but his best work is in pathetic poems, as

Der Tod und das Mädchen, where death comforts the frightened maiden, the "Lied am Grabe meines Vaters," and in the humorous stories of

Urians Reise um die Welt, beginning with the often quoted words: "Wenn jemand eine Reise thut, so kann er was verzählen," and

Geschichte von Goliath und David, "War einst ein Riese Goliath, gar ein gefährlich Mann!"

While Gottsched, having arrogated to himself the dictatorship of the German stage, found that the Swiss attacked him, and that Germany ceased to follow his cast-iron opinions, while Klopstock wrote his "Messias" and Wieland his manifold works, and the Göttinger Hain deified the one and blackened the name of the other, another name was making itself heard, a name which, especially in the drama, was to take a high place in the literature of the country.

Gotthold Ephraim Lessing was born in Saxony in 1729. His busy life ended in 1781. He continued on other and broader lines the work of Gottsched; his literary career differs from that of Klopstock, in that he did not, like Klopstock, determine on the object of his life at its outset and remain firm to his early resolution; it has greater resemblance with the development of Wieland, but does not present the sharp contrast of Wieland's change from exaggerated affectation of piety to licentiousness in tone,

followed by the purer art of his later and better works.
Lessing was never narrowly strict in his religious views.
It is possible that he showed too great laxity, that his large
toleration may have had its source in religious indifference
rather than in charity, but he is throughout the writer of
noble works, containing grand thoughts and high ideals.
His popularity and rise to fame were far from being the
work of a moment. As a boy, he showed that fondness for
books which is possibly more frequently found in Germany
than in any other country. He early grasped the meaning
of the tendency, and saw its potential result—pedantry.
And the knowledge, or the fear, of that pedantry caused him
to write his first very mediocre play " Der junge Gelehrte.''

Lessing left Leipzig, with the idea of seeking wider
scope for his own development, and went to Berlin, where
Frederick II. at last persuaded Voltaire to visit him.
Lessing obtained an introduction to Voltaire, and the
veteran of brilliant reputation frequently invited the young
man to visit him, and advised him freely on literary style
and matter. The rupture came after a time, as with the
majority of Voltaire's friends. He had shown the MS.
of " Le Siècle de Louis XIV." to Lessing, and Lessing
allowed others to see it. Voltaire taxed him with dishonest motives, and the two parted with considerable
ill-feeling.

Meanwhile Lessing was writing with great application.
His early plays, after the " Junge Gelehrte," were : " Der
Misogyn," and " Der Freigeist," where the freethinker is
brought to change his views by a very upright and straight-
forward theologian. The " Jude " preaches that religious
toleration which was afterwards to find its full expression
in his masterpiece " Nathan der Weise," and censures the
cruel prejudices entertained by Christians against the Jews.

One of Lessing's friends, Moses Mendelssohn, was a very
noble and broad-minded man, and showed the best side of

the Jewish intellect and character. This friendship no doubt confirmed him in his tolerant views.

Lessing felt that an attempt to depart from the stereo-typed tragedy of historical character, and the introduction of a more familiar element, the tragedy or the comedy of daily life in the middle classes, would be likely to meet with success. This, as possessing the larger proportion of interest for the every-day spectator, was greeted with enthusiasm, and Lessing made his first essay at this "bürgerliche" tragedy in his somewhat painful play,

Miss Sara Sampson. The actors bear English names, though that is their only claim to distinctively English character, and the plot is founded on the novel "Clarissa Harlowe." The hero has deserted his first love for the sake of the unhappy "Miss Sara Sampson." The deserted woman threatens to kill herself and her child, but in reality kills her rival; and the whole story is a mournful tragedy without the grandeur of one noble action to relieve its gloom.

In 1755 Lessing returned to Leipzig, the theatre there being superior to the theatre in Berlin, and after the end of the Seven Years' War (1756-1763), he wrote the first of his three dramatic masterpieces,

Minna von Barnhelm (1767). The time for the publica-tion of this comedy was wholly favourable. The Seven Years' War was at an end, but military life and fortune occupied all minds. Saxony had been conquered, and Frederick the Great was again triumphant, but many of the officers who had served under him were rich in the memory of their brave deeds alone, for the king's ex-chequer was exhausted. Lessing's idea was to produce a national military drama—right from the heart of daily life as it were—a play which should be a tribute to the valour and honour of the Prussian officer, and should also in a manner typify the ultimate friendly relations of

Prussia and Saxony, by the marriage of a Prussian major with a Saxon lady. The hero, Major von Tellheim, a noble, generous man, experiencing the reverses of fortune, and reaping only ingratitude for having risked his life for his country, had before the close of the war become betrothed to the heroine, a young Saxon lady of great fortune, Minna von Barnhelm. Discharged from the army, and in distress for money, he thinks himself no longer worthy of her ; but she, knowing the disinterestedness and modesty of his character, comes to Berlin to find him, and insists on preventing him from sacrificing himself. Her maid, Franziska, and his "Wachtmeister," Paul Werner, are two delightful characters ; Franziska, with her unfailing repartee and quickness of comprehension, contrasting with the slow and honest Paul, who would lay down his life for his major. The king in the end rights Tellheim's wrongs, and the close of the play, with its two pairs of lovers happy, is in every way satisfactory. "Minna von Barnhelm" was the first national comedy performed on the German stage, and was a brilliant success.

The second of Lessing's greater plays, recognised by Goethe himself as the first great German tragedy, is

Emilia Galotti (1772), a tragedy intended as a lively protest against the tyranny of princes. Lessing's prince is represented as ruling over a small Italian state, a man dabbling in art and literature, not in himself especially tyrannical or vicious, but accustomed to deny himself nothing, whether allowable or not, and wholly guided and influenced by a most villainous favourite, the chamberlain Marinelli. The Prince sees Emilia Galotti, who is the affianced bride of a brave soldier, Count Appiani, falls in love with her, and determines, on the advice of his evil counsellor, to prevent the marriage. Then the plot unfolds itself on the lines of the history of the Roman maiden, Virginia. Emilia's father, in order to save her from the prince's power, plunges his sword into his daughter's heart, and in response to his wild cry as he sees her fall, " Gott, was hab' ich gethan," she answers,

"Eine Rose gebrochen, ehe der Sturm sie entblättert.
Lassen Sie mich sie küssen, diese väterliche Hand."

Nathan der Weise, Lessing's third and greatest dramatic masterpiece, was published in 1779. If in "Minna von Barnhelm" and "Emilia Galotti" we admire the unalterable beauty of diction, the purity of taste in words, which is one of Lessing's most salient points, we find in "Nathan," the culminating perfection of this wonderful mastery of language in the faultless five-footed iambic verse, here first introduced into the German drama and destined to a noble future.

The clearness and force, the directness and elegance, which mark Lessing's writings above all others, are the more remarkable because by no means common in German —even in writers of great genius. It is probable that his early association with Voltaire, who, faulty as he often is in subject-matter, has an almost perfect style of his own, may have contributed towards this high excellence in Lessing. However that may be, his readers can only be thankful that he attained it, from whatever source it came.

There is no doubt that "Nathan" cost its author more thought and more serious effort than his other plays. It is the gravest and the most uniformly elevated in style. Its centre-point and leading idea is that religious toleration which Lessing—sometimes with unchristian bitterness— had always striven to inculcate; but the setting is in itself picturesque and interesting, the glamour of that noble theme of song, the Crusades, lies over it, and a great historic hero, Saladin, is one of the actors. In Nathan, Lessing portrayed his friend Moses Mendelssohn, and he neglected nothing which could give worth and dignity to the character of the noble Jew.

Nathan, surnamed among his people the Wise, is a merchant possessing great wealth, and living at Jerusalem with his adopted daughter, Recha, and her nurse, Daja. He has gone on a journey; during his absence a fire consumes his house, and Recha would have perished had she not been rescued by a Knight Templar, who saves her from the flames and disappears from sight, but not from the memory of the maiden. The Jew returns, and is summoned before Saladin, who is in need of money and accepts a loan from him; and in this scene the story of the " Three Rings," beginning, "Vor grauen Jahren lebt' ein Mann im Osten," which is the keynote of the whole piece, is told by Nathan to the Sultan.

Lessing did not invent the story himself. Boccaccio tells nearly the same tale of Saladin, and in the eleventh century it was attributed to a Spanish king.

Saladin in Lessing's play, asks which is the preferable of the three religions, Mohammedanism, Judaism, or Christianity? And Nathan in reply tells his story:

There was once a man who possessed a ring, which had the secret property of making its wearer agreeable to God and man.

This ring passed on through generations, from father to best-loved son, until its possessor for the time was the father of three sons, whom he loved equally. He would not exalt one above the two others, and therefore before his death he caused two other rings to be made, so exactly similar to the original that they could not be distinguished from it. Then he died, the three sons were each in possession of a ring, and each claimed that his was the original. The sons appealed to a judge who heard their claims, and pronounced judgment. Their father, he said, had proved that he loved them equally by giving them each a ring. If the real ring possessed the property of making him, who wore it with that intention, agreeable to God and man, let each prove the genuineness of his ring by the fulfilment of the purpose of the giver—let him prove himself agreeable to God and man—and, after thousands of years, a wiser judge would pronounce the final sentence on the relative merits of the three.

Saladin was struck with the story, and treated Nathan with high honour. Meanwhile Recha, nursing her enthusiastic admiration of the Templar, whom she at first believes to be an angel in human form, and who loves her in secret, is proved to be the daughter of a Christian ; and the Patriarch—a caricature of Lessing's bitter opponent Göze, an orthodox pastor—interferes to take her away from her adopted father. In the end, it is discovered that she and the Templar are brother and sister, and the children of Saladin's younger brother, who had married a Frankish lady and disappeared years ago.

The minor characters in the play are drawn with great skill. There is a dervish of wild and lawless temperament, who can bear the utmost destitution of poverty, but not the slightest restraint; a timid "Klosterbruder," the cowardly, almost dishonest Christian nurse, Daja, and the Patriarch, who has all the characteristics of a Grand Inquisitor. The fault of the detail of the play—from the standpoint of justice—is the inferiority of the Christians as compared with Saladin, his sister Sittah, and Nathan. Lessing fell into an error, too common in writers who cry out against intolerance among Christians—they are themselves intolerant of the Christians. That, however, does not interfere with the artistic value of a great literary masterpiece.

Side by side with the drama, Lessing had done excellent work in other fields of literature. As a critic, his unfailing accuracy of judgment, keenness, and breadth of view, and perfect literary taste, entitle him to the very highest rank. Lessing is indeed the real founder of æsthetic criticism in Germany, and Macaulay has justly called him "the first critic of Europe." The æsthetic writings couched in his clear language and full of his irrefutable arguments are worthy of all praise. Such are the essays:

Wie die Alten den Tod gebildet, a wonderfully keen and intelligent criticism of classic art, and the deservedly celebrated "Laokoon," in which Lessing established principles until then unthought of in Germany. The

Laokoon was called into being by the work of Winckelmann, a talented writer on art. Lessing, always inclined to controversy, in which his unrivalled critical faculty invariably allowed him to shine, combated many of the principles laid down by Winckelmann. Then, starting from the criticism of the celebrated Laokoon group in statuary, where he describes and explains every contortion of the writhing figure, and every line in the martyred brow—the "Sitz des Ausdrucks," as he styles it—he proceeds from plastic to poetic art, and lays down the most excellent rules for epic poetry. He insists on the avoidance of long descriptions, enumeration of qualities, and attractions, pointing out the superiority of Homer over Virgil in that particular, and, as a general principle, the preferability of action to mere words. The "Laokoon" is worthy of a high place not only for its style, but also for the value and soundness of its artistic teaching.

Lessing's versatile genius found manifold expression. We may mention

Fabeln und Sinngedichte, almost epigrammatical in their conciseness,

Anmerkungen über das Epigramm,

Briefe antiquarishen Inhalts, and the

Hamburgische Dramaturgie.

Lessing's life, as far as worldly success is concerned, was

by no means fortunate. The remembrance of his early quarrel with Voltaire, which was almost all the king could be persuaded to know of Lessing, prevented Frederick II. from sanctioning his appointment as librarian in Berlin. Lessing went to Hamburg, attempted there to reform the theatre, and published periodically the "Hamburgische Dramaturgie." The enterprise failed, most likely for want of money, but what was written of the "Dramaturgie" was of the highest excellence. It was an "Art of the Drama," calculated to extinguish the false ideas then prevailing; it pointed out the serious defects of the French school, and their wrong interpretation of Aristotle's "Three Unities," insisted on the paramount necessity of action, and set up as models Sophocles and Shakespeare. Lessing's reform of the drama had begun with Miss Sara Sampson. In the "Dramaturgie" he produced a masterpiece of criticism, and the most important work on poetry of the eighteenth century.

After leaving Hamburg Lessing was at last made librarian at Wolfenbüttel (Brunswick). Here the least praiseworthy part of his literary work was accomplished in his bitter controversial writings against Pastor Göze, and the strictly dogmatical party. He had lately lost his wife and infant child, and his grief may have embittered his thought and warped his judgment. The controversy was stopped officially, and Lessing wrote as a noble expression of his views, "Nathan der Weise." Three years after, in 1781, he died.

It is fitting to mention here besides *Moses Mendelssohn* (died 1786), author of "Phädon oder über die Unsterblichkeit der Seele," Lessing's other friend,

Nicolai, died 1811, one of the principal agents in the German revival of letters. He published chiefly in the "Allgemeine deutsche Bibliothek," and wrote a novel, "Magister Sebaldus Nothanker."

CHAPTER IX.

THE period was full of new awakening. The glory of the Second Golden Age of German Literature shone in multifarious lustre, every branch of study, every field of thought, found its respective workers, and among those who opened up new paths, disseminated new ideas in other minds and scattered everywhere fruitful seed, was

Johann Gottfried Herder.—He was born in East Prussia in 1744, and died at Weimar in 1803. Educated for the Church, he hoped through his calling to influence the great, and make himself a lasting reputation. He was full of ambition, of high aims and great thoughts, but a certain incapability of finishing the work in hand, haunted him, and prevented the realization of his greatest plans, possibly on account of their vast scope and difficulty of fulfilment, for his central idea, throughout his varied work, was the progress of the human into harmony with the divine. Herder's genius as a linguist and as a translator has never been surpassed. He possessed the rare talent of grasping the inner meaning of foreign song—of putting himself in the place of the writer, of seeing with his eyes. He studied with wonderful perseverance the sources of the most diverse kinds of poetry. His splendid linguistic talent opened to him an unexplored mine of rich treasure; he reproduced not the words alone, but the living spirit of

Hebrew, Greek, Italian, Spanish, French, English folk-lore
and song, as well as the songs and legends of the less
cultured peoples of other parts of the world. He admired
Ossian, translated the Norse Edda, and interpreted Old
German poetry anew. An assemblage of these varied
elements is contained in his
Stimmen der Völker in Liedern, and in the same groove
of study he wrote
Vom Geiste der hebräischen Poesie.
Prior to these in date, Herder's important works were
Fragmente zur deutschen Litteratur (1767), and
Kritische Wälder (1769), the latter bearing in many re-
spects a resemblance to Lessing's " Laokoon." In his
Blätter von deutscher Art und Kunst, he eulogized Shake-
speare and Ossian ; and he appeared as an apostle of ortho-
doxy, as the defender of Revelation and the priesthood, in
Die älteste Urkunde der Menschheit, and in
*Auch eine Philosophie der Geschichte zur Bildung der
Menschheit.*
From 1784 to 1791 his longer work, which, like most of
his more voluminous writings, remained unfinished,
Ideen zur Philosophie der Geschichte der Menschheit, was
published. Herder brought to bear on it a wonderful power of
imaginative description, and vast stores of knowledge. One
of his leading ideas is the survival of right among humanity.
The right lives, the wrong dies. He overflows with admiration for the civilization and culture of the Greeks, but the
work breaks off when it reaches mediæval times. The
Briefe zur Beförderung der Humanität contain portraits of
great historical characters, whom Herder holds up as types
and models of virtue. Among others, he draws a striking
picture of the genius of Frederick the Great.
Herder wrote also " Legenden," a subject long neglected
in Germany.
In his poetical work *Der Cid* (1801), he germanized

Spanish Romances. According to R. Köhler, the greater part of "Der Cid" is imitated from a French prose text.

In summing up Herder's work and influence, it may be said that his labours in the study of language were the most extensive and the most fruitful. An essay written in the earlier period of his career, to which a prize was awarded, in 1772, by the Berlin Academy,

Über den Ursprung der Sprache, opened an entirely new course of study, and gave ideas by which the philologians of to-day profit. He recognised in its full significance the intimate connection between language and thought, and, going back to the origin of literature, found the antiquity of poetry to be greater than that of prose. Hence his wonderful collection of songs of all nations, and the importance he ascribed to poetry as the "mother-tongue of the human race."

For many years Herder filled the office of General-Superintendent (of the clergy) in Weimar, and it was there that he became intimately associated with Goethe, who learnt much from him. It is in Weimar that he lies buried with the inscription on his tomb, "Licht, Liebe, Leben."

Among Herder's friends in early life, one from whom he drew many of his poetical ideas, was the talented but rather obscure writer called the "Magus des Nordens,"

Johann Georg Hamann (1730-1788), who was a native of Königsberg, and wrote

Sokratische Denkwürdigkeiten.

Hamann gloried in the abasement of human reason, human logic, before the mysteries of life and death, which no philosophy can explain. He placed poetry before science, and maintained that faith is better than knowledge, since knowledge is necessarily limited by the limits of human intelligence. He it was who called poetry the "Muttersprache des menschlichen Geschlechts," and Herder followed in his steps when he wrote the "Litteraturbriefe" and "Über den Ursprung der Sprache."

Hamann, and *Lavater* (died 1801), the author of "Physiognomische Fragmente"—"Physiognomik," was a whimsical system of face-reading,—may be classed among the representative writers of the so-called

Sturm und Drang ("Storm and Stress") group, styled by Lewes the "Stormsters." The name was given to those writers who pinned their faith to originality above all things, and to genius, with its eccentricities. They were revolutionary in literature and in politics, and intolerant of all barriers. They "stormed" through life, hence the name which, originally the title of a play by Maximilian Klinger, came to be distinctive of the writers themselves, who were called "Stürmer und Dränger." The models which they followed with more or less fidelity were Shakespeare, old Germanic poetry, the Volkslied, Ossian,— or, more correctly, the pretended Ossian written by Macpherson,—and a work received at its publication with great enthusiasm in Germany, "Bishop Percy's Reliques," that excellent collection of old ballads which was, indeed, an acquisition to all literature. Herder, when writing with the fervour which sometimes distinguished him, was classed among the Stürmer und Dränger. Goethe, when he wrote "Götz von Berlichingen," was one of them, as also Schiller at the time of his writing the "Räuber." Goethe, in later life, repudiated his literary past, and Schiller also quieted down after the violent "fermentation period" of his youth. "Stürmer und Dränger" in all their works are:

Jacob Reinhold Lenz (1751-1792), who possessed undoubted genius, tainted by the insanity in which his life ended. He was for a time at the Court in Weimar with Goethe, but his culpable foolishness in writing a pasquinade on the Duchess Amalia, of which his incipient mental malady was the cause, compelled him to leave it. Lenz wrote

touching lyrics, but in his dramatic attempts, such as
" Der Hofmeister " and " Die Soldaten," the most extravagant ideas run riot, relieved by occasional excellence
of character-drawing.

Maximilian Klinger (1752-1831) wrote wild and inflated
plays, such as " Sturm und Drang,"—which, although it
gave the name to the whole period, is inferior to " Die
Zwillinge," his best work—" Der Schwur " and " Die
falschen Spieler," which are filled with declamatory hatred
of tyranny, and treated again the popular theme: " Fausts
Leben, Thaten und Höllenfahrt."

Friedrich Müller (1749-1825), called " Maler " Müller,
for he was a painter as well as a poet, wrote another
" Faust," and " Golo und Genovefa," in which the horrible
is fully depicted. His other works are " Niobe," " Idyllen,"
and " Soldatenabschied " (" The Soldier's Farewell ").

One of the impassioned enemies of tyranny under whose
influence Schiller fell in his early days was the poet and
musician,

Daniel Friedrich Schubart (1739-1791). He was a
typical Stürmer und Dränger. His

Fürstengruft (" Sepulchre of Princes ") was a stormy
invective against royal tyranny, and full of bitter reproaches
of the crimes of rulers. Some of Schubart's songs are good.
He admired Frederick the Great, in whose honour he wrote
" Hymnus auf Friedrich den Grossen." One of his best
known works was " Der ewige Jude "—the Wandering Jew
of the oft-treated legend.

With the foregoing poets must be classed Goethe and
Schiller in their youth. Both were animated by the aims
and aspirations of the revolutionaries in literature and
politics, and this phase of their development was embodied
in their early writings, which shall be mentioned here
before the account of their later works, to be given in the
two following chapters.

Johann Wolfgang Goethe

was born at Frankfort-on-the-Main August 28th, 1749 ;
died March 22nd, 1832, at Weimar. He was intended by
his father for the law. The father, a grave, perhaps commonplace man, had not the lively sympathy for his gifted
son which the mother felt. It was to his mother that
Goethe owed the training of his imagination, and the
charm of bright companionship. Shakespeare early became his idol. In 1773, when twenty-four years of age,
he made himself famous by the publication of his first play,
Götz von Berlichingen, written with Shakespearian freedom from dramatic rules, and in the revolutionary spirit
of the rising generation. The "Götz" of history, "der
Ritter mit der eisernen Hand," was probably more of a
freebooting noble than a champion of ideal liberty ; Goethe,
however, makes him a defender of the oppressed, and the
victim of cruel tyranny, and draws a vivid picture of the
lawlessness of the German princes, and of the inability of
the emperor to cope with the disturbances of his realm.

Götz is a model husband and father, a hero of somewhat
rough stamp, but of noble if rugged nature, contrasting
with the polished effeminacy of the weak and treacherous
Weislingen, who had formerly been his friend. An attempt
to quell a rising of the peasantry is construed into an
attempt at insurrection on his part, and he dies while
imprisoned, murmuring " Freiheit ! "

A storm of applause greeted the play. It is the anti-
podes of Goethe's later style, drastic, coarse in its original
editions, but in many parts true to nature, as was Shakespeare, the great master, whose leadership he followed,
and it appealed to—for it was the outcome of—the spirit
of the times.

Clavigo was published in 1774. It is the story of the
infidelity of a lover to his betrothed—adapted from a

subject of Beaumarchais'—and earlier in the same year appeared

Die Leiden des jungen Werther—the "Sorrows of Young Werther"—formerly so much beloved by the admirers of the sentimental style in literature. The book, written in a series of letters by the hero, Werther, is false in morality and sentiment, but possesses great and remarkable beauties. The descriptions of nature are among the finest Goethe ever penned. The motive of the tale is the suicide of the young Jerusalem, which had just occurred at Wetzlar, blended with the story of his own love for Charlotte Buff. But with that discretion which is undoubtedly, in such a case, the better part of valour, Goethe refrained from the decisive pistol-shot by which his hero ended his moaning, and as an alternative wrote the history of his sorrows.

Werther loves Charlotte. She is already betrothed to Albert, and in due course marries him. Werther tries to tear himself away from the scene of his unhappy love, tries to feel friendship only for the wife of his friend, but the effort is beyond his strength. He determines on suicide. Under the pretext of starting on a journey, he sends to borrow Albert's pistols, reflecting as he does so that Charlotte will take them down and dust them before sending them to him, and with these desirably-dusted weapons he shoots himself, after much deliberation and attention to accessories.

The affectation of the book, its mawkish sentimentality and unmanly weakness are apparent enough to us now, but at the time of its publication it created a *fureur*, and exercised an incredible, and, we must add, baneful influence. A principal reason of this was that it was a work of genius —unmistakable, though misapplied.

Goethe himself mocked his own "Werther" in after life. It had served his purpose; by writing the story of his unfortunate affection he had cured himself of it.

" Götz " and " Werther " are his two principal works of the " Sturm und Drang " period.

The other great dramatist of Germany,

Johann Christoph Friedrich von Schiller,

born November 10th, 1759, at Marbach, died May 9th, 1805, at Weimar, was in a greater degree than Goethe driven to revolutionary ideas, by his early experience of petty tyranny in his native Würtemberg. He was an army-surgeon in Stuttgart, and to avoid imprisonment without trial fled from the territory of the duke, whose anger was excited by Schiller's poetical work.

In 1781 Schiller's first play,

Die Räuber, was published, bearing a lion on the title-page and the inscription, " In tyrannos." The whole play was the cry of the oppressed against the oppressor, of the victim of social order against social order, and, with the immaturity of youthful judgment, the good is dashed away with the bad, and the just and the unjust are united in one sweeping condemnation.

The hero, Karl Moor, becomes the chief of a band of robbers. He is driven to this by a diabolically wicked brother Franz, who ousts him from his father's house and from his father's love, then attempts to kill the father and win the affections of Karl's betrothed, the indifferently drawn heroine, Amalia. The father dies, a victim of the abominable cruelty of Franz. Karl stabs Amalia. Franz, in abject terror at the retribution threatening his heavily-laden soul, puts an end to his own life, so that the sequel is wholly tragic. Karl Moor, with a price of a thousand Louis d'or on his head, goes to put himself in the power of a starving workman with the words, " Dem Mann kann geholfen werden."

This heroic robber, Karl Moor—the type of a noble

youth driven by injustice to wrong-doing—cries out against the state of his country, and openly calls for a republic. Some scenes in the play are coarse and repellent, the whole is exaggerated and crude; but Schiller's dramatic genius made itself felt from the first. He may shock, but he never wearies.

The poet's absence without leave in order to be present at the first performance of "Die Räuber" at Mannheim in 1782, was the climax of his offences in the Duke's eyes, and the immediate cause of his flight from Würtemberg territory.

Schiller produced another tragedy in 1783, *Fiesco*, the story of a brilliant conspiracy against tyrannical power in Genoa. Again the hero is endowed with the ideal beauty of character and nobility of purpose which distinguished all Schiller's heroes, again the horrors of despotic power are depicted with a powerful hand.

"Fiesco" was followed the next year by *Kabale und Liebe*, a tragedy in which the abuses of the petty German courts were handled mercilessly. President von Walter, the unscrupulous minister of the prince, and his villainous secretary, together with an unprincipled favourite, Lady Milford, unite against and cause the ruin of the hero and heroine—the son of the minister, and a "Bürgermädchen," Luise Miller.

In addition to the ignoble court intrigues, another abuse censured here is the "Soldatenhandel"—the traffic in soldiers, by which bands of unfortunate young men were drafted off by their prince to serve in foreign armies—simply sold as slaves, and slaves whose duty was to fight, and shed their blood for strangers.

These three tragedies were the principal products of Schiller's "Sturm und Drang" period. The ideal of liberty, chastened and refined, and rather poetic than practical, remained the constant inspiration of Schiller's works;

but the crudities and exaggerations were softened away, and only the imaginings of a pure and noble soul, tried by suffering, struggling against petty domestic cares, but filled with the worship of a beauty for which reality was too low, lived on in Schiller's unchangeable and sublime idealism.

CHAPTER X.

THE name of Goethe is one of the few enrolled in the first rank of the poets of all nations, those poets who have given to the world works which will endure while language lasts. It is not by any means in all his writings that he has attained this pre-eminent rank. Among his voluminous works there is much which posterity has already ceased to value; much which was forced, written with divided heart, without spontaneity, or under the influence of a passing style. But though his genius may occasionally be obscured, it is never wholly hidden, and it bursts forth at times with dazzling splendour and almost overwhelming force. No one will deny to the first part of "Faust" its place among the masterpieces of all ages.

A comparison between the two men, Goethe and Schiller, as *men*, certainly shows Schiller the purer, the nobler. A comparison between them as *poets* gives the higher place to Goethe. Schiller, in his essay "Über naive und sentimentalische Dichtung," says: "Der Dichter *ist* entweder Natur, oder er wird sie suchen. Jenes macht den naiven, dieses den sentimentalischen Dichter." In his own opinion he himself is the "sentimental poet," Goethe the "naïve poet," therefore nature itself, while Schiller only seeks nature. This distinction, which establishes Goethe's superiority as a writer, accounts, perhaps, for Schiller's greater moral worth. Schiller was in many ways above the failings of humanity, an ascetic and an idealist; Goethe was a man of the world, a realist swayed by many passions, with a belief in the sanctifying power of labour indeed, but otherwise with no very earnest faith. It was not without cause that Heine called him "der grosse Heide."

It was inevitable that such a man should pass through many phases. There was first the fermentation of the "Sturm und Drang," the first fruits of his youth, on which we have touched. Then the healing of his love for Charlotte Buff (the heroine of "Werthers Leiden"), his desertion of Friederike Brion, the daughter of the pastor of Sesenheim, which, though devoid of the actively tragic element in "Faust," gave the foundation to his Gretchen tragedy—the finest of all his creations ; then his summons to Weimar by the young Duke Karl August, and the beginning of a new epoch.

The court of Weimar had a great literary past. The patronage of letters was a tradition among its rulers. Left a widow with a young son, whose inheritance was precarious in unsettled times, the Duchess Amalia did her utmost for the well-being and the culture of her court. Wieland and Herder were both summoned to Weimar, and, finally, when the young Duke Karl August had assumed the government, the author of "Götz" and the celebrated "Werther," was invited to his court as a guest.

During the early part of his stay in Weimar, Goethe behaved like a student in holiday time, and Karl August followed his lead. This came to an end, however. The duke's affection for, and confidence in, Goethe increased rapidly. He appointed him to one office after another, and responsibility brings wisdom. It was at this time that he formed his enthusiastic friendship for Frau von Stein, a friendship which was the principal influence in his life

for several years, and which had the effect of quieting his
boisterous passions, and teaching the ungoverned youth the
dignity befitting the man.

An interval elapsed before another drama appeared from
Goethe's pen. He was still writing, but in a more or less
desultory way, for, as minister of state, even in so small a
princedom as Weimar, he lacked full leisure for the completion of great poems. Two minor plays, " Clavigo," already
mentioned, and " Stella," had succeeded " Götz." In 1782
appeared the poem " Das Göttliche," beginning : " Edel sei
der Mensch, hilfreich und gut " ; and " Prometheus," first
intended for a drama, then compressed into a monologue,
had been published earlier. The plots of "Egmont" and
" Faust " had been roughly sketched soon after " Götz,"
but not until about the time of Goethe's return from his
long-wished-for journey in Italy (1786-1788) did the
former appear. A romanticism, which Goethe afterwards
abandoned, was still visible in

Egmont. The struggle of the heroic central figure of
the play against a relentless despotism and bigotry—personified in Alba—with which he is wholly unable to cope,
the touching picture of Clärchen, with her great love for
Egmont, have a warm human interest which cannot fail of
its effect. Goethe's Egmont is not the Egmont of history.
Goethe's Egmont is unmarried, high-minded, patriotic, but
rash and childish in his unconquerable optimism. We see
the influence of Shakespeare in the Brussels mob—in their
criticisms of passing events, and in their unwillingness to
incur danger in an attempt to rescue the man who had
been their idol. Clärchen tries to incite them to demand
Egmont's release. She fails, and drinks poison not to
survive her lover. Egmont dies, but the vision of Clärchen
awaiting him takes away the bitterness of death. Clärchen
bears a strong resemblance to Gretchen in " Faust " in her
perfect love for, and trust in her lover, as a being of a

G

higher order, whose condescension makes her paradise. Her love-song is a perfect little poem:

> "Freudvoll
> Und leidvoll,
> Gedankenvoll sein;
> Hangen
> Und bangen
> In schwebender Pein;
> Himmelhoch jauchzend,
> Zum Tode betrübt;
> Glücklich allein
> Ist die Seele, die liebt."

But Goethe had been learning in Weimar, and continued to learn in Italy, a far severer style in drama. He now was a convert to the most austere classicism, and the perfection of artistic beauty was seen when he published *Iphigenie* in 1787. This was the first of his dramas in iambic verse, and is faultless in its calm grandeur and smooth versification. It is a drama of atonement and reconciliation, ending in the peaceful return of Iphigenie, Orestes, and Pylades to that land of Greece which Iphigenie had "sought with her soul"—in the words of the poem, "Das Land der Griechen mit der Seele suchend." The Furies cease to trouble Orestes, all ends in harmony and peace.

There are no sharp contrasts in the play; Thoas, King of Tauris, is not drawn as a barbarous tyrant. He had wished to make Iphigenie his wife, and when the whole truth is told him—for Iphigenie is incapable of subterfuge, and fails utterly when she attempts it—he allows her and her companions to depart unmolested. It was said of the play that it was *not* Greek, "it only wore a Greek garb," and that is in a measure true, for Iphigenie is acknowledged to be Frau von Stein, and the Furies tormenting Orestes are the passions which she calmed in Goethe's breast. But Goethe had nevertheless returned to the noble simplicity of the Greeks, and the poem is worthy of its subject.

Suited for scenic representation it certainly is not, the want of action and the length of the speeches render it unfit, but apart from that, as a work of poetic art, " Iphigenie " is a pure and noble harmony.

After " Iphigenie " came

Torquato Tasso, published in 1790, still showing the influence of Frau von Stein.

Tasso is at the court of Ferrara. The Prince, Alfonso, shows him the greatest consideration and affection. The noble lady who inspires in him an enthusiastic passion is the Princess Leonore. Tasso finishes the " Gerusalemme Liberata," and she sets on his brow the laurel-crown. Then the secretary of state, Antonio, arrives at the court, and an innate antipathy comes to expression between Antonio, the realist, and Tasso, the idealist. They fight within the precincts of the palace. Then Tasso, to complete his disgrace, in a moment of wild rapture dares to declare his love to the princess. His banishment from Ferrara is the result, and his agony is terrible. Yet he has one consolation in his misery—he has the power of expressing it:

> " Und wenn der Mensch in seiner Qual verstummt,
> Gab mir ein Gott, zu sagen, wie ich leide ! "

Goethe's contemporaries again furnished him with models: Alfonso, the patron of the arts, is, of course, Karl August of Weimar, the princess once more Frau von Stein, Tasso partly, but not wholly the unfortunate poet Lenz, already growing insane, who, as has been said, came to Weimar and had to be expelled from court, Antonio in some degree Goethe himself, as minister of state. The lifelike reproduction, side by side, of two characters so entirely dissimilar as Tasso and Antonio, is the highest possible art, and the excellence of " Tasso " is above criticism.

Unfortunately the poet's dramatic work now came to a standstill again. He occupied himself in scientific study,

and gave utterance to great thoughts in his writings, but
he had neither the mathematical training nor the bent of
mind to do work of the highest order in scientific research.
He was wasting his time, for the poet is not successful as a
man of science.   His

Metamorphose der Pflanzen, 1790, a harbinger of the
Darwinian theory of evolution, and the

Farbenlehre, a treatise on colour, published years later,
may be named.

In 1790 a fragment of "Faust" appeared.

In 1791 Goethe assumed the management of the theatre
in Weimar.   In 1794 he published his new version of the
old satirical "Tierepos,"

Reineke Fuchs, written in hexameters, and in 1795, the
novel,

Wilhelm Meister's Lehrjahre.   The hero is desirous of
becoming an actor contrary to his father's wishes.   He
joins a company of players, fills at last the *rôle* of Hamlet,
then discovers that his supposed vocation was a mis-
take, abandons the stage and forms a close connection
with a nobleman.   The end is hurried.   Goethe had tired
of the work and wished to get it off his hands at any
price.   The sequel,

Wilhelm Meister's Wanderjahre, did not appear until
1821, eleven years before Goethe's death, and is not equal
to the earlier work.   Its main idea is that of renunciation of
one's own aims and affections, and it is rich in knowledge
and experience, but the episodes are wanting in the cohesion
necessary to a novel as a whole.   The "Lehrjahre" possesses many beauties; extensive knowledge of the world
and of human character is shown in it; the bohemianism
of the actors is true to life, and the mysterious figures of
the Harper and Mignon introduce a touch of the deepest
tragic poetry.   Mignon's homeless life and pathetic love,
her beautiful song, "Kennst du das Land," with its refrain

—" Dahin ! dahin ! möcht' ich mit dir, o mein Geliebter, ziehn ! "—will be remembered even if the remainder of the book should be forgotten.

In 1790 Goethe had finished his

Römische Elegien, in which another phase breaks the dignified calm of the " Iphigenie " and " Tasso " period. The intellectual and high-minded Frau von Stein had ceased to occupy the highest place in his imagination, and he had formed an attachment to Christine Vulpius, the sister of Vulpius, the author of " Rinaldo Rinaldini," a tedious robber-tale.

She may or may not have been unworthy of Goethe—he married her years after, in 1806—but it is to his love for her that we owe the exquisite little lyric " Gefunden," beginning

" Ich ging im Walde so für mich hin."

The " Römische Elegien " show what we may term a return to nature, after the classic severity of the dramas in iambic verse. In 1796 appeared the first part of

Briefe aus der Schweiz, the record of Goethe's journeyings in Switzerland in 1779. The

Italienische Reise, which is the more celebrated of the two, and contains beside the record of his travels, reflections, descriptions, æsthetic criticism, human portraiture, the reproduction of his own thoughts and feelings—a work only capable of proceeding from such a mind as Goethe's— was not published until much later, the first volume in 1816, the second the following year.

Schiller, who held a professorship at the University of Jena, became intimately acquainted with Goethe in 1794. In 1799 he moved to Weimar. A friendship, the continuity of which remained unbroken till Schiller's death, sprang up between the two poets, and was in the highest degree beneficial to both. The two united were more than a match for all literary antagonists. Together they published the

Xenien, couplets in distichs, some harmlessly sarcastic, others bitterly satirical and capable of grievously wounding even the most thick-skinned victims. These "Xenien" were published in Schiller's periodical the "Musenalmanach," and they effectually silenced opposition to any undertaking or opinion of the poet-friends.

Hermann und Dorothea.—The great German idyllic epic, "Hermann und Dorothea," appeared in 1797. The simplicity of subject clothed in majestic hexameters, the perfect truth to nature of the unpretentious figures, the patriotic sentiment which touches the heart of every German, made and make it a highly valued poem. Goethe founded "Hermann und Dorothea" on an incident of the expulsion of a band of protestants from Salzburg in 1731, but he transplanted it into the present, the time of the French Revolution, for which his antipathy was marked. A band of German emigrants leave their homes beyond the Rhine, to save themselves from being harassed and pillaged by French troops. Among them is Dorothea, the heroine, an orphan and alone, but "hilfreich und gut" as Goethe wished mankind to be. In her is personified that "infinitely variable modesty of service" which Ruskin considers the crowning glory of woman. The emigrants pass by the little town where lives the host of the "Golden Lion," proud of his possessions and anxious to add to his prosperity and distinction by the advancement of his son, Hermann. Hermann is too diffident, too little given to boasting to satisfy his father, but his mother understands and sympathises with him. He has hitherto declined to choose a wife for himself, but at the sight of Dorothea—tending a sick woman—his mind is made up instantly. Sure of his mother's sympathy he tells her his decision, she obtains the father's consent, and—in a description of idyllic beauty

—he leads his bride home. However, Hermann's friends have previously acted with due caution; all necessary enquiries are made concerning Dorothea, there is no romantic slurring over of details, nor any wearisome enumeration of them; they explain themselves spontaneously in the action, after the grand model of Homer. The old German ideal of constancy reappears in the character of Hermann; he will not be driven out by foreign foe, but remain firm, defend his right, and die for his own.

Faust.—In 1808 Faust, Part I., was published at last. It is the finest achievement of Goethe's immortal genius. The story of Dr. Faustus had been told and retold in German, sometimes a miserable failure, sometimes with some approach to interest, but this was something else—it was the vivification of dry bones. It typified the final purification and apotheosis of the erring seeker after knowledge. All that was in Goethe of insight into human thought and action, all his vast store of knowledge of men and things, his one firm belief in the sanctifying power of labour, joined to the inspiration and tenderness of his youth, meet in his great work. The First Part has the merit of at least partial unity; though its composition stretched over a period of years, it was finished before age diminished the firmness of touch of the master-hand. The second Part, which was not completed until 1831, shortly before Goethe's death, contains many obscure passages which a host of commentators have attempted to explain without success, but the spirit which animated his work shines out brightly to the end—the redeeming virtue of work for the sake of humanity—not *prayer* without ceasing, but *labour* without ceasing. The plot may, perhaps, be shortly told here, but any superficial prose narration is of necessity inadequate to give the merest idea of the work itself.

With the boldness of the writers of the old religious

plays, Goethe placed his Prologue in Heaven. There
Mephistopheles receives from the Almighty the permission to try his servant Faust, but is at the same time
reminded—

> " Ein guter Mensch in seinem dunkeln Drange
> Ist sich des rechten Weges wohl bewufst."

In the first scene of the play Faust, having summoned and
failed to quell the spirits, wearied of the hopeless search
for knowledge, is in the act of putting an end to the vanity
of it all by a draught of poison, when the sound of the
Easter chimes, the Easter chant,

> "Christ ist erstanden,"

stays his hand. On Easter-day Mephistopheles comes to him,
appearing first in the form of a poodle, and the compact
between them is signed with a drop of blood, in accordance
with tradition ; Mephistopheles is to obey Faust until Faust,
satisfied at last, shall say to the passing moment—" Ver-
weile doch! Du bist so schön!" Then his service shall
cease, and the soul of Faust be forfeited. Having made
this compact, Mephistopheles takes Faust away from his
books to mix with men—" Die schlechteste Gesellschaft
läfst dich fühlen, dafs du ein Mensch mit Menschen bist."
They visit the rowdy students in Leipzig and afterwards
the Witch's kitchen, where Faust drinks the draught which
is to make him young again. Then the Gretchen tragedy
begins. Faust wins the girl's innocent love at once, but her
innate purity shrinks from Mephistopheles. She recognises evil instinctively, and with the simplicity of childlike
faith she questions Faust about his religion. But it is no
part of Mephistopheles' scheme that happiness should come
to Gretchen or to Faust. A sleeping-draught given her by
Faust for her mother is deadly poison. She is betrayed
and deserted. With the tenderest pathos Goethe shows
her agony of grief before the Mater Dolorosa:

" Ach neige,
Du Schmerzensreiche,
Dein Antlitz gnädig meiner Not ! "

Madness and death as the murderer of her child are to be her
fate. Meanwhile Mephistopheles has enticed Faust away
to the Witches' Carnival on the Brocken ; but a phantom of
Gretchen appears to him, he appeals to Mephistopheles to
provide means to save her. They enter the dungeon where
Gretchen lies in the last tragic scene. She is mad, but she
recognises her lover :

" O weh ! Deine Lippen sind kalt,
Sind stumm.
Wo ist dein Lieben
Geblieben ?
Wer brachte mich drum ? "

Still he cannot prevail on her to accompany him outside.
Then Mephistopheles becomes impatient, for the day is
breaking — he shows himself. Gretchen knows him at
once, cries out to God to save her, "Dein bin ich, Vater, rette
mich !" and tears herself away from Faust. A voice from
Heaven declares her saved, Mephistopheles drags Faust
away, and Gretchen's voice in the distance dies away :

" Heinrich ! Heinrich ! "

That ends the first part.

The *Second Part* contains the heterogeneous subject-
matter of the "Volksdrama" which no dramatic skill
could mould into a harmonious whole. Goethe displays
in it his stores of classic learning, and remains true at
least to the unity of the principal idea.

Faust and Mephistopheles are at the court of an Emperor,
to whom they give all kinds of assistance. Helen of Troy
is conjured from Hades, her beauty works on Faust as on
her lovers of old ; he swears to possess her.

Then follow scenes in which classic mythology plays
the greater part. Helen is brought to the world again

without memory of the past. 'A son is born to Faust and her, but the boy, impatient of the limitations of human existence, springs into space and vanishes. This boy—Euphorion— has been said to represent Lord Byron. The mother in despair follows her child, and Faust is alone again.

Then we see him once more at the emperor's court. In return for his services he receives from the emperor land to reclaim from the sea, to render fruitful for mankind. The good of humanity is now his sole aim and wish. He grows old and is struck blind, but his will remains as strong as ever. All his energies are set on draining the marshland whence pestiferous vapours infect the surrounding country. The sound of spades digging in the ground rejoices his heart—but it is not the work he has ordered— it is his grave that they are digging. In imagination he sees the good arising from the completion of this great work. If it were once finished, he says, he could bid the moment tarry; and as his mind dwells on the good to come, the happiness, the satisfaction which was to terminate his compact with the Evil One, fills his soul:

> "Im Vorgefühl von solchem hohen Glück
> Geniefs ich jetzt den höchsten Augenblick."

So the end has come—the bond to Mephistopheles is due, Faust falls back and dies. But angels driving back the evil spirits carry his soul away, with the words:

> "Wer immer strebend sich bemüht,
> Den können wir erlösen."

Gretchen, purified and redeemed, receives the spirit in heaven, and Faust, the seeker after truth, is saved, because he has worked and striven for the good of his fellow-men. So the trickster Mephistopheles, has lost his prey, and the "guter Mensch" has found the "rechten Weg" spoken of in the Prologue in Heaven. The innate nobility of soul has not deserted him through all his errors and temptations.

Nor does Mephistopheles, the indefatigable agitator in mischief, the common, vile jester, the low and slanderous spirit of gross passions, without enough grandeur to make him terrible, ever vary from his native baseness. The fallen archangel has no part in Mephistopheles; he is much more the comic devil of the old Mysteries, whose discomfiture was a subject of mirth. Perhaps a more thoroughly diabolic nature could not be conceived. No shadow of the despairing defiance of Milton's Satan is left to him; all sense of loss and shame has vanished from Mephistopheles, sorrow and sin, and the destruction of the higher nature are sport to him; not for one instant is he moved by other than the lowest and vilest impulses; the vain endeavour, the broken heart, the lost soul, are to him no more than a jest. Of Gretchen's sorrow and shame he only says: "Sie ist die erste nicht." Lower than Mephistopheles no spirit could fall.

The workmanship of the wonderful poem is very unequal. This could not be otherwise, for Goethe projected the play in early youth and completed it in old age. Scenes which he had schemed remained unwritten, so that the connection between the different episodes is, in many cases, left to the imagination, not only in the second but also, though less visibly, in the first part. The "Walpurgisnacht" scene was first left unfinished, then patched up with literary satire very much out of place in such connection. But, with all its imperfections of construction, Faust is a great and immortal work and the brightest glory of its author.

Die natürliche Tochter, a drama in five acts had been produced at the Weimar Theatre in 1803. Goethe intended it to form the first part of a trilogy, but the succeeding parts were never added, and the play, notwithstanding the grandeur and power of its eloquent language, failed to attain wide popularity.

Shortly after the completion of Part I. of "Faust" the novel *Die Wahlverwandtschaften*, the story of love which found the beloved object too late—ending in tragic death in one case, and in noble renunciation in the other—was published; and, 1811-1831,

Aus meinem Leben, Wahrheit und Dichtung, which is the author's autobiography from childhood, but extends only to the year 1775. The half-title," Dichtung," prepares us for idealism as well as plain fact, so that the incidents may sometimes be fairly considered to have received a certain poetic glamour in the telling. Like all Goethe's prose, these books are masterpieces of style.

Lyrics. The greatest Dramatist of Germany was also the greatest Lyric Poet. Numberless short poems are simply perfection, which one word more or less would spoil. Known to everyone are the "Erlkönig," "Der Sänger," "Der Fischer," "Des Schäfers Klagelied; " and "Wandrers Nachtlied," ("Über allen Gipfeln ist Ruh,") the peacefulness in deep sadness of the last being beyond praise.

It is impossible to enumerate here all the works of a writer so voluminous as Goethe, but the most celebrated have been touched on. It was on March 22nd, 1832, that the busy hand fell idle at last, and the far-seeing eye closed for ever. We know the cry, "Mehr Licht," which was among the last murmurs of the aged poet. May not the words addressed to his own creation, "Faust" have been uttered also to him :

> " Wer immer strebend sich bemüht,
> Den können wir erlösen ? "

The strife and the search after truth were over forever : he was laid to rest at Weimar, near his friend Schiller, who had preceded him to the tomb, in the prime of manhood, twenty-seven years before. The words were fulfilled at last which he had written to his own heart in earlier years :

> " Warte nur, balde
> Ruhest auch du."

CHAPTER XI.

In the square of Weimar they stand side by side, Goethe and Schiller, the two greatest poets of Germany; and, as symbolized in the bronze statue, they lived in the harmony of perfect friendship from 1779, when Schiller went to Weimar, till 1805, when death struck him down in the midst of his labours. The influence of the one was beneficial to the other: in many ways they represented different schools of thought, and the one was the complement of the other. Goethe was the realist, Schiller the idealist; but they never clashed, and the death of the younger man was a severe blow to Goethe.

Schiller's first fervour and heat of imagination had found vent in " Die Räuber," and in " Kabale und Liebe." He moderated his style, and the crudities of his first crusade against tyranny were refined away by a more perfected taste, but he remained the apostle of liberty till the last, and this is the mainspring of the power he exercises over his countrymen.

Don Carlos was the next tragedy, in polished iambic verse, full of noble thoughts in noble speech, but still a young man's work, and displeasing to the older and riper man, Goethe.

The titular hero—for the Marquis Posa is the actual hero—Don Carlos, son of Philip II. of Spain, has an unhappy attachment to his stepmother, Elisabeth of Valois, who had first been betrothed to him, before his father took her for his own bride.

This unfortunate passion is suspected, and the prince accused of treasonable designs, and in spite of the devotion of his friend, the Marquis Posa, one of those ideally perfect dreamers whom Schiller painted with such love—for he himself was of the same stamp—Carlos is ruined, and Posa dies for him in vain. They are both victims of the Inquisition, and the whole poem is a polemic against its cruel tyranny and the despotic power of the king; but the crude scene-painting of "Die Räuber" has disappeared, there is no exaggerated declamatory eloquence; Posa's harangues are long indeed, but his ideal of freedom and humane government for the persecuted Netherlands is just and right, though impractible by a Philip II. or an Alba. Elisabeth, in her difficult position, is dignified and calm without being callous. She pities Carlos, though she does not return his passion. If she could be swayed from her duty to her husband and to her own dignity, it would be by her admiration of Posa, not of Carlos. One glimpse only of this is shown us in the scene where, as he persists in the sacrifice of himself for the prince, she cries: "Ich schätze keinen Mann mehr!" and Posa—until then without regret in his self-abnegation—murmurs: "Das Leben ist doch schön!"

"Don Carlos" was published in 1787, the same year as "Iphigenie," and during the twelve succeeding years Schiller finished no drama. He began the

Geisterseher, but that was left uncompleted. Meanwhile he was seeking higher culture, learning to reverence new models, and perfecting his own productive faculty. Like Goethe, he studied the Greek drama. He was at this time Professor at Jena, and in 1794 became intimately associated with Goethe. In 1799 he removed to Weimar. The same year another dramatic work appeared at last, "Wallensteins

Lager," which was put on the stage at the Weimar Theatre, where, under Goethe's management, lasting from 1791 to 1817, Schiller's plays, except those of his earliest period, were acted one after the other.

Wallenstein. The short "Vorspiel," "Wallensteins Lager," is written with a truth to nature, and an insight into character more realistic than Schiller's usual manner. Though the period of the Thirty Years' War afforded him scope enough for the description of horrors he would have given unsparingly in his youth, he now avoids the exclusively dark view, and his comprehensive picture of the motley assemblage leaves, on the whole, a fresh and exhilarating impression of the soldiery. "Wallensteins Lager" gives a definite idea of the ascendency of the great general over the mind of his troops, of their implicit belief in him and his invincibility. The "erste Jäger" blames the Wachtmeister's attempted imitation of Wallenstein as a sort of sacrilege—

> "Wie er räuspert und wie er spuckt,
> Das habt ihr ihm glücklich abgeguckt;
> Aber sein Genie, ich meine sein Geist,
> Sich nicht auf der Wachparade weist."

The sermon preached by the Capuchin Friar is in the popular style of the celebrated preacher, Abraham a Santa Clara, and the whole picture of the camp is brilliantly finished. The most idealistic of the characters is the "Kürassier" of Pappenheim's regiment commanded by Max Piccolomini, who throws a poetic glamour over war and the soldier's life, and awakens the slumbering spirit of his brothers in arms with his stirring song:

> "Wohl auf Kameraden, aufs Pferd, aufs Pferd!"

—a song which, under the name of "Schillers Reiterlied" (Trooper's Song), has become a national favourite.

Die Piccolomini and *Wallensteins Tod.*—The real character of Wallenstein himself could inspire no warm sympathy in Schiller; he was able to judge the man on his merits, unblinded by prejudice. But, in order to arouse the necessary interest, he allows the circumstances in which he places the general, if not to justify his actions, at least to palliate his offences. His own aggrandisement is his one aim, and the devotion of a great army renders that aggrandisement temptingly easy. It has become so much a part of his nature as to be, to some extent, a fixed idea. The stars have foretold it, and his belief in astrology is as firm as the Mahometan's fatalism. In the unscrupulous furtherance of his aims—finally by treason to his master, the emperor—the Gräfin Terzky, his sister-in-law, is his evil counsellor. The lovers, Thekla, Wallenstein's daughter, and Max Piccolomini, are the two entirely single-minded and unworldly characters, not historical, but beautiful poetical conceptions. Both are dear to Wallenstein, both leave him at the last, the one to be trampled under the horses' feet, in a wild charge against the Swedes to vindicate his own honour, and prove his faith to his emperor, meeting thus, as Thekla says, "Das Loos des Schönen auf der Erde," the other, unable to face life when her lover is no more, to seek his grave and meet the death she feels is near.

There is a grand sorrow in Schiller's Wallenstein which cannot leave the reader unmoved. He betrays his emperor, but is himself betrayed by his generals, above all by Octavio Piccolomini, the father of Max, whom he trusted implicitly, and of Max's death he says: "Er ist der Glückliche. Er hat vollendet." The murder of Wallenstein is not actually represented on the stage, but described with such skill, that we realize it as vividly as though it took place before our eyes, and immediately after the perpetration of the deed, the body is borne across the stage. In the "Picco-

lomini " and " Wallensteins Tod " Schiller idealizes freely.
He allows his personages to utter long and majestic speeches,
sometimes with a sublimity of language to which he
alone could attain, and glories in his embellishment of
the reality. This, indeed, was Schiller's almost invariable
custom ;—idealization, rather than the natural reproduction
of everyday life, he considered to be the province of poetic
art.

Maria Stuart followed " Wallenstein " in 1800. Schiller,
while not extenuating the gravity of the crimes attributed to
the unfortunate queen, represents her as so intensely human,
so infinitely unhappy, that she wholly arouses the sympathy
claimed by a heroine of tragedy. The comparison with Elizabeth is all in Mary's favour. Vain, crafty, bitterly envious,
incapable of generous feeling, the Queen of England is
morally far below the Queen of Scots, though the latter is
acknowledged to have murdered her husband. Of idealized
characters, dear to Schiller's heart, there are none in " Maria
Stuart." Mary herself is purified by suffering; she rises
at last above things earthly to the abnegation of self, and
resigns herself to the sacrifice of her life, forfeited on an
unjust charge, as an expiation of the old crime of Darnley's
death, but she has been hitherto no ideally perfect character—she is a woman with more than all a woman's
failings. The minor characters are depicted with master
touches. Leicester, weak, indecisive, afraid to avow his
love for Mary, and giving her up for the more powerful
Elizabeth with a cowardice which renders him contemp-
tible ; Shrewsbury, honest, and abhorrent of Elizabeth's
double-dealing and cruelty; Mortimer, Paulet's nephew,
who — commissioned to murder Mary—is really blindly
devoted to her cause. One of the finest scenes is that in
the garden at Fotheringay, in the third act, where the imprisoned queen, intoxicated with the unwonted liberty of
the free air, speaks the well-known words :

> " Laſs mich der neuen Freiheit genieſsen,
> Laſs mich ein Kind sein, sei es mit,
> Und auf dem grünen Teppich der Wiesen
> Prüfen den leichten, geflügelten Schritt."

The—to Mary—unexpected appearance of Elizabeth brings about the catastrophe. The light and sunshine long denied her have filled the captive queen with a reckless disregard of consequences. She overwhelms her cousin with a storm of vituperation, humbles the proud queen in Leicester's presence, and by so doing brings about her own long-deferred doom, the pathetic ending of an unhappy life.

Schiller's dramas were becoming true in touch and execution; "Maria Stuart" is an almost faultless work of art. It was followed by

Die Jungfrau von Orleans, a romantic tragedy, recognizing the supernatural element, and wholly idealistic in treatment. Schiller has ennobled his characters and beautified history, and who shall say that he was not right in doing so ? The shameful death of the heroine is changed in the poem— Johanna dies victorious on the battle field. All her suffering, all her sorrow, is the result of her failing in truth to her own high standard. She has devoted herself to heaven and to the love of her country, and then earthly love for Lionel, an Englishman and her enemy, comes between her and her aim, and destroys her singleness of purpose. She spares his life and feels a curse upon her own. Therefore, when accused of witchcraft, she answers nothing, but accepts disgrace as the just punishment of heaven. Shame and misery and imprisonment are her portion. At the last she rushes into the midst of battle, conquers for the king, and, wounded to the death, asks for her banner:

> " Nicht ohne meine Fahne darf ich kommen,
> Ich darf sie zeigen, denn ich trug sie treu ! "

The flag is given her: she stands upright with eyes fixed on the sky :

"Seht ihr den Regenbogen in der Luft?
Der Himmel öffnet seine goldnen Thore ....
Hinauf—hinauf—die Erde flieht zurück—
Kurz ist der Schmerz, und ewig ist die Freude!"

It has been said that the warriors on both sides—French and English—are characterless, and only a repetition of one type. However that may be, it was not Schiller's object to attempt that analysis of every-day character and literal truth to nature to which his genius seldom devoted itself. A type of English common-sense and courage is given in Talbot, who utters the oft-quoted line

"Mit der Dummheit kämpfen Götter selbst vergebens,"

and the one utterly wicked character is Charles' mother, Isabeau, while Agnes Sorel matches Joan in fidelity and unselfishness.

Artistically the most perfect of Schiller's plays is *Die Braut von Messina, oder die feindlichen Brüder*, a tragedy where the classical ideal of an irresistible destiny is revived, and joined to the motive of the two hostile brothers, which had already appeared in literature, in Fletcher's "Rollo." The representation of the antique chorus, which Schiller utilized for the most eloquent lyrical expression, was blamed as an unsuccessful attempt, but Schiller justly avers the chorus, as used by the Greeks, was far preferable to the ever-recurring, garrulous confidant of the French stage and its admirers. The chorus is formed by two bands of followers, belonging respectively to Don Manuel and Don Cesar. These are the brothers, the ill-fated victims of a tragic destiny.

Their father, the Prince of Messina, robbed *his* father of his betrothed wife, and so brought a curse upon his house. Two sons are born who hate each other from infancy, then a daughter. The father dreams that she causes the destruction of her brothers, but the mother has a vision concerning the daughter, signifying "that the 'brothers shall be united in love of her." The father orders the girl-child to be thrown into the sea. The queen, however, contrives to save her, and has her brought up secretly in a secluded convent. But it happens that both brothers see her, and not knowing who she is, each seeks her for his bride. After the death of the father the princess succeeds in reconciling her sons, and tells them that their sister lives. Beatrice is to be brought home by an old and faithful servant—but she has disappeared from the convent. The brothers severally seek her. Don Cesar finds her in Don Manuel's arms, and not realizing that she is their sister, not the bride he hoped for, Don Cesar stabs his brother to the heart. When he hears the truth from his mother's lips, Don Cesar avenges on himself his brother's death, and stabs himself to expiate his crime.

> "Das Leben ist der Güter höchstes nicht,
> Der Übel gröfstes aber is die Schuld."

The poet's brilliant dramatic work was drawing to an end. Not inspiration, or poetic power, was to fail him, but life itself. Struggling against disease with that pure philosophy which rises superior to physical ease and mere earthly happiness, Schiller had fought the good fight, but his remaining strength was all too soon to leave him. His "Demetrius," a tragedy of highest promise, remained a fragment. But before the brilliant roll was ended, he won his highest title to the lasting love and honour of his countrymen by his

Wilhelm Tell.—This, the greatest work of this great dramatist, appeared in 1804.

From the early days of his Würtemberg experiences till his quiet years in Weimar, from the extravagances of his early plays to the ripe taste and chastened beauty of his last great drama, the same idea had actuated him—the cult of an ideal and glorified liberty.

The subject of the Swiss struggle was necessarily attractive to him, and furnished matter worthy of his masterpiece. In the "Braut von Messina," Schiller had departed from the invariable rule in all his plays since its introduction in "Don Carlos,"— a certain historical foundation. In "Wilhelm Tell" he returned to history, authentic or legendary, as we may choose to regard it. His conception of the Swiss hero is high. He entirely justifies the murder of Gessler, the tyrant whose life brought daily ruin to thousands, and contrasts Tell's deed of righteous vengeance in the sacred cause of liberty with Johannes Parricida's murder of his uncle—

"Zum Himmel heb' ich meine reinen Hände,
Verfluche dich und deine That ! "

Stauffacher and his wife are two of the most grandly drawn characters. The heroic Gertrud, who would dare all for her Fatherland, and in the last extremity put an end to her own life—

—" Ein Sprung von dieser Brücke macht mich frei ! "—

is contrasted with Tell's own wife, Hedwig, a far less courageous woman, fearing for her husband, accusing him of hard-heartedness and cruelty, fearing for her children, but a faithful wife at heart. Through all the telling of the well-known story, Schiller's splendid flow of language equals his splendid flow of iambic verse. "Wilhelm Tell" is one of the great masterpieces of European literature.

We have still to consider Schiller's ballads and lyrics, as well as his fine achievements in prose. The two best known of the latter are

Abfall der Niederlande, a subject to which the author had been led by his play of "Don Carlos," and

Der dreissigjährige Krieg, which led to the tragedy of "Wallenstein." Both show Schiller to have been not a poet alone, but a brilliant historian, not always reliable in his facts as he himself admits, but admirable in his style. His "Essays" on various literary and artistic subjects are in every way excellent, and his

Über die ästhetische Erziehung des Menschen contains valuable ideas for a philosophy of the Beautiful.

Schiller's earlier lyrical poems have that tendency to gorgeous word-painting and high-sounding language which characterized his youth;

Hektors Abschied is an example. "Die Götter Griechenlands" shows development both in form and language. In later ballads, such as "Der Taucher," "Der Ring des Polykrates," "Die Kraniche des Ibykus," "Der Kampf mit dem Drachen," Schiller earned well his unexampled popularity. He is equal to all the varying subjects, his epical power of description, his dramatic handling of the action, enchain the imagination without flagging. Nor is the sentimental poem, such as "Der Ritter Toggenburg," foreign to his genius; and the charming little lyric, "Das Mädchen aus der Fremde," is known to every reader of German. It is impossible to enumerate many here, but one of Schiller's best known poems,

Das Lied von der Glocke is a masterpiece in its style—of which Longfellow's "Building of the Ship" is the best of many weak reproductions—an unstrained and perfectly harmonious blending of the poetry and pathos of human life, with the materialistic description of the "Casting of the Bell."

It was in 1805 that Schiller's song sank into silence. The beginning of our century saw the disappearance of many great names in German literature; but the men who died then, such as Kant and Klopstock, might consider their work ended. They died full of years and honours, but Schiller was cut off in his prime. The death of the friend whose loyalty had never wavered, was a hard blow to Goethe. The elder man had still years of life before him, but the younger, who had borne year-long suffering with the heroism of a Spartan and the resignation of a martyr, who had allowed no bodily suffering to dim the serene light of his genius, was taken away from his long struggle when only forty-six, and his loss awakened infinite regret.

CHAPTER XII.

WHILE Goethe, abandoning the greater licence of his early days, was returning more closely to classical models and inculcating such a return by all the weight of his great name and example, the so-called "Romantiker" had formed a new school, of which the University of Jena was the starting-point, and the philosophy of Fichte, in opposition to that of Kant, the groundwork. Old Germanic poetry, Folk-songs, and Folk-lore, inspired the romantic poets; they were thoroughly subjective, and held themselves bound by no rules; for the imagination, as sovereign over reason, was allowed full sway.

The Romantic School showed its influence in all departments of literature and science, but some writers only can be considered here.

The group of men called "ältere Romantiker" was composed of Friedrich von Hardenberg, the brothers Schlegel, and Ludwig Tieck.

Friedrich von Hardenberg (1772-1801), better known by his pseudonym

Novalis, possessed many of the characteristics of the old Mystics. He is marked by purity of thought, mystical piety, and unbounded imaginative faculty. He wrote "Gedichte," "Geistliche Lieder" and "Hymnen an die Nacht." His prose work is the fragment of a novel,

"Heinrich von Ofterdingen,"—the mythical poet said to have taken part in the Wartburg "Battle of the Bards."

August Wilhelm von Schlegel (1767-1845), established, with the collaboration of his brother, the organ of the Romantiker, the "Athenäum." He was a notable critic and writer on literature, but his great work is the masterly translation of Shakespeare. The elder Schlegel also wrote the tragedy "Ion." His younger brother

Friedrich von Schlegel (1772-1829) wrote "Geschichte der alten und neuen Litteratur" and "Über die Sprache und Weisheit der Inder," the latter a favourite subject of the period.

A very prolific, though on the whole mediocre writer was

Ludwig Tieck (1773-1853), the most influential of the older romantic poets. Plays and novels—many of the last excellent—flowed from his pen. "Franz Sternbalds Wanderungen" is one of the most important. "Abdallah" and "William Lovell" may also be named, and among the satirical dramas, "Blaubart," "Der gestiefelte Kater," and "Prinz Zerbino oder die Reise nach dem guten Geschmack."

Two of his plays are: "Leben und Tod der heiligen Genoveva," and "Kaiser Octavianus." He published "Minnelieder aus dem schwäbischen Zeitalter," and an adaptation of Ulrich von Lichtenstein's "Frauendienst," both of which visibly aided the revival of interest in old German poetry, a subject which had a great fascination for Tieck. His "Phantasus" is a collection of old tales, to which he added the fairy-drama (Märchenschauspiel) "Fortunat." His interest in the English drama led him to revise the translation of many of Shakespeare's plays—the translations themselves were actually made by his daughter and Graf Wolf von Baudissin, although they passed as Tieck's own. Tieck also translated "Don Quixote" into German.

Between the two groups, known as the Elder and Younger Romantic Writers, we will place the Brothers Grimm, Alexander and Wilhelm von Humboldt, and Jean Paul Richter, who were all more or less affected by the " Romantic " wave of thought.

Jakob Grimm (1785-1863), the celebrated philologian —one of the pioneers of the scientific study of language— and his brother,

Wilhelm Grimm (1786-1859), wrote frequently together. They published together the

Kinder und Hausmärchen—a wonderful adaptation of old German nursery-tales in a language of their own, and written with full knowledge of what really appeals to the child-mind.

Wilhelm Grimm turned his attention more especially to the study of sagas, fairy tales, and ballads of German and Norse origin. Jacob published as well his "Deutsche Grammatik," which was a history of all Germanic languages, and his "Deutsche Mythologie," and both together worked at the compilation of the "Deutsches Wörterbuch," which remained unfinished.

As types of patient pious-minded scholars, and as authors of those fairy-tales known to every child, the memory of the Brothers Grimm is very dear to the German heart.

Wilhelm von Humboldt (1767-1835) was a close friend of Goethe and Schiller. He wrote

Ästhetische Versuche and " Über die Verschiedenheit des menschlichen Sprachbaues," which is his chief scientific work. His aim was the spread of knowledge for the good of humanity.

Alexander von Humboldt (1769-1859) was a traveller and natural philosopher of a high order. He sought in his writings to give a complete and harmonious picture of the universe. His great work is

Kosmos, which attempted to collect and unite all the results of previous researches in natural science.

A somewhat eccentric genius, celebrated among his contemporaries, was

Jean Paul Richter (1763-1825), usually known as *Jean Paul,* the name under which he wrote. He was a great master of satire, and full of comic power; his influence on the literature of his time was considerable ; as a humorist he has few equals. The defects of his novels lie in his inability to bring his wealth of ideas into coherent form, in the endless length of his sentences, and in the too great exuberance of metaphor, often far-fetched and strained, which hinders the reader from following his thought, and is out of place in progressive narration. Still Carlyle's high opinion of Jean Paul's wonderful humour—"that vast World-Mahlstrom of Humour," as he characteristically calls it—was probably not exaggerated. In his wholly comic works, such characters as the schoolmaster, Fibel, who considers himself a genius because he is the author of an A. B. C. book, and the chemist, Nicolaus Marggraf, who tries to enrich humanity by the manufacture of diamonds, are drawn with wonderful realism. In that class of Jean Paul's works, all the characters have some absurd fixed idea ; in his other writings, the hero is almost invariably placed in too narrow a sphere for his temperament and intellect, his discontent grows, and at the end he finds more congenial surroundings, more enlightened companions. Such is the case in

Siebenkäs. His first satirical writings were the

Grönländische Prozesse. The novels, "Die unsichtbare Loge" and "Hesperus," are founded on his own experiences and intellectual development. "Quintus Fixlein" is the history of a poor schoolmaster, who is finally appointed minister of a country parish. Jean Paul's two best works are :

Titan, whose hero, Prince Albano, shows the develop-

ment of a praiseworthy and highly-gifted man, surrounded
by the discontented and eccentric characters typical of
Jean Paul's conceptions, and the

Flegeljahre, in his best humorous style, but unfortunately
left unfinished.

Jean Paul consistently espoused the cause of liberty. He
advocated the freedom of the press, and sought to reanimate
German courage under the Napoleonic yoke. Numbers of
ideas, expressed in unwieldly terms, and scattered about
his works with a large contempt for the opportune, are fit
food for serious reflection.

Jüngere Romantiker. The band of writers to whom
the title "Jüngere Romantiker" was given had their head-
quarters in Heidelberg.

Clemens Brentano (1778-1842), in conjunction with
Achim von Arnim, published a collection of German songs
and ballads to which was given the name

Des Knaben Wunderhorn. He wrote also "Godwi oder
das steinerne Bild," which he styled "ein verwilderter
Roman," "Die lustigen Musikanten," and the charmingly
told "Geschichte vom braven Kasperl und dem schönen
Annerl." His style is light and pleasing, and possesses
natural grace and wit, though he revels in the most
fantastic ideas.

Ludwig Achim von Arnim (1781-1831) wrote the novels,
"Gräfin Dolores," and "Die Kronenwächter," besides
many shorter tales. Arnim wished to re-establish the old
popular German style in literature, and wrote in excellent
language, with a strong predilection for the marvellous.
His wife,

Bettina von Arnim, who was the sister of Clemens
Brentano, had, with her brother, played as a child in the
house of Goethe's mother. Bettina had an enthusiastic
affection for the great poet, and published

Goethes Briefwechsel mit einem Kinde, in which it is

impossible to distinguish what is really founded on fact from the outcome of her too lively imagination.

Ernst Theodor Amadeus (Wilhelm) Hoffmann (1776-1822) was one of the most celebrated story-writers of the Romantic School. Wonderful imaginative power, combined with a carefully artistic style, enabled him to represent supernatural horrors with surprising resemblance to real events, aud so to enthral the fancy of the reader. His subjects are drawn from various sources, but all bear the impress of his individual genius. Characteristic works are : " Die Serapions-Brüder " and " Nachtstücke," which are both collections of independent stories slightly strung together. Some of the most popular of his tales are : " Meister Martin, der Küfner, und seine Gesellen," "Der Nufsknacher," "Das Fräulein von Scudéry," "Der Kampf der Sänger," another rendering of the Wartburg "Battle of the Bards," probably suggested to Hoffman by Novalis' unfinished novel, "Heinrich von Ofterdingen," and the " Lebensansichten des Katers Murr "—a forerunner of Scheffel's cat "Hiddigeigei," in the "Trompeter von Säkkingen."

Friedrich de la Motte-Fouqué (1777-1843) wrote dramas founded on Norse myths, as " Sigurd der Schlangentöter," the hero of the north ; the " Ritterroman," "Der Zauberring," and the well-known fairy-tale

Undine, his best work. Undine, a water-nymph, can win an immortal soul if a human being loves and weds her. She lives with two old fisher-folk as a beautiful maiden ; a knight comes and takes her for his bride, but the interference of Bertalda, who had hoped to marry Huldbrand, is fatal to their happiness. The knight is assailed by suspicions of Undine's supernatural origin, and she vanishes in the waves of the Danube. The story is tenderly told, in part with old-world quaintness, and is founded on legends of the water-sprites.

A poet who did much to render Romanticism ridiculous was

Zacharias Werner (1768-1823). He had an original strain of oriental mysticism, but his imagination ran riot; the most unnatural and sensational exaggerations were piled one on the other. Werner wrote, "Die Söhne des Thals," a drama of the destruction of the Templars' Order, "Martin Luther oder die Weihe der Kraft," "Die Weihe der Unkraft," and, in 1809, he began the series of the so-called

Schicksalstragödien, Tragedies of Destiny, by the publication of

Der vierundzwanzigste Februar. This absurdly sensational play has for its centre-point what might be termed hereditary crime, committed on the same date, with the same instrument, by an involuntary agent in the hands of an inexorable fate. The 24th February is of course the fatal day, an ill-omened knife is the weapon, and the catastrophe is the murder of a son by his father who does not recognize him—the last of a series of similar crimes committed in this doomed family. Werner lost no opportunity of rendering his horrible subject more horrible by harrowing details, and it is an instance of the remarkable aberrations of literary taste that his example was followed, and similar tragedies appeared in considerable number.

Adolf Müllner (1774-1829), wrote as an improvement on Werner's "24th February,"

Der neunundzwanzigste Februar and *Die Schuld*. It was suggested that the last line of Schiller's "Braut von Messina" should be quoted in reference to the latter play, "Der Übel gröfstes aber is die Schuld"—and it certainly is bad enough—the outcome of a diseased imagination wholly devoid of a saving sense of humour. That sense of humour, however, was keenly alive in a poet who may be mentioned here as the adversary of the "Schicksalstragödien," and of the romantic school in general, a man of brilliant parts but restless temperament,

August, Graf von Platen, born 1796, died 1835. He was a lyrical poet of note, and attempted to compete with Goethe himself. His attainments as a linguist have been equalled by few; he possessed facility and correctness in all metrical composition, so that his verse is in all cases flowing and easy, but his poetry is not of the kind which appeals directly to the heart. Platen excelled in satire. His *Verhängnisvolle Gabel*, the "fatal fork," which burlesqued the weapon of tragic destiny beloved by Werner and his followers, went far to improve the public taste, as did also " Der romantische Ödipus." The comedies written against the Romantic School contain some of his finest work. Platen wrote the odes " An Franz II." and " An Karl X.," idylls, such as

Die Fischer auf Capri; Sonnets; and the long epic poem relating the adventures of the sons of Haroun-al-Raschid, in the style of Wieland's " Oberon,"

Die Abbassiden. Platen's restless nature was incapable of a tranquil life in his own country. He died at Syracuse.

Austrian Poets. Frans Grillparzer (1791-1872) was the most celebrated Austrian dramatist of his time. He wrote a " Schicksalstragödie " more powerful and far less absurd than those of Werner and Müllner,

Die Ahnfrau, in which, as in Müllner's " Schuld," eight-syllabled rhymed trochaics in imitation of Calderon are used. The Ancestress appears in the play when any evil is about to happen to the ill-fated race, and Grillparzer's genius was powerful enough to give interest to the gruesome tale; some scenes are among the most thrilling of their kind. In " Sappho " and in the trilogy,

Das goldene Vliess (the three parts are named: 1. Der Gastfreund. 2. Die Argonauten. 3. Medea) classical subjects are treated, but the desire to be true to nature has led the poet to reproduce contemporary types rather than possible figures of antiquity. Sappho's unhappy love and tragic death are told with a certain modern sentiment which detracts from the artistic value of the play, and the character of Medea, wild in her jealousy and thirst for revenge on Jason's unfaithfulness, though drawn with a certain grandeur in its unsexed cruelty, is too inhuman to retain sympathy.

Des Meeres und der Liebe Wellen (" Hero and Leander ") is another tragedy drawn from a classical source, and " Der Traum ein Leben " introduces once more the subject of an irresistible destiny.

Grillparzer's method of literary procedure, in general, may be said to be in harmony with that of the romantic dramatists, though after the "Ahnfrau," his taste was purified, and he attained heights which they never reached.

One of the most unhappy of German poets, also an Austrian, was Nikolaus Niembsch, Edler von Strehlenau, 1802-1850, who wrote as

Nikolaus Lenau, and has been called "deutscher Dichter des Schmerzes." His beautiful lyrics are the finest of his work, especially the exquisitely touching

Schilflieder, and such poems as " Die Rose der Erinnerung," " Der Urwald," " Meeresstille," and " Sturmesmythe."

" Der Postillon," " Das Posthorn," and " Die Drei Indianer " are well known.

Lenau's chief dramatic and epic poems are " Faust," "Savonarola," "Die Albigenser," and "Don Juan." Melancholia, threatening insanity, haunted his whole life. In 1844, shortly before the date fixed for his marriage, madness declared itself, and he died in a lunatic asylum in 1850. The wish for death to end his sufferings and his life-long melancholy had been expressed years before

in "Der Seelenkranke," a moving sonnet to his dead
mother:

> " So laſs mich bald aus diesem Leben scheiden !
> Ich sehne mich nach einer stillen Nacht ;
> O hilf dem Schmerz Dein müdes Kind entkleiden."

Joseph, Freiherr von Zedlitz (1790-1862) was another
Austrian poet to whom the thought of death gave frequent
inspiration, but comparing him with Lenau, we feel that
he takes the inspiriting, where Lenau takes the hopeless
view ; his poems do not breathe the ineffable sadness
characteristic of the poet of the " Schilflieder." The
Totenkränze, a eulogy of men who have lived and died
nobly, is Zedlitz's best poem. The drama " Kerker und
Krone," treating of Tasso's last days, is celebrated, as are
the ballads " Die nächtliche Heerschau," " Das Geister-
schiff," " Das Weib des Räubers," and " Mariechen." " Das
Waldfräulein " is a delightful fairy tale.

Anastasius Grün, whose real name was Anton, Graf von
Auersperg (1806-1876), wrote graceful and witty verse.
He had in his mind ideal reforms for the benefit of the
people, and embodied his theories in his poems. Some of
his works are: "Der letzte Ritter" in praise of Maximilian I., of which " Die Martinswand," forms a part, and
the "Spaziergänge eines Wiener Poeten," a collection of
verses which rendered him celebrated. Three narrative
poems, the two first entirely comic, " Die Nibelungen im
Frack," " Der Pfaff' vom Kahlenberg " and "Robin Hood"
show Grün's graceful gaiety and wealth of picturesque
language. A few more Austrian poets may be mentioned
very shortly:

Friedrich Halm (1806-1871), a Viennese dramatist,
wrote " Griseldis," " Der Sohn der Wildnis," and " Der
Fechter von Ravenna."

Nepomuk Vogl (1802-1866) made his reputation espe-

I

cially by his ballads. He wrote "Das Erkennen" and "Herr Heinrich sitzt am Vogelherd."

Egon Ebert (1801-1882) attained some celebrity as a lyric poet. His chief works are the Bohemian national epic, "Wlasta," and "Fromme Gedanken eines weltlichen Mannes."

Gabriel Seidl (1804-1875) wrote ballads occasionally marked by warm feeling. Such are "Das Glücksglöcklein," "Der Falschmünzer" and "Der tote Soldat."

Ernst von Feuchtersleben (1806-1849) held closely to the German classics, and eschewed the vagaries of the Romantic school. He wrote "Zur Diätetik der Seele," and "Lieder."

One Austrian prose-writer, of great merit in purity of language and graceful style, shall close the list,

Adalbert Stifter (1806-1868), the author of excellent idylls and tales under the title of "Studien."

Though the interest in his books is never thrilling, his mastery of description, high tone and poetic thought, should· render them popular. The best are "Abdias," "Der Kondor," "Der Hochwald," and "Der Hagestolz." "Bunte Steine," "Der Nachsommer," and the historical novel, "Witiko" are his other chief works.

CHAPTER XIII.

THE term " Gesundete Romantiker " has been applied to those writers who, while following in the path of Tieck, Brentano, and their fellows, in choice and treatment of subject, and in general mode of thought, abandoned the extravagances which were the blots on much of the work of their predecessors, and so won lasting fame among the German people.

Adalbert von Chamisso (1781-1838), a Frenchman by birth, but a German by adoption, is one of the great lyrical poets of modern times. The freshness and brightness of his humorous poems, his power of expressing simple, natural feeling simply and naturally, the tenderness with which he treats the loves and sorrows of everyday life, have long established his fame among general readers. Chamisso may be reproached with too strong a predilection for sensational subjects, and for painful descriptions of horrors which too nearly resemble the defects of modern realism. This is especially visible in his ballads, but usually he entrances without shocking.

Salas y Gomez, one of the longest and perhaps the best of his poems, transports the reader to a desert island in the ocean, and shows wonderful descriptive power. The well-known

Frauen-Liebe und Leben tells the joys and sorrows of

maiden, wife, and mother, and gives the cry of the widow's heart:

> "Nun hast du mir den ersten Schmerz gethan,
> Der aber traf.
> Du schläfst, du harter, unbarmherz'ger Mann,
> Den Totenschlaf."

One of Chamisso's best known poems is "Das Schlofs Boncourt," a tenderly expressed lament for the loss of his birthplace, the Château Boncourt, in Champagne.

Many shorter poems, such as "Der Bettler und sein Hund," "Die Sonne bringt es an den Tag," "Das Riesenspielzeug," "Die alte Waschfrau," are deservedly popular, while the humorous "Tragische Geschichte" of the discontented man whose pigtail persisted in hanging behind, in spite of all his contortions and changes of position, "Der Zopf, der hängt ihm hinten!" is in Chamisso's gayest style.

Read by everyone is the prose story *Peter Schlemihl*, founded on the popular superstition of the possibility of selling one's shadow to the Evil One. The apparently artless style leads from incident to incident with unflagging interest. Chamisso also wrote an excellent description of his travels.

Joseph von Eichendorff (1788-1857), the last eminent "Romantiker," is noted for his fresh pictures of wood and valley, mountain and lake, inspired by an enthusiastic love of nature and a pure and innocent mind.

Aus dem Leben eines Taugenichts, his celebrated prose story, is a charming little work, interspersed with spirited songs. "Lucius," a narrative poem, is also excellent of its kind, and his "Wanderlieder," such as "Wer hat dich, du schöner Wald?" and "Durch Feld und Buchenhallen," are known to all, as is also "In einem kühlen Grunde." The short poems, written on the death of his child, are among the most moving of the kind in the German language.

Wilhelm Müller (1794-1827), the father of Professor Max Müller, wrote love-songs worthy to become real Volkslieder, spoken from the heart and speaking to the heart. Their true poetic simplicity gives them a place among the brightest lyrical gems of the century. We may name "Ich schnitt es gern in alle Rinden ein," "Bächlein, lafs dein Rauschen sein ! "; and of his "Wanderlieder eines rheinischen Hand- werkburschen," the two famous songs, "Das Wandern ist des Müllers Lust," and "Im Krug zum grünen Kranze." Müller also wrote the ballad, "Der Glockengufs zu Breslau."

August Kopisch (1799-1853) took as his favourite subject, goblins, dwarfs, elves, and " Heinzelmännchen." He was, like his friend

Robert Reinick (1805-1852), the author of " Sonntags- morgen," " Dem Vaterlande," and " Käferlied," a painter as well as a poet. Kopisch and Reinick both spent years in Italy. The former is almost as great a master of versification as Platen, but his happiest efforts are in the bright and sparkling verse with which he writes of the fairies and the elves. Of humorous poems by Kopisch we may name "Die Heinzelmännchen," " Die Zwerge auf dem Baum," and "Der Süntelstein zu Halberstadt;" of serious, " Der Trompeter," " Psaumis und Puras," and the little poem learnt by the German children, "Blücher am Rhein," beginning :

> "Die Heere blieben am Rheine stehn,
> Soll man hinein nach Frankreich gehn?"

Karl Immermann (1796-1840), who was satirized by Platen as " Nimmermann," wrote in the romantic style "Das Thal von Ronceval," " König Periander und sein Haus," and " Cardenio und Celinde," the subject treated by Andreas Gryphius. His historical plays, "Trauerspiel in Tyrol," and " Kaiser Friedrich II.," justified Platen in his satirical criticisms, to which Immermann replied by his heroic poem, "Tulifäntchen." He wrote also the tale "Die Epigonen," and

Münchhausen, his best work. The Westphalian village story "Der Oberhof" is unsurpassed of its kind, and the Vorspiel to the dramatic myth "Merlin" is a production of the very highest merit.

One of the great lyric poets of Germany, Heine, may be named in this place, for his genius was firmly rooted in the romantic soil. Although his ultimate identification of himself with France has lost him much of the honour which he would otherwise receive from German writers, it is unjust to deny a very high place in literature to the poet, however the man may be judged. His writings contain many defects: the inner bitterness, the scathing sarcasm, the laxity of religious or moral principle in the man, tainted his writings as his life; yet none can deny that he reached lyric heights to which few have attained.

Heinrich Heine (1797-1856) was a Jew who was baptized because as a Jew he laboured under social disadvantages. Early in life he published

Das Buch der Lieder, a celebrated collection of love-songs, which acted as a revelation of his genius, though in many of them the passion is more affected than real; then the

Reisebilder, in which bitterly satirical references to literary contemporaries—to Count Platen in particular— brought him into universal disfavour. Political references also caused the book to be severely censured. Heine left Germany for Paris, where he spent the remainder of his life, and during his last years received a pension from the French government, for which he has often been blamed.

Heine's political prose-writings have lost something of the interest they possessed for contemporaries, but his mastery of language is admirable, his style brilliantly clear, his invective cutting, and his satire merciless. Much of his poetry is marred by a defect which he shared in common with Byron, the constantly recurring sudden transition from pathos to satire, a transition which, effective at first, becomes wearisome from its frequency. He sometimes strove after brilliancy rather than sincerity, and cultivated wit at the expense of truth. Poems which are free from this shallowness of feeling are pearls indeed, such as " An meine Mutter," and the almost rhymeless verses on the " Fichtenbaum," the mere suggestion of a poem, and yet how poetical !

> " Ein Fichtenbaum steht einsam
> Im Norden auf kahler Höh'.
> Ihn schläfert ; mit weifser Decke
> Umhüllen ihn Eis und Schnee.
>
> Er träumt von einer Palme,
> Die fern im Morgenland
> Einsam und schweigend trauert
> Auf brennender Felsenwand."

For eight years before his death Heine was the victim of cruel bodily suffering, and unable to rise from his bed. It was then that he showed a species of heroism by his continuous literary work, and his great tenderness for his old mother in Hamburg by hiding his sufferings from her. During these last years he was cheered by the touchingly affectionate care of a lady whom he called " la Mouche." The truest and most heartfelt of all his love-poems was written of her—the beautiful " Passion-Flower," speaking of a mystic union between himself, dying, and this girl, the passion-flower :

> " Frag', was er strahlet, den Karfunkelstein,
> Frag', was sie duften, Nachtviol' und Rosen—
> Doch frage nie, wovon im Mondenschein
> Die Marterblume und ihr Toter kosen !"

Another of Heine's poems, " Die Wallfahrt nach Kevlaar," bears no trace of his mocking lightness. " Das Meer hat

seine Perlen " (translated by Longfellow), " Du bist wie
eine Blume," and " Auf Flügeln des Gesanges," are perfect
love-songs, "Die Grenadiere " is universally popular, and
the well-known

Lorelei, the story of the syren of the Rhine, told with
Heine's characteristic brevity, is probably the most sung of
all the much-sung German songs. It is a variation of a
ballad by Brentano, rather than directly founded on an
ancient legend. The wonderful cleverness of Heine's prose,
as in the

Harzreise, will always be fascinating in spite of the writer's
superficiality and frequent insincerity, for his style possesses inimitable originality.

Friedrich Rückert, 1788-1866, wrote in his youth stirring
battle-songs, such as " O wie ruft die Trommel so laut!"
the ode, " Auf die Schlacht von Leipzig," "Barbarossa,"
"Die Riesen und die Zwerge," and " Geharnischte Sonette."
As a linguist he may be placed beside Platen. Eastern
languages were his especial study. Under the influence of
Goethe's " West-östlicher Divan," he imitated Persian
poetry, but his taste was not equal to his facility of versification.

Die Weisheit des Brahmanen clothes Rückert's own philosophy in Eastern garb. Another oriental subject is "Nal
und Damajanti." A cycle of love-poems, expressive of his
own feelings for his bride, and called

Liebesfrühling, contains some really poetic lines in a
mass of commonplace sentimentality. Another cycle of
sonnets, called

Amaryllis, is inspired by idyllic village-life.

Kind Horn and *Rostem und Suhrab* are epic poems;
" Herodes der Große," "Saul und David," "Christofero
Colombo," and " Kaiser Heinrich IV.," dramas. Rückert
was a prolific writer, and attained great popularity, but his
weakness lies in his inability to distinguish always between

the poetic and the prosaic—the want of an inherent sense of the fitness of things.

As the author of " Geharnischte Sonette " and " Kranz der Zeit," Rückert takes his place among the Poets of the War of Liberation.

The reaction against Napoleonic oppression produced strong patriotic feeling in Germany. This enthusiasm naturally expressed itself in song, and to the group of poets, whose utterances were chiefly inspired by the hope of liberating the Fatherland, the name of

Dichter der Befreiungskriege has been given. Chief among them is

Ernst Moritz Arndt (1769-1860), the work of whose life was to awaken the people to a sense of the necessity of casting off the foreign yoke. His first book against Napoleon and the cowardice of the German princes,

Germanien und Europa, appeared in 1803 ; the second, " Der Geist der Zeit " (1806-9), was universally read and caused his banishment. The patriotic songs, " Lieder für Deutsche " and " Kriegs- und Wehrlieder " had surprising effect. Such songs as " Was ist des Deutschen Vaterland ? " " Der Gott, der Eisen wachsen liefs,"

> " Was blasen die Trompeten ?
> Husaren heraus ! "

" Scharnhorst," beginning " Wer ist würdig unsrer grofsen Toten ? " and " Sind wir vereint zur guten Stunde," show his fresh and stirring style. His heart and soul were given to the cause during the whole of a long life, and the truth and sincerity of the singer go to the hearer's heart.

Theodor Körner (1791-1813) is a more brilliant and picturesque figure, burning with youthful enthusiasm for a great cause through his short but glorious career, dying the hero's death for his country. His battle-songs are full of the fire of a noble purpose, written in camp, sung by his

soldiers. It was only after his death that they were collected, and published in a volume called

Leier und Schwert.—Perhaps the most celebrated of all
is the " Schwertlied : "

> "Du Schwert an meiner Linken,
> Was soll dein heitres Blinken ? "

It was composed on the morning of his death. He had
just finished reading aloud the last verse—

> "Nun laſst das Liebchen singen,
> Daſs helle Funken springen !
> Der Hochzeitsmorgen graut.
> Hurrah ! Du Eisenbraut !
>   Hurrah ! "

when the signal for action was given. He fell at Gade-
busch in Mecklenburg, when only twenty-two years of age.

Körner's other well-known battle-songs are : " Herz !
laſs dich nicht zerspalten," " Lützows wilde Jagd,"
"Vater, ich rufe Dich ! " and the " Abschied vom Leben,"
the last written as he lay wounded after action, and believed
that his last hour had come. His plays and stories are of
unequal merit. Körner's early death hindered what might
have been the development of a great genius. His drama,

Zriny, however, is widely read.

A man whose destiny contrasts darkly with that of
Körner is the unhappy dramatist,

Heinrich von Kleist (1777-1811).—Equally inspired
by patriotic enthusiasm, but doomed to repeated disappoint-
ment and want of sympathy, Kleist ended his life by
suicide in the best years of his manhood. It was unfortunate that Goethe from the first judged Kleist hardly.
He expressed his antipathy openly and unjustly, for the
freer dramatic methods which he blamed in Kleist had been
his own in his youthful days, before his return to the
traditions of the past. Kleist's early works were :

Die Familie Schroffenstein and *Penthesilea*, which showed considerable dramatic ability, and the very popular *Käthchen von Heilbronn*.   The sparkling comedy,

Der zerbrochene Krug, in which the judge himself is finally discovered to be the culprit, is one of the best in the German language.   The story,

Michael Kohlhaas, is also excellent.   With the exception of these works, and of some short stories, such as the thrilling tale " Das Erdbeben in Chili," Kleist's one inspiration and purpose was the task of writing against the foreign invader, and foretelling the vengeance which should befall him.   The lyrics, " An die Königin Luise von Preußen," " An den Kaiser Franz den Ersten," and " Germania an ihre Kinder," are among the finest in this class of poetry.   Kleist's two great patriotic dramas are

Prinz Friedrich von Homburg, and the

Hermannsschlacht, which breathe throughout the enthusiastic desire for freedom from the foreign yoke and vengeance on the oppressor.   The style has a peculiar charm of its own; it is concise, clear, and always to the point.   It was long before Heinrich von Kleist won the renown he merits, but he is now acknowledged to rank as a dramatist below Goethe, Schiller, and Lessing alone.

Max von Schenkendorf (1783-1817) also stands among the greatest of the poets of the " Befreiungskriege."   The youthful boldness of Körner, the sharp invective of Kleist, are replaced in him by a melodious intensity of feeling, and an inner piety, which make it possible to compare him with Novalis.   The " Landsturmlied," "Soldatenmorgenlied," "Das Lied vom Rhein," and the poems, "Das Münster," "Wenn alle untreu werden," and " Auf Scharnhorsts Tod," beginning :

> " In dem wilden Kriegestanze
> Brach die schönste Heldenlanze,
> Preußen, euer General—"

are well known ; but best known of all is the melodious,
heartfelt little song, beginning :

> "Freiheit, die ich meine,
> Die mein Herz erfüllt,
> Komm' mit deinem Scheine,
> Süfses Engelsbild !"

That was the aspiration of all the poets of the War of
Liberation, the one cry of all their hearts and voices.

CHAPTER XIV.

It is not alone in our own century that a number of poets almost contemporary have sung in Suabia. The country round the Upper Rhine and the Neckar had been the province of the German troubadours, the Minnesänger. Hartmann von Aue and Gottfried von Strafsburg, sang in the south-west of Germany, and in the middle of our own century the glory of Suabia was revived in what is termed the "Schwäbische Dichterschule." The poets so styled drew their inspiration from the woods, mountains, and rivers of their beautiful "Schwabenland," from the sunshine and the song of birds over the vineyard and the golden cornfield, as Justinus Kerner wrote:

" Wo der Winzer, wo der Schnitter singt ein Lied durch Berg und
    Flur :
Da ist schwäbischer Dichter Schule, und ihr Meister heifst—
    Natur."

The most celebrated of this group of poets is.
Ludwig Uhland (1787-1862), the writer of many of the most popular German ballads and songs. Of the former, which are very numerous, known to everyone are
Taillefer, Bertran de Born, Das Glück von Edenhall, and "Des Sängers Fluch," the last named one of the most effective and striking of ballads. Its popularity is almost unexampled. The picture of the stony-hearted king—"so

finster und so bleich "—who alone is unmoved by the
minstrel's song, of the old bard's despair at the youth's
cruel death, and finally the utterance of the curse, with its
ultimate fulfilment, are familiar to us all. Uhland himself,
like his own " Sänger," sang of :

> "— Lenz und Liebe, von sel'ger goldner Zeit,
> Von Freiheit, Männerwürde, von Treu' und Heiligkeit."

Such songs as *Ich hatt' einen Kameraden* and *Es zogen
drei Burschen wohl über den Rhein* are universally sung.
As a dramatist, Uhland has not attained the fame which
is justly his as a lyric poet. His
Ernst, Herzog von Schwaben and *Ludwig der Baier*,
couched in noble language and full of noble thought, are
well worthy to be read, but are not adaptable for representation. Uhland mixed with great earnestness in Würtemberg politics; his " Wanderung" is a political poem,
crying out for the freedom of his Fatherland. As a
writer of fresh, simple love-songs, charming in their
natural expression of happiness, he is beyond praise, as in
" Die Zufriedenen," beginning, " Ich saſs bei jener Linde."
True emotion, not rich in words but strong in feeling, is
to be found in his sorrowful poems, such as those written
to his dead mother, entitled " Nachruf," in one of which he
describes a quiet grave for her, and ends :

> " Ich grub dir dieses Grab in meinem Herzen."

A friend of Uhland's, a man distinguished by great
charm of manner and warmth of heart, was
Gustav Schwab (1792-1850). He possessed a simple,
happy nature, and had great poetical talent, but perhaps
too great facility of expression without sufficient critical
faculty, so that occasional want of taste renders him, in
most of his work, inferior to Uhland. Excellent, however,
are the two poems,

Das Gewitter, founded on a real incident, when four persons, great-grandmother, grandmother, mother, and daughter were killed by one flash of lightning, and

Der Reiter und der Bodensee, a ballad of breathless interest. Others equally good are " Das Mahl zu Heidelberg," and " Der Riese von Marbach," and a popular student-song is his " Lied eines abziehenden Burschen " :

> " Bemooster Bursche zieh' ich aus,
> Behüt' dich Gott, Philisterhaus !
> Zur alten Heimat geh' ich ein,
> Mufs selber nun Philister sein ! "

Justinus Kerner (1786-1862) was a poet of more tragic cast than Uhland or Schwab. The thought of death is present in the majority of his poems, and he says himself,

> " Mein Lied erzeugt der Schmerz,
> Schnell stirbt es hin in Thränen."

He has the great merit of sincerity, and the power of writing what are real Volkslieder, such as

Der Wandrer an der Sägemühle.—Having, after various vicissitudes, become a doctor, Kerner turned his attention to the half-visionary, half-scientific investigation of somnambulism, and was carried away by what we should now call spiritualism.   This led to his writing

Die Seherin von Prevorst.—A poem showing his taste for the horrible is

Die vier wahnsinnigen Brüder; but the song, " Wohlauf, noch getrunken den funkelnden Wein " is in Kerner's brightest style.

Kaiser Rudolfs Ritt zum Grabe, is a ballad which may be worthily classed with Schiller's " Graf von Habsburg," and " Der reichste Fürst " is another of Kerner's best. The novel,

Reiseschatten von dem Schattenspieler Luchs, an early work, is written in the style of Jean Paul, and contains many whimsical figures, such as the Gravedigger, who,

sitting in the church-yard, works at the invention of a
flying- machine, and the man who imagines himself to be
on a galloping horse, when he is only rushing along on
foot.

The last of the four most considerable Suabian poets is
Eduard Mörike (1804-1875), but he is not as general a
favourite as the three with whom he is classed. Only two
of his ballads are very popular,

Die Geister am Mummelsee, and a merrier poem,

Schön-Rohtraut.—His "Lieder" are greatly superior;
the splendid "Lied vom Winde" has an iresistible
swing—

> "Fort! Wohlauf! Auf!
> Halt' uns nicht auf!
> Fort über Stoppel und Wälder und Wiesen!
> Wenn ich dein Schätzchen seh',
> Will ich es grüfsen,
> Kindlein, ade!

Storchenbotschaft, Das Liebesvorzeichen, and *Die Schwestern*
are also bright and gay, whilst " Das verlassene Mägdlein "
is a simple and touching expression of a deserted girl's
misery.

Mörike wrote a novel in the Romantic style,

Maler Nolter, and a charming tale,

Mozart auf der Reise nach Prag.

An older Suabian poet, not classed with those of whom
Uhland is the chief, was the unfortunate

Friedrich Hölderlin (1770-1843), the lover of Greece and
classic antiquity, the last thirty-seven years of whose life
were passed in hopeless insanity.

Hyperion oder der Eremit in Griechenland is one of the
finest examples of German prose. Hölderlin's chief poems
are

Griechenland, Die Heimat, Der Wandrer, and *An die
Natur.*

Modern Poets.—A few poets, who might be roughly classed as belonging to the middle of our own century, shall be referred to shortly, before we pass to a cursory notice of the chief novelists.

Heinrich August Hoffmann von Fallersleben (1798-1874) lost his professorship at the University of Breslau, in 1843, on account of his radicalism. He was a really great lyrical poet, possessed unusual facility in versification, and often attained the excellence of real " Volkslieder " by simplicity, depth of feeling, and playfulness of tone combined. His " Kinderlieder," " Wanderlieder," " Liebeslieder," and " Lieder der Landsknechte," have all attained well-deserved popularity. " Deutschland, Deutschland über alles," " Zwischen Frankreich und dem Böhmerwald," " Alle Vögel sind schon da," and " O glücklich, wer ein Herz gefunden," are characteristic.

Ferdinand Freiligrath (1810-1876) lived for some years in London, owing to political difficulties, brought about by his liberal views boldly expressed in the forties, but ended an honoured old age in his own country. Freiligrath gives marvellous word-pictures. Richness of colouring is his most striking characteristic ; the poet Kinkel called him " den Rubens unsrer Poesie." Well known among many others are " Löwenritt," " Unter den Palmen," " Gesicht des Reisenden," " Der Blumen Rache ; " but of all that he has written those words from the lament for his father are the most often quoted :

> " O lieb', so lang Du lieben kannst !
> O lieb', so lang Du lieben magst !
> Die Stunde kommt, die Stunde kommt,
> Wo Du an Gräbern stehst und klagst ! "

Gottfried Kinkel (1815-1882), another political victim, was imprisoned in 1849, but escaped the following year. After a short sojourn in America he lived in London until

K

1866. He then became professor at the Polytechnic and University of Zurich, where he remained until his death.

Kinkel wrote the well-known epic poems, " Otto der Schütz," " Der Grobschmied von Antwerpen," and " Tanagra."

Otto der Schütz, by far the most popular, is a story of the Rhine in twelve "adventures," and tells with charming vivacity the story of Otto, a younger son of Landgrave Henry of Thuringia, who, refusing to become a monk in accordance with his father's wish, escapes to the Rhine, becomes a famous archer, and finally wins the beautiful daughter of the Count of Cleves for his bride.

Kinkel's most charming village tale is " Margret," and he has also written many lyrics. All his works are marked by mingled grace and strength, and great power of observation as well as of feeling.

Friedrich Hebbel (1813-1863) was a dramatist of great original genius, revelling in emotional subjects, and of unsurpassed ability in awakening excitement and awe. His most powerful dramas are " Judith," " Agnes Bernauer," and—his masterpiece—" Die Nibelungen."

Hebbel's excellent narrative poem is " Mutter und Kind."

Karl Gutzkow (1811-1878), a highly-gifted dramatist and novelist, repeats in his works the oft-heard cry for liberty and toleration, but his writings are sometimes marred by bitterness, and by hard judgment of his contemporaries, as well as by sceptical impatience of the existing moral and social code. Gutzkow's three great novels are " Die Ritter vom Geist," " Der Zauberer von Rom," and " Hohenschwangau." One of his best short tales is " Der Sadducäer von Amsterdam," showing the same train of thought as his most successful drama, the celebrated " Uriel Acosta "—a protest in favour of freedom of opinion.

Uriel Acosta treats a tragic subject with tragic power, and produces overwhelming effect on the stage.

Zopf und Schwert, a historical comedy of intrigue, treating of the time of Friedrich Wilhelm I. of Prussia, is frequently played.

An eminent lyrical poet is

Emanuel Geibel (1815-1884). Full of poetic possibilities, he never, or rarely, fails in producing the effect he desires. Of his voluminous work, " Zeitstimmen," " Heroldsrufe," " Spanische Volkslieder und Romanzen," and " Klassisches Liederbuch," form a small portion only. Widely known among many others are the poems, " Der Zigeunerbube im Norden," " Zigeunerleben," and

Der Tod des Tiberius, the last a tragically effective description of the remorse - haunted Emperor's last hours,

> " O gieb mir Lethe, Lethe, mich zu tränken ! "

König Sigurds Brautfahrt, is Geibel's most important epic poem, and of his plays the most celebrated are " Sophonisbe " and " Brunhild," the latter a thoroughly successful attempt to introduce the grand old heroic figures into the modern drama.

To close this imperfect list of modern poets, *Friedrich von Bodenstedt*, born 1819, shall be named. He attained great and immediate popularity by his

Lieder des Mirza Schaffy, which are full of quaint wisdom and playful philosophy, and very attractive in form. " Tausend und ein Tag im Orient " is one of Bodenstedt's best prose-works.

Novelists.—While possessing one of the grandest and richest of literatures, Germany, it must be confessed by any unprejudiced student, has not in modern days been as happy as England or France in the production of the novel.

It is not purposed to attempt here any systematic biographical notice or criticism of modern novelists, but a few of the principal works of fiction which have real literary value may be shortly mentioned, as a conclusion to this little book.

Gustav Freytag is indisputably one of the greatest German novelists. His "Soll und Haben," "Verlorene Handschrift," and the historical series, "Die Ahnen," are standard works. "Soll und Haben" is the most finished picture of German middle-class life and manners which has even yet appeared. High moral tone, great command of language, vast imaginative power, and thorough mastery of his subject distinguish Freytag; but he is fond of long dissertations on social and political matters in works of fiction, and these digressions are out of place in novels, judged from the English standpoint.

Hauff's "Lichtenstein," on the model of Sir Walter Scott's novels, is an excellent historical romance, with sufficient humour to save it from the charge of tediousness; and

Scheffel's "Ekkehard" is a book which cannot be too highly praised. The picture drawn of the young monk, Ekkehard, the author of "Walther von Aquitanien," is not historically correct. In the novel the unhappy love for the beautiful but unprincipled Hadwig, Duchess of Suabia, against which he struggles in vain, is the cause of his fleeing into the solitude where he writes his poem; whereas the poem was really written in the calm of the cloister of St. Gallen, and Ekkehard was undisturbed by love of a princess. But it is permitted to an author to treat facts with poetical licence when he is capable of presenting to his readers as quaint and humorous, and withal powerfully passionate a work as Scheffel's "Ekkehard."

Felix Dahn, the author of the "Kampf um Rom," is a writer who has attained a wide popularity, but his much read book lacks the unity in its several parts necessary to the novel proper. It is rather a series of episodes loosely strung together, and its hero, Cethegus, immovable in his schemes of vengeance and ambition, is certainly not a natural or even a possible character.

Georg Ebers, too, is an author of wide celebrity who lacks the truth to nature indispensable to lasting fame.

" Homo sum " deserves perhaps the highest praise of all his many books, and " Eine ägyptische Königstochter," and " Uarda," stand next to it. There is necessarily a difficulty in reproducing probable characters from a distant past and a far-off country, and it is in his women especially that Ebers fails the most signally. " Ein Wort," " Die Frau Bürgermeisterin," " Der Kaiser," " Die Nilbraut," " Serapis," much read as they have been, will surely never be highly prized by posterity.

The greatest modern Humorist of Germany is incontestibly **Fritz Reuter**, whose writings in Plattdeutsch are perfect of their kind. " Ut mine Stromtid," and " Ut de Franzosentid," are both founded on incidents in the author's early life. The immortal figure of Onkel Bräsig, as well as such characters as Fritz Triddelfitz and Frau Nüssler, is inimitably drawn, and Reuter fulfils to the utmost the humorist's task of representing and mingling the laughter and tears of human nature.

Two German-Swiss writers have reached a high place in modern fiction. These are *Gottfried Keller*, and *Konrad Ferdinand Meyer*. The former is especially famed for his novelettes, of which " Romeo und Julia auf dem Dorfe," from " Die Leute von Seldwyla," is generally considered the best. It is a perfectly drawn picture of two village children whose fathers have an irreconcilable quarrel. The story is faultlessly told in the most artistically simple language, but its ending puts it outside the pale of entirely pure and healthy literature. Keller first made his reputation by his novel "Der grüne Heinrich." Other of his stories are "Die Leute von Seldwyla," mentioned before, "Züricher Novellen" and "Das Sinngedicht," which are among the minor literary triumphs of the century.

Keller's countryman, *Conrad Ferdinand Meyer*, has done stately and majestic work in the historical tale. His books cannot be considered "light literature," they are serious and profitable reading, and their literary value is indisputable. "Georg Jenatsch" was his first tale; "Der Heilige" is the story of Thomas à Becket. Other tales are "Das Amulet," "Der Schuss von der Kanzel," and perhaps best of all "Die Versuchung des Pescara." All of these can be unreservedly praised.

Berthold Auerbach earned his celebrity by "Dorfgeschichten." He sometimes allows his villagers unnatural sentimentality, but, on the whole, his representation of the peasant of the Black Forest is wonderfully realistic. His two longer books, "Auf der Höhe," and "Das Landhaus am Rhein," may be classed as somewhat sensational. The tendency in the former is the spread of liberal ideas; "Das Landhaus" pleads the social and official re-habilitation of the Jews. Auerbach was himself a Jew.

Friedrich Spielhagen's most widely read book is "Problematische Naturen," which has for its sequel "Durch Nacht zum Licht." The prejudices of a democrat are not always quite invisible in his works, so that clergy and nobility are occasionally hardly judged—an inartistic partiality which may detract from his permanent fame. "Die von Hohenstein," "In Reih und Glied," "Hammer und Amboss," are powerfully conceived. Spielhagen has also written shorter tales, such as "Clara Vere," which is a not very happy adaptation of the story of Tennyson's "Lady Clara Vere de Vere," and "Quisisana," which is really interesting.

The Austrian *Rosegger* is a quaint and charming story-writer. He brings the life of the Alps clearly before our eyes. Deep thought and earnest study of humanity underlie his apparently simple words, and the true pathos of his famous book, "Die Schriften des Waldschulmeisters," is free from all sentimentality and affectation ; the story of a child-like, self-denying nature, painted in simple colours by a finished artist. Two other of Rosegger's best works are " Der Gottsucher " and " Meine Ferien."

Heinrich Riehl is celebrated as a writer of short stories. "Aus der Ecke," " Am Feierabend," " Lebensrätsel," are the names given to some of his volumes of tales. His writings show a high standard of morality ; he expressed his intention of writing nothing which could not be read aloud to his children, and considered that a book unfit for general reading was artistically false. "Die Gerechtigkeit Gottes," " Die Vierzehn Nothelfer," " Der stumme Ratsherr," and " Das Spielmannskind," are all charming stories, and the "Kulturgeschichtliche Novellen " are especially well known.

Paul Heyse, one of the most popular German writers of our day, a master of style and a distinguished novelist, has written many social novels of that modern type which takes our follies, weaknesses and sins as the worthiest sub-ject of narration, and treats them as justifiable and, under certain circumstances, even meritorious. All Heyse's writings have beauty of style, and those which are free from the de-fect referred to are graceful and pleasing tales. Such are " L'Arrabiata," an Italian love-story ; " Nerina," also an Italian story, with a sad ending; " Anfang und Ende," and " Er soll dein Herr sein." The " Roman der Stiftsdame " is a serious and very moving story, told with Heyse's accus-tomed skill. Books which in their time excited much com-ment are " Die Kinder der Welt," and " Im Paradiese."

Another author of very great popularity at the present day is the brilliant *Hermann Sudermann*—the dramatist of the extraordinarily successful play " Die Ehre "—charming in style, though often unblushingly realistic ; striking in emotional power, but, like Heyse, essentially modern in his view of social questions. With him the end justifies the means, no action is culpable in itself if the goal aimed at is desirable. The novels, "Frau Sorge," by many considered Sudermann's best, and "Der Katzensteg" may be mentioned. Shorter stories are, "Im Zwielicht," "Die Geschwister," and "Jolanthes Hochzeit."

LIST OF AUTHORITIES.

BAECHTHOLD, Jakob. "Geschichte der deutschen Litteratur in der Schweiz." Frauenfeld, 1892.

BINDER, W. "Sprichwörterschatz der deutschen Nation." Stuttgart, 1873.

BREUL, Karl. "A Handy Bibliographical Guide to the Study of the German Language and Literature." London, 1895.

BRINK, B. ten, und W. SCHERER. "Quellen und Forschungen zur Sprach-und Kulturgeschichte der germanischen Völker." Strassburg, 1874, etc.

BROCKHAUS' "Konversations-Lexikon," 16 Bände. Leipzig, 1887.

DUDEN, Konrad. "Vollständiges orthographisches Wörterbuch." Leipzig, 1894.

ECHTERMEYER, Theodor. "Auswahl deutscher Gedichte." Halle, 1893.

ERCK, Ludwig. "Deutscher Liederhort." Leipzig, 1894.

ETTMÜLLER, L. "Handbuch der deutschen Litteraturgeschichte von den ältesten bis auf die neuesten Zeiten, mit Einschlufs der angelsächs., altskandinav. und mittelniederländ. Schrifwerke." Leipzig, 1847.

—— "Gûdrûnlieder." Zürich, 1841.

FISCHER, Kuno. "G. E. Lessing als Reformator der deutschen Litteratur." Stuttgart, 1881.

—— "Goethe-Schriften." Heidelberg, 1890.

—— "Schiller-Schriften." Heidelberg, 1892.

FREHSE, F. "Wörterbuch zu Fritz Reuters sämtlichen Werken." Wismar, 1867.

GENÉE, R. "Lehr-und Wanderjahre des deutschen Schauspiels." Berlin, 1882.

GOEDEKE, Karl. "Grundrifs zur Geschichte der deutschen Dichtung." Hannover, 1859-91.

GÖTZINGER, M. W. "Deutsche Dichter." Aarau, 1876.

GOTTSCHALL, Rudolf v. "Die deutsche National-Litteratur des neunzehnten Jahrhunderts." Breslau, 1892.

GRIMM, Jakob. "Deutsche Mythologie." Berlin, 1878. English translation by J. S. Stallybrass, London. 1882-1888.

GRIMM, Jakob und Wilhelm GRIMM. "Deutsches Wörterbuch." Leipzig, 1854, etc.

GRIMM, Wilhelm. "Die deutsche Heldensage." Gütersloh, 1889.

HUB, Ignaz. "Deutschlands Balladen-und Romanzendichter." Würzburg, 1860.

KLUGE, Friedrich. "Etymol. Wörterbuch der deutschen Sprache." Strassburg, 1894. English translation by J. F. Davis.

KLUGE, Hermann. "Geschichte der deutschen National-Litteratur." Altenburg, 1894.

KOBERSTEIN, Karl August. "Grundrifs zur Geschichte der deutschen National-Litteratur, bearbeitet von K. Bartsch." Leipzig, 1872.

KURZ, Heinrich. "Geschichte der deutschen Litteratur." Leipzig, 1892.

LACHMANN, Karl. "Der Nibelungen Not und die Klage." Berlin, 1881.

LEWES, George H. "The Life and Works of Goethe." London, 1875.

MEYERS "Konversations-Lexikon," 19 Bände. Leipzig, 1892.

MORSIER, E. de. "Romanciers allemands contemporains." Paris, 1890.

MÜLLENHOFF, C. V. "Denkmäler deutscher Poesie und Prosa aus dem VIII.-XII. Jahrh." Berlin, 1873.

MÜLLER, F. Max. "The German Classics from the 4th to the 19th Century." Adapted to W. Scherer's "Hist. of Germ. Liter." Oxford, 1886.

PALLESKE, Emil. "Schillers Leben und Werke." Stuttgart, 1891.

"PUBLICATIONS of the English Goethe Society." London, 1886, etc.

SANDERS, Daniel. "Geschichte der deutschen Sprache und Litteratur bis zu Goethes Tod." Berlin, 1887.

SCHERER, Wilhelm. "Geschichte der deutschen Litteratur." Berlin, 1882. English translation by Mrs. F. C. Conybeare, edited by F. Max Müller. Oxford, 1885-1891.

SCHERR, Johannes. "Allgemeine Geschichte der Litteratur." Stuttgart, 1875.

SCHMECKEBIER, Oskar. "Deutsche Verslehre." Berlin, 1886.

SIMROCK, Karl Jos. "Handbuch der deutschen Mythologie." Bonn, 1887.

STAHR, Adolf. "Ed. Schurés Geschichte des deutschen Liedes." Minden, 1884.

WACKERNAGEL, Philipp. "Das deutsche Kirchenlied." Leipzig, 1877.

WEINHOLD, Karl. "Die deutschen Frauen in dem Mittelalter." Wien, 1882.

ZARNCKE, Friedrich. "Beiträge zur Erläuterung einer Geschichte des Nibelungenliedes. Leipzig, 1857.

CHRONOLOGICAL SUMMARY.

L

INDEX OF AUTHORS WITH THEIR CHIEF WORKS.

CHISWICK PRESS :—CHARLES WHITTINGHAM AND CO.
TOOKS COURT, CHANCERY LANE, LONDON.

A

CLASSIFIED CATALOGUE

OF

EDUCATIONAL WORKS

PUBLISHED BY

GEORGE BELL & SONS

LONDON: YORK STREET, COVENT GARDEN
NEW YORK: 66, FIFTH AVENUE; AND BOMBAY
CAMBRIDGE: DEIGHTON, BELL & CO
FEBRUARY, 1895

CONTENTS.

GREEK AND LATIN CLASSICS.

ANNOTATED AND CRITICAL EDITIONS.

AESCHYLUS. Edited by F. A. PALEY. M.A., LL.D., late Classical Examiner to the University of London. *4th edition, revised.* 8vo, 8s.
[*Bib. Class.*

— Edited by F. A. PALEY, M.A., LL.D., 6 vols. fcap. 8vo, 1s. 6d.
[*Camb. Texts with Notes.*

Agamemnon.	Persae.
Choephoroe.	Prometheus Vinctus.
Eumenides.	Septem contra Thebas.

ARISTOPHANIS Comoediae quae supersunt cum perditarum fragmentis tertiis curis, recognovit additis adnotatione critica, summariis, descriptione metrica, onomastico lexico HUBERTUS A. HOLDEN, LL.D. [late Fellow of Trinity College, Cambridge]. Demy 8vo.

Vol. I., containing the Text expurgated, with Summaries and Critical Notes, 18s.

The Plays sold separately :

Acharnenses, 2s.	Aves 2s.
Equites, 1s. 6d.	Lysistrata, et Thesmophoriazu-
Nubes, 2s.	sae, 4s.
Vespae, 2s.	Ranae, 2s.
Pax, 2s.	Plutus, 2s.

Vol. II. Onomasticon Aristophaneum continens indicem geographicum et historicum 5s. 6d.

— The Peace. A revised Text with English Notes and a Preface. By F. A. PALEY, M.A.. LL.D. Post 8vo, 4s. 6d. [*Pub. Sch. Ser.*

— The Acharnians. A revised Text with English Notes and a Preface. By F. A. PALEY, M.A., LL.D. Post 8vo, 4s. 6d. [*Pub. Sch. Ser.*

— The Frogs. A revised Text with English Notes and a Preface. By F. A. PALEY, M.A., LL.D. Post 8vo, 4s. 6d. [*Pub. Sch. Ser.*

CAESAR De Bello Gallico. Edited by GEORGE LONG, M.A. *New edition.* Fcap. 8vo, 4s.

Or in parts, Books I.-III., 1s. 6d. ; Books IV. and V., 1s. 6d. ; Books VI. and VII., 1s. 6d. [*Gram. Sch. Class.*

— De Bello Gallico. Book I. Edited by GEORGE LONG, M.A. With Vocabulary by W. F. R. SHILLETO, M.A. 1s. 6d. [*Lower Form Ser.*

— De Bello Gallico. Book II. Edited by GEORGE LONG, M.A. With Vocabulary by W. F. R. SHILLETO, M.A. Fcap. 8vo, 1s. 6d.
[*Lower Form Ser.*

— De Bello Gallico. Book III. Edited by GEORGE LONG, M.A. With Vocabulary by W. F. R. SHILLETO, M.A. Fcap. 8vo. 1s. 6d.
[*Lower Form Ser.*

— Seventh Campaign in Gaul. B.C. 52. De Bello Gallico, Lib. VII. Edited with Notes, Excursus, and Table of Idioms, by REV. W. COOK-WORTHY COMPTON, M.A., Head Master of Dover College. With Illustrations from Sketches by E. T. COMPTON, Maps and Plans. *2nd edition.* Crown 8vo, 2s. 6d. net.

" A really admirable class book."—*Spectator.*

" One of the most original and interesting books which have been published in late years as aids to the study of classical literature. I think

CAESAR—*continued.*
it gives the student a new idea of the way in which a classical book may
be made a living reality."—*Rev. J. E. C. Welldon*, Harrow.
— **Easy Selections from the Helvetian War.** Edited by A. M. M. STED-
MAN, M.A. With Introduction, Notes and Vocabulary. 18mo. 1*s.*
[Primary Classics.
**CALPURNIUS SICULUS and M. AURELIUS OLYMPIUS
NEMESIANUS.** The Eclogues, with Introduction, Commentary,
and Appendix. By C. H. KEENE, M.A. Crown 8vo, 6*s.*
CATULLUS, TIBULLUS, and PROPERTIUS. Selected Poems.
Edited by the REV. A. H. WRATISLAW, late Head Master of Bury St.
Edmunds School, and F. N. SUTTON, B.A. With Biographical Notices of
the Poets. Fcap. 8vo, 2*s. 6d.* *[Gram. Sch. Class.*
CICERO'S Orations. Edited by G. LONG, M.A. 8vo. *[Bib. Class.*
Vol. I.—In Verrem. 8*s.*
Vol. II.—Pro P. Quintio—Pro Sex. Roscio—Pro. Q. Roscio—Pro M.
Tullio—Pro M. Fonteio—Pro A. Caecina—De Imperio Cn. Pompeii—
Pro A. Cluentio—De Lege Agraria—Pro C. Rabirio. 8*s.*
Vols. III. and IV. *Out of print.*
— **De Senectute, De Amicitia, and Select Epistles.** Edited by GEORGE
LONG, M.A. *New edition.* Fcap. 8vo, 3*s.* *[Gram. Sch. Class.*
— **De Amicitia.** Edited by GEORGE LONG, M.A. Fcap. 8vo, 1*s. 6d.*
[Camb. Texts with Notes.
— **De Senectute.** Edited by GEORGE LONG, M.A. Fcap. 8vo, 1*s. 6d.*
[Camb. Texts with Notes.
— **Epistolae Selectae.** Edited by GEORGE LONG, M.A. Fcap. 8vo, 1*s. 6d.*
[Camb. Texts with Notes.
— **The Letters to Atticus.** Book I. With Notes, and an Essay on the
Character of the Writer. By A. PRETOR, M.A., late of Trinity College,
Fellow of St. Catherine's College, Cambridge. 3*rd edition.* Post 8vo,
4*s. 6d.* *[Pub. Sch. Ser.*
CORNELIUS NEPOS. Edited by the late REV. J. F. MACMICHAEL,
Head Master of the Grammar School, Ripon. Fcap. 8vo, 2*s.*
[Gram. Sch. Class.
DEMOSTHENES. Edited by R. WHISTON, M.A., late Head Master of
Rochester Grammar School. 2 vols. 8vo, 8*s.* each. *[Bib. Class.*
Vol. I.—Olynthiacs—Philippics—De Pace—Halonnesus—Chersonese
—Letter of Philip—Duties of the State—Symmoriae—Rhodians—Mega-
lopolitans—Treaty with Alexander—Crown.
Vol. II.—Embassy—Leptines—Meidias—Androtion—Aristocrates—
Timocrates—Aristogeiton.
— **De Falsa Legatione.** By the late R. SHILLETO, M.A., Fellow of St.
Peter's College, Cambridge. 7*th edition.* Post 8vo, 6*s.* *[Pub. Sch. Ser.*
— **The Oration against the Law of Leptines.** With English Notes.
By the late B. W. BEATSON, M.A., Fellow of Pembroke College. 3*rd
edition.* Post 8vo, 3*s. 6d.* *[Pub. Sch. Ser.*
EURIPIDES. By F. A. PALEY, M.A., LL.D. 3 vols. 2*nd edition, revised.*
8vo, 8*s.* each. Vol. I. *Out of print.* *[Bib. Class.*
Vol. II.—Preface—Ion—Helena—Andromache—Electra—Bacchae—
Hecuba. 2 Indexes.
Vol. III. — Preface — Hercules Furens—Phoenissae—Orestes—Iphi-
genia in Tauris—Iphigenia in Aulide—Cyclops. 2 Indexes.

EURIPIDES. Electra. Edited, with Introduction and Notes, by C. H. KEENE, M.A., Dublin, Ex-Scholar and Gold Medallist in Classics. Demy 8vo, 10s. 6d.
— Edited by F. A. PALEY, M.A., LL.D. 13 vols. Fcap. 8vo, 1s. 6d. each.
[*Camb. Texts with Notes.*

Alcestis.	Phoenissae.
Medea.	Troades.
Hippolytus.	Hercules Furens.
Hecuba.	Andromache.
Bacchae.	Iphigenia in Tauris.
Ion (2s.).	Supplices.
Orestes.	

HERODOTUS. Edited by REV. J. W. BLAKESLEY, B.D. 2 vols. 8vo, 12s.
[*Bib. Class.*
— **Easy Selections from the Persian Wars.** Edited by A. G. LIDDELL, M.A. With Introduction, Notes, and Vocabulary. 18mo, 1s. 6d.
[*Primary Classics.*

HESIOD. Edited by F. A. PALEY, M.A., LL.D. *2nd edition, revised.* 8vo, 5s.
[*Bib. Class.*

HOMER. Edited by F. A. PALEY, M.A., I.L.D. 2 vols. 2nd edition, revised. 14s. Vol. II. (Books 13-24) may be had separately, 6s.
[*Bib. Class.*
— Iliad. Books I.-XII. Edited by F. A. PALEY, M.A., LL.D. Fcap. 8vo, 4s. 6d.
Also in 2 Parts. Books I.-VI. 2s. 6d. Books VII.-XII. 2s. 6d.
[*Gram. Sch. Class.*
— Iliad. Book I. Edited by F. A. PALEY, M.A., LL.D. Fcap. 8vo, 1s.
[*Camb. Text with Notes.*

HORACE. Edited by REV. A. J. MACLEANE, M.A. *4th edition,* revised by GEORGE LONG. 8vo, 8s. [*Bib. Class.*
— Edited by A. J. MACLEANE, M.A. With a short Life. Fcap. 8vo, 3s. 6d. Or, Part I., Odes, Carmen Seculare, and Epodes, 2s.; Part II., Satires, Epistles, and Art of Poetry, 2s. [*Gram. Sch. Class.*
— Odes. Book I. Edited by A. J. MACLEANE, M.A. With a Vocabulary by A. H. DENNIS, M.A. Fcap. 8vo, 1s. 6d. [*Lower Form Ser.*

JUVENAL : Sixteen Satires (expurgated). By HERMAN PRIOR, M.A., late Scholar of Trinity College, Oxford. Fcap. 8vo, 3s. 6d.
[*Gram. Sch. Class.*

LIVY. The first five Books, with English Notes. By J. PRENDEVILLE. A new edition revised throughout, and the notes in great part re-written, by J. H. FREESE, M.A., late Fellow of St. John's College, Cambridge. Books I. II. III. IV. V. With Maps and Introductions. Fcap. 8vo. 1s. 6d. each.
— Book VI. Edited by E. S. WEYMOUTH, M.A., Lond., and G. F. HAMILTON, B.A. With Historical Introduction, Life of Livy, Notes, Examination Questions, Dictionary of Proper Names, and Map. Crown 8vo, 2s. 6d.
— Book XXI. By the REV. L. D. DOWDALL, M.A., late Scholar and University Student of Trinity College, Dublin, B.D., Ch. Ch. Oxon. Post 8vo, 3s. 6d. [*Pub. Sch. Ser.*
— Book XXII. Edited by the REV. L. D. DOWDALL, M.A., B.D. Post 8vo, 3s. 6d. [*Pub. Sch. Ser.*

LIVY. Easy Selections from the Kings of Rome. Edited by A. M. M. STEDMAN, M.A. With Introduction, Notes, and Vocabulary. 18mo, 1s. 6d. 　　　　　　　　　　　　　　　　　　*[Primary Class.*

LUCAN. The Pharsalia. By C. E. HASKINS, M.A., Fellow of St. John's College, Cambridge, with an Introduction by W. E. HEITLAND, M.A., Fellow and Tutor of St. John's College, Cambridge. 8vo, 14s.

LUCRETIUS. Titi Lucreti Cari De Rerum Natura Libri Sex. By the late H. A. J. MUNRO, M.A., Fellow of Trinity College, Cambridge. *4th edition, finally revised.* 3 vols, demy 8vo. Vols. I., II., Introduction, Text, and Notes, 18s. Vol. III., Translation, 6s.

MARTIAL: Select Epigrams. Edited by F. A. PALEY, M.A., LL.D., and the late W. H. STONE, Scholar of Trinity College, Cambridge. With a Life of the Poet. Fcap. 8vo, 4s. 6d. 　　　　　*[Gram. Sch. Class.*

OVID: Fasti. Edited by F. A. PALEY, M.A., LL.D. *Second edition.* Fcap. 8vo, 3s. 6d. 　　　　　　　　　　　　　*[Gram. Sch. Class.*
　Or in 3 vols, 1s. 6d. each [*Grammar School Classics*], or 2s. each [*Camb. Texts with Notes*], Books I. and II., Books III. and IV., Books V. and VI.

— **Selections from the Amores, Tristia, Heroides, and Metamorphoses.** By A. J. MACLEANE, M.A. Fcap. 8vo, 1s. 6d.
　　　　　　　　　　　　　　　　　[Camb. Texts with Notes.

— **Ars Amatoria et Amores.** A School Edition. Carefully Revised and Edited, with some Literary Notes, by J. HERBERT WILLIAMS, M.A., late Demy of Magdalen College, Oxford. Fcap. 8vo, 3s. 6d.

— **Heroides XIV.** Edited, with Introductory Preface and English Notes, by ARTHUR PALMER, M.A., Professor of Latin at Trinity College, Dublin. Demy 8vo, 6s.

— **Metamorphoses, Book XIII.** A School Edition. With Introduction and Notes, by CHARLES HAINES KEENE, M.A., Dublin, Ex-Scholar and Gold Medallist in Classics. *3rd edition.* Fcap. 8vo, 2s. 6d.

— **Epistolarum ex Ponto Liber Primus.** With Introduction and Notes, by CHARLES HAINES KEENE, M.A. Crown 8vo, 3s.

PLATO. The Apology of Socrates and Crito. With Notes, critical and exegetical, by WILHELM WAGNER, PH.D. *12th edition.* Post 8vo, 3s. 6d. A CHEAP EDITION. Limp Cloth. 2s. 6d. 　[*Pub. Sch. Ser.*

— **Phaedo.** With Notes, critical and exegetical, and an Analysis, by WILHELM WAGNER, PH.D. *9th edition.* Post 8vo, 5s. 6d. [*Pub. Sch. Ser.*

— **Protagoras.** The Greek Text revised, with an Analysis and English Notes, by W. WAYTE, M.A., Classical Examiner at University College, London. *7th edition.* Post 8vo, 4s. 6d. 　　　　　[*Pub. Sch. Ser.*

— **Euthyphro.** With Notes and Introduction by G. H. WELLS, M.A., Scholar of St. John's College, Oxford; Assistant Master at Merchant Taylors' School. *3rd edition.* Post 8vo, 3s. 　　　[*Pub. Sch. Ser.*

— **The Republic.** Books I. and II. With Notes and Introduction by G. H. WELLS, M.A. *4th edition,* with the Introduction re-written. Post 8vo, 5s. 　　　　　　　　　　　　　　　　　[*Pub. Sch. Ser.*

— **Euthydemus.** With Notes and Introduction by G. H. WELLS, M.A. Post 8vo, 4s. 　　　　　　　　　　　　　　　[*Pub. Sch. Ser.*

— **Phaedrus.** By the late W. H. THOMPSON, D.D., Master of Trinity College, Cambridge. 8vo, 5s. 　　　　　　　　　[*Bib. Class.*

— **Gorgias.** By the late W. H. THOMPSON, D.D., Master of Trinity College, Cambridge. *New edition.* 6s. 　　　　　[*Pub. Sch. Ser.*

PLAUTUS. **Aulularia.** With Notes, critical and exegetical, by W..
WAGNER, PH.D. *5th edition.* Post 8vo, 4*s.* 6*d.* [*Pub. Sch. Ser.*
— **Trinummus.** With Notes, critical and exegetical, by WILHELM
WAGNER, PH.D. *5th edition.* Post 8vo, 4*s.* 6*d.* [*Pub. Sch. Ser.*
— **Menaechmei.** With Notes, critical and exegetical, by WILHELM
WAGNER, PH.D. *2nd edition.* Post 8vo, 4*s.* 6*d.* [*Pub. Sch. Ser.*
— **Mostellaria.** By E. A. SONNENSCHEIN, M.A., Professor of Classics at
Mason College, Birmingham. Post 8vo, 5*s.* [*Pub. Sch. Ser.*
— **Captivi.** Abridged and Edited for the Use of Schools. With Intro-
duction and Notes by J. H. FREESE, M.A., formerly Fellow of St. John's
College, Cambridge. Fcap. 8vo, 1*s.* 6*d.*

PROPERTIUS. **Sex. Aurelii Propertii Carmina.** The Elegies of
Propertius, with English Notes. By F. A. PALEY, M.A., LL.D. *2nd
edition.* 8vo, 5*s.*

SALLUST : **Catilina and Jugurtha.** Edited, with Notes, by the late
GEORGE LONG. *New edition, revised,* with the addition of the Chief
Fragments of the Histories, by J. G. FRAZER, M.A, Fellow of Trinity
College, Cambridge. Fcap. 8vo, 3*s.* 6*d,* or separately, 2*s.* each.
[*Gram. Sch. Class.*

SOPHOCLES. Edited by REV. F. H. BLAYDES, M.A. Vol. I. Oedipus
Tyrannus—Oedipus Coloneus—Antigone. 8vo, 8*s.* [*Bib. Class.*
Vol. II. Philoctetes—Electra—Trachiniae—Ajax. By F. A. PALEY,
M.A., LL.D. 8vo, 6*s.*, or the four Plays separately in limp cloth, 2*s.* 6*d.*
each.
— **Trachiniae.** With Notes and Prolegomena. By ALFRED PRETOR, M.A.,
Fellow of St. Catherine's College, Cambridge. Post 8vo, 4*s.* 6*d.*
[*Pub. Sch. Ser.*
— **The Oedipus Tyrannus of Sophocles.** By B. H. KENNEDY, D.D.,
Regius Professor of Greek and Hon. Fellow of St. John's College, Cam-
bridge. With a Commentary containing a large number of Notes selected
from the MS. of the late T. H. STEEL, M.A. Crown 8vo, 8*s.*
— — A SCHOOL EDITION, post 8vo, 5*s.* [*Pub. Sch. Ser.*
— Edited by F. A. PALEY, M.A., LL.D. 5 vols. Fcap. 8vo, 1*s.* 6*d.* each.
[*Camb. Texts with Notes.*

Oedipus Tyrannus. | Electra.
Oedipus Coloneus. | Ajax.
Antigone. |

TACITUS : **Germania and Agricola.** Edited by the late REV. P. FROST,
late Fellow of St. John's College, Cambridge. Fcap. 8vo, 2*s.* 6*d.*
[*Gram. Sch. Class.*
— **The Germania.** Edited, with Introduction and Notes, by R. F. DAVIS,
M.A. Fcap. 8vo, 1*s.* 6*d.*

TERENCE. With Notes, critical and explanatory, by WILHELM WAGNER,
PH.D. *3rd edition.* Post 8vo, 7*s.* 6*d.* [*Pub. Sch. Ser.*
— Edited by WILHELM WAGNER, PH.D. 4 vols. Fcap. 8vo, 1*s.* 6*d.* each.
[*Camb. Texts with Notes.*

Andria. | Hautontimorumenos.
Adelphi. | Phormio.

THEOCRITUS. With short, critical and explanatory Latin Notes, by
F. A. PALEY, M.A., LL.D. *2nd edition, revised.* Post 8vo, 4*s.* 6*d.*
[*Pub. Sch. Ser.*

THUCYDIDES, Book VI. By T. W. DOUGAN, M.A., Fellow of St. John's College, Cambridge; Professor of Latin in Queen's College, Belfast. Edited with English notes. Post 8vo, 3s. 6d.   [*Pub. Sch. Ser.*

— **The History of the Peloponnesian War.** With Notes and a careful Collation of the two Cambridge Manuscripts, and of the Aldine and Juntine Editions. By the late RICHARD SHILLETO, M.A., Fellow of St. Peter's College, Cambridge. 8vo. Book I. 6s. 6d. Book II. 5s. 6d.

VIRGIL. By the late PROFESSOR CONINGTON, M.A. Revised by the late PROFESSOR NETTLESHIP, Corpus Professor of Latin at Oxford. 8vo.
      [*Bib. Class.*
    Vol. I. The Bucolics and Georgics, with new Memoir and three Essays on Virgil's Commentators, Text, and Critics. 4th edition. 10s. 6d.
    Vol. II. The Aeneid, Books I.-VI. 4th edition. 10s. 6d.
    Vol. III. The Aeneid, Books VII.-XII. 3rd edition. 10s. 6d.

— Abridged from PROFESSOR CONINGTON's Edition, by the REV. J. G. SHEPPARD, D.C.L., H. NETTLESHIP, late Corpus Professor of Latin at the University of Oxford, and W. WAGNER, PH.D. 2 vols. fcap. 8vo, 4s. 6d. each.   [*Gram. Sch. Class.*
    Vol. I. Bucolics, Georgics, and Aeneid, Books I.-IV.
    Vol. II. Aeneid, Books V.-XII.
    Also the Bucolics and Georgics, in one vol. 3s.

Or in 9 separate volumes (*Grammar School Classics, with Notes at foot of page*), *price* 1s. 6d. *each.*

Bucolics.	**Aeneid,** V. and VI.
Georgics, I. and II.	**Aeneid,** VII. and VIII.
Georgics, III. and IV.	**Aeneid,** IX. and X.
Aeneid, I. and II.	**Aeneid,** XI. and XII.
Aeneid, III. and IV.	

Or in 12 separate volumes (*Cambridge Texts with Notes at end*), *price* 1s. 6d. *each.*

Bucolics.	**Aeneid,** VII.
Georgics, I. and II.	**Aeneid,** VIII.
Georgics, III. and IV.	**Aeneid,** IX.
Aeneid, I. and II.	**Aeneid,** X.
Aeneid, III. and IV.	**Aeneid,** XI.
Aeneid, V. and VI. (price 2s.)	**Aeneid,** XII.

    Aeneid, Book I. CONINGTON's Edition abridged. With Vocabulary by W F. R. SHILLETO, M.A. Fcap. 8vo, 1s. 6d.   [*Lower Form Ser.*

XENOPHON : Anabasis. With Life, Itinerary, Index, and three Maps. Edited by the late J. F. MACMICHAEL. *Revised edition.* Fcap. 8vo, 3s. 6d.   [*Gram. Sch. Class.*
    Or in 4 separate volumes, price 1s. 6d. *each.*
    Book I. (with Life, Introduction, Itinerary, and three Maps)—Books II. and III.—Books IV. and V.—Books VI. and VII.

— **Anabasis.** MACMICHAEL's Edition, revised by J. E. MELHUISH, M.A., Assistant Master of St. Paul's School. In 6 volumes, fcap. 8vo. With Life, Itinerary, and Map to each volume, 1s. 6d. each.
      [*Camb. Texts with Notes.*
    Book I.—Books II. and III.—Book IV.—Book V.—Book VI.—Book VII.

XENOPHON. Cyropaedia. Edited by G. M. GORHAM, M.A., late Fellow of Trinity College, Cambridge. *New edition.* Fcap. 8vo, 3*s.* 6*d.*
[*Gram. Sch. Class.*
Also Books I. and II., 1*s.* 6*d.* ; Books V. and VI., 1*s.* 6*d.*
— Memorabilia. Edited by PERCIVAL FROST, M.A., late Fellow of St. John's College, Cambridge. Fcap. 8vo, 3*s.* [*Gram. Sch. Class.*
— Hellenica. Book I. Edited by L. D. DOWDALL, M.A., B.D. Fcap. 8vo, 2*s.* [*Camb. Texts with Notes.*
— Hellenica. Book II. By L. D. DOWDALL, M.A., B.D. Fcap. 8vo, 2*s.*
[*Camb. Texts with Notes.*

TEXTS.

AESCHYLUS. Ex novissima recensione F. A. PALEY, A.M., LL.D. Fcap. 8vo, 2*s.* [*Camb. Texts.*
CAESAR De Bello Gallico. Recognovit G. LONG, A.M. Fcap. 8vo, 1*s.* 6*d.* [*Camb. Texts.*
CATULLUS. A New Text, with Critical Notes and an Introduction, by J. P. POSTGATE, M.A., LITT.D., Fellow of Trinity College, Cambridge, Professor of Comparative Philology at the University of London. Wide fcap. 8vo, 3*s.*
CICERO De Senectute et de Amicitia, et Epistolae Selectae. Recensuit G. LONG, A.M. Fcap. 8vo, 1*s.* 6*d.* [*Camb. Texts.*
CICERONIS Orationes in Verrem. Ex recensione G. LONG, A.M. Fcap. 8vo, 2*s.* 6*d.* [*Camb. Texts.*
CORPUS POETARUM LATINORUM, a se aliisque denuo recognitorum et brevi lectionum varietate instructorum, edidit JOHANNES PERCIVAL POSTGATE. Tom. I.—Ennius, Lucretius, Catullus, Horatius, Vergilius, Tibullus, Propertius, Ovidius. Large post 4to, 21*s.* net. Also in 2 Parts, sewed, 9*s.* each, net.
.*.* To be completed in 4 parts, making 2 volumes.
CORPUS POETARUM LATINORUM. Edited by WALKER. Containing :—Catullus, Lucretius, Virgilius, Tibullus, Propertius, Ovidius, Horatius, Phaedrus, Lucanus, Persius, Juvenalis, Martialis, Sulpicia, Statius, Silius Italicus, Valerius Flaccus, Calpurnius Siculus, Ausonius, and Claudianus. 1 vol. 8vo, cloth, 18*s.*
EURIPIDES. Ex recensione F. A. PALEY, A.M., LL.D. 3 vols. Fcap. 8vo, 2*s.* each. [*Camb. Texts.*
Vol. I.—Rhesus — Medea — Hippolytus— Alcestis —Heraclidae—Supplices—Troades.
Vol. II.—Ion—Helena—Andromache—Electra—Bacchae—Hecuba.
Vol. III.—Hercules Furens—Phoenissae—Orestes—Iphigenia in Tauris —Iphigenia in Aulide—Cyclops.
HERODOTUS. Recensuit J. G. BLAKESLEY, S.T.B. 2 vols. Fcap. 8vo, 2*s.* 6*d.* each. [*Camb. Texts.*
HOMERI ILIAS I.-XII. Ex novissima recensione F. A. PALEY, A.M., LL.D. Fcap. 8vo, 1*s.* 6*d.* [*Camb. Texts.*
HORATIUS. Ex recensione A. J. MACLEANE. A.M. Fcap. 8vo, 1*s.* 6*d.*
[*Camb. Texts.*
JUVENAL ET PERSIUS. Ex recensione A. J. MACLEANE, A.M. Fcap. 8vo, 1*s.* 6*d.* [*Camb. Texts.*

LUCRETIUS. Recognovit H. A. J. MUNRO, A.M. Fcap. 8vo, 2s.
[*Camb. Texts.*

PROPERTIUS. Sex. Propertii Elegiarum Libri IV. recensuit A.
PALMER, collegii sacrosanctae et individuae Trinitatis juxta Dublinum
Socius. Fcap. 8vo, 3s. 6d.

SALLUSTI CRISPI CATILINA ET JUGURTHA, Recognovit
G. LONG, A.M. Fcap. 8vo, 1s. 6d. [*Camb. Texts.*

SOPHOCLES. Ex recensione F. A. PALEY, A.M., LL.D. Fcap. 8vo, 2s. 6d.
[*Camb. Texts.*

TERENTI COMOEDIAE. GUI. WAGNER relegit et emendavit. Fcap.
8vo, 2s. [*Camb. Texts.*

THUCYDIDES. Recensuit J. G. DONALDSON, S.T.P. 2 vols. Fcap.
8vo, 2s. each. [*Camb. Texts.*

VERGILIUS. Ex recensione J. CONINGTON, A.M. Fcap. 8vo, 2s.
[*Camb. Texts.*

XENOPHONTIS EXPEDITIO CYRI. Recensuit ᵀ F. MACMICHAEL.
A.B. Fcap. 8vo, 1s. 6d. [*Camb. Texts.*

TRANSLATIONS.

AESCHYLUS, The Tragedies of. Translated into English Prose. By
F. A. PALEY, M.A., LL.D., Editor of the Greek Text. *2nd edition
revised*, 8vo, 7s. 6d.
— **The Tragedies of.** Translated into English verse by ANNA SWANWICK.
4th edition revised. Small post 8vo, 5s.
— **The Tragedies of.** Literally translated into Prose, by T. A. BUCKLEY, B.A.
Small post 8vo, 3s. 6d.
— **The Tragedies of.** Translated by WALTER HEADLAM, M.A., Fellow of
King's College, Cambridge. [*Preparing.*

ANTONINUS (M. Aurelius), The Thoughts of. Translated by
GEORGE LONG, M.A. *Revised edition.* Small post 8vo, 3s. 6d.
Fine paper edition on handmade paper. Pott 8vo, 6s.

APOLLONIUS RHODIUS. The Argonautica. Translated by E. P.
COLERIDGE. Small post 8vo, 5s.

AMMIANUS MARCELLINUS. History of Rome during the
Reigns of Constantius, Julian, Jovianus, Valentinian, and Valens. Translated by PROF. C. D. YONGE, M.A. With a complete Index. Small post
8vo, 7s. 6d.

ARISTOPHANES, The Comedies of. Literally translated by W. J.
HICKIE. *With Portrait.* 2 vols. small post 8vo, 5s. each.
Vol. I.—Acharnians, Knights, Clouds, Wasps, Peace, and Birds.
Vol. II.—Lysistrata, Thesmophoriazusae, Frogs, Ecclesiazusae, and
Plutus.
— **The Acharnians.** Translated by W. H. COVINGTON, B.A. With Memoir
and Introduction. Crown 8vo, sewed, 1s.

ARISTOTLE on the Athenian Constitution. Translated, with Notes
and Introduction, by F. G. KENYON, M.A., Fellow of Magdalen College,
Oxford. Pott 8vo, printed on handmade paper. *2nd edition.* 4s. 6d.
— **History of Animals.** Translated by RICHARD CRESSWELL, M.A. Small
post 8vo, 5s.

ARISTOTLE. Organon: or, Logical Treatises, and the Introduction of Porphyry. With Notes, Analysis, Introduction, and Index, by the REV. O. F. OWEN, M.A. 2 vols. small post 8vo, 3s. 6d. each.

— **Rhetoric and Poetics.** Literally Translated, with Hobbes' Analysis, &c., by T. BUCKLEY, B.A. Small post 8vo, 5s.

— **Nicomachean Ethics.** Literally Translated, with Notes, an Analytical Introduction, &c., by the Venerable ARCHDEACON BROWNE, late Classical Professor of King's College. Small post 8vo, 5s.

— **Politics and Economics.** Translated, with Notes, Analyses, and Index, by E. WALFORD, M.A., and an Introductory Essay and a Life by DR. GILLIES. Small post 8vo, 5s.

— **Metaphysics.** Literally Translated, with Notes, Analysis, &c., by the REV. JOHN H. M'MAHON, M.A. Small post 8vo, 5s.

ARRIAN. Anabasis of Alexander, together with the Indica. Translated by E. J. CHINNOCK, M.A., LL.D. With Introduction, Notes, Maps, and Plans. Small post 8vo, 5s.

CAESAR. Commentaries on the Gallic and Civil Wars, with the Supplementary Books attributed to Hirtius, including the complete Alexandrian, African, and Spanish Wars. Translated by W. A. M'DEVITTE, B.A. Small post 8vo, 5s.

— **Gallic War.** Translated by W. A. M'DEVITTE, B.A. 2 vols., with Memoir and Map. Crown 8vo, sewed. Books I. to IV., Books V. to VII., 1s. each.

CALPURNIUS SICULUS, The Eclogues of. The Latin Text, with English Translation by E. J. L. SCOTT, M.A. Crown 8vo, 3s. 6d.

CATULLUS, TIBULLUS, and the Vigil of Venus. Prose Translation. Small post 8vo, 5s.

CICERO, The Orations of. Translated by PROF. C. D. YONGE, M.A. With Index. 4 vols. small post 8vo, 5s. each.

— **On Oratory and Orators.** With Letters to Quintus and Brutus. Translated by the REV. J. S. WATSON, M.A. Small post 8vo, 5s.

— **On the Nature of the Gods.** Divination, Fate, Laws, a Republic, Consulship. Translated by PROF. C. D YONGE, M.A., and FRANCIS BARHAM. Small post 8vo, 5s.

— **Academics, De Finibus, and Tusculan Questions.** By PROF. C. D. YONGE, M.A. Small post 8vo, 5s.

— **Offices;** or, Moral Duties. Cato Major, an Essay on Old Age; Laelius, an Essay on Friendship; Scipio's Dream; Paradoxes; Letter to Quintus on Magistrates. Translated by C. R. EDMONDS. *With Portrait,* 3s. 6d.

— **Old Age and Friendship.** Translated, with Memoir and Notes, by G. H. WELLS, M.A. Crown 8vo, sewed, 1s.

DEMOSTHENES, The Orations of. Translated, with Notes, Arguments, a Chronological Abstract, Appendices, and Index, by C. RANN KENNEDY. 5 vols. small post 8vo.

    Vol. I.—The Olynthiacs, Philippics. 3s. 6d.

    Vol. II.—On the Crown and on the Embassy. 5s.

    Vol. III.—Against Leptines, Midias, Androtion, and Aristocrates. 5s.

    Vols. IV. and V.—Private and Miscellaneous Orations. 5s. each.

— **On the Crown.** Translated by C. RANN KENNEDY. Small post 8vo, sewed, 1s., cloth, 1s 6d.

DIOGENES LAERTIUS. Translated by PROF. C. D. YONGE, M.A. Small post 8vo, 5s.

EPICTETUS, The Discourses of. With the **Encheiridion** and Fragments. Translated by GEORGE LONG, M.A. Small post 8vo, 5*s*. Fine Paper Edition, 2 vols. Pott 8vo, 10*s*. 6*d*.

EURIPIDES. A Prose Translation, from the Text of Paley. By E. P. COLERIDGE, B.A. 2 vols., 5*s*. each.

Vol. I.—Rhesus, Medea, Hippolytus, Alcestis, Heraclidæ, Supplices, Troades, Ion, Helena.

Vol. II.—Andromache, Electra, Bacchae, Hecuba, Hercules Furens, Phoenissae, Orestes, Iphigenia in Tauris, Iphigenia in Aulis, Cyclops.

.*.* The plays separately (except Rhesus, Helena, Electra, Iphigenia in Aulis, and Cyclops). Crown 8vo, sewed, 1*s*. each.

— Translated from the Text of Dindorf. By T. A. BUCKLEY, B.A. 2 vols. small post 8vo, 5*s*. each.

GREEK ANTHOLOGY. Translated by GEORGE BURGES, M.A. Small post 8vo, 5*s*.

HERODOTUS. Translated by the REV. HENRY CARY, M.A. Small post 8vo, 3*s*. 6*d*.

— **Analysis and Summary of.** By J. T. WHEELER. Small post 8vo, 5*s*.

HESIOD, CALLIMACHUS, and **THEOGNIS.** Translated by the REV. J. BANKS, M.A. Small post 8vo, 5*s*.

HOMER. The Iliad. Translated by T. A. BUCKLEY, B.A. Small post 8vo, 5*s*.

— **The Odyssey, Hymns, Epigrams, and Battle of the Frogs and Mice.** Translated by T. A. BUCKLEY, B.A. Small post 8vo, 5*s*.

— **The Iliad.** Books I.-IV. Translated into English Hexameter Verse, by HENRY SMITH WRIGHT, B.A., late Scholar of Trinity College, Cambridge. Medium 8vo, 5*s*.

HORACE. Translated by Smart. *Revised edition.* By T. A. BUCKLEY, B.A. Small post 8vo, 3*s*. 6*d*.

— **The Odes and Carmen Saeculare.** Translated into English Verse by the late JOHN CONINGTON, M.A., Corpus Professor of Latin in the University of Oxford. 11*th edition*. Fcap. 8vo. 3*s*. 6*d*.

— **The Satires and Epistles.** Translated into English Verse by PROF. JOHN CONINGTON, M.A. 8*th edition*. Fcap. 8vo, 3*s*. 6*d*.

— **Odes and Epodes.** Translated by SIR STEPHEN E. DE VERE, BART. 3*rd edition, enlarged.* Imperial 16mo. 7*s*. 6*d*. net.

ISOCRATES, The Orations of. Translated by J. H. FREESE, M.A., late Fellow of St. John's College, Cambridge, with Introductions and Notes. Vol. I. Small post 8vo, 5*s*.

JUSTIN, CORNELIUS NEPOS, and **EUTROPIUS.** Translated by the REV. J. S. WATSON, M.A. Small post 8vo, 5*s*.

JUVENAL, PERSIUS, SULPICIA, and **LUCILIUS.** Translated by L. EVANS, M.A. Small post 8vo, 5*s*.

LIVY. The History of Rome. Translated by DR. SPILLAN, C. EDMONDS, and others. 4 vols. small post 8vo, 5*s*. each.

— Books I., II., III., IV. A Revised Translation by J. H. FREESE, M.A., late Fellow of St. John's College, Cambridge. With Memoir, and Maps. 4 vols., crown 8vo, sewed, 1*s*. each.

— Book V. A Revised Translation by E. S. WEYMOUTH, M.A., Lond. With Memoir, and Maps. Crown 8vo, sewed, 1*s*.

— Book IX. Translated by FRANCIS STORR, B.A. With Memoir. Crown 8vo, sewed, 1*s*

LUCAN. The Pharsalia. Translated into Prose by H. T. RILEY. Small post 8vo, 5s.

— The Pharsalia. Book I. Translated by FREDERICK CONWAY, M.A. With Memoir and Introduction. Crown 8vo, sewed, 1s.

LUCIAN'S Dialogues of the Gods, of the Sea-Gods, and of the Dead. Translated by HOWARD WILLIAMS, M.A. Small post 8vo, 5s.

LUCRETIUS. Translated by the REV. J. S. WATSON, M.A. Small post 8vo, 5s.

— Literally translated by the late H. A. J. MUNRO, M.A. *4th edition.* Demy 8vo, 6s.

MARTIAL'S Epigrams, complete. Literally translated into Prose, with the addition of Verse Translations selected from the Works of English Poets, and other sources. Small post 8vo, 7s. 6d.

OVID, The Works of. Translated. 3 vols., small post 8vo, 5s. each.
Vol. I.—Fasti, Tristia, Pontic Epistles, Ibis, and Halieuticon.
Vol. II.—Metamorphoses. *With Frontispiece.*
Vol. III.—Heroides, Amours, Art of Love, Remedy of Love, and Minor Pieces. *With Frontispiece.*

PINDAR. Translated by DAWSON W. TURNER. Small post 8vo, 5s.

PLATO. Gorgias. Translated by the late E. M. COPE, M.A., Fellow of Trinity College. *2nd edition.* 8vo, 7s.

— Philebus. Translated by F. A. PALEY, M.A., LL.D. Small 8vo, 4s.

— Theaetetus. Translated by F. A. PALEY, M.A., LL.D. Small 8vo, 4s.

— The Works of. Translated, with Introduction and Notes. 6 vols. small post 8vo, 5s. each.
Vol. I.—The Apology of Socrates—Crito—Phaedo—Gorgias—Protagoras—Phaedrus—Theaetetus—Euthyphron—Lysis. Translated by the REV. H. CARY.
Vol. II.—The Republic—Timaeus—Critias. Translated by HENRY DAVIS.
Vol. III.—Meno—Euthydemus—The Sophist—Statesman—Cratylus —Parmenides—The Banquet. Translated by G. BURGES.
Vol. IV.—Philebus—Charmides—Laches—Menexenus—Hippias—Ion —The Two Alcibiades—Theages—Rivals—Hipparchus—Minos—Clitopho—Epistles. Translated by G. BURGES.
Vol. V.—The Laws. Translated by G. BURGES.
Vol. VI.—The Doubtful Works. Edited by G. BURGES. With General Index to the six volumes.

— Apology, Crito, Phaedo, and Protagoras. Translated by the REV. H. CARY. Small post 8vo, sewed, 1s., cloth, 1s. 6d.

— Dialogues. A Summary and Analysis of. With Analytical Index, giving references to the Greek text of modern editions and to the above translations. By A. DAY, LL.D. Small post 8vo, 5s.

PLAUTUS, The Comedies of. Translated by H. T. RILEY, B.A. 2 vols. small post 8vo, 5s. each.
Vol. I.—Trinummus—Miles Gloriosus—Bacchides—Stichus—Pseudolus —Menaechmei—Aulularia—Captivi—Asinaria—Curculio.
Vol. II.—Amphitryon—Rudens—Mercator—Cistellaria—Truculentus —Persa—Casina—Poenulus—Epidicus—Mostellaria—Fragments.

— Trinummus, Menaechmei, Aulularia, and Captivi. Translated by H. T. RILEY, B.A. Small post 8vo, sewed, 1s., cloth, 1s. 6d.

PLINY. The Letters of Pliny the Younger. Melmoth's Translation, revised, by the REV. F. C. T. BOSANQUET, M.A. Small post 8vo, 5*s.*

PLUTARCH. Lives. Translated by A. STEWART, M.A., late Fellow of Trinity College, Cambridge, and GEORGE LONG, M.A. 4 vols. small post 8vo, 3*s.* 6*d.* each.

— **Morals.** Theosophical Essays. Translated by C. W. KING, M.A., late Fellow of Trinity College, Cambridge. Small post 8vo, 5*s.*

— **Morals.** Ethical Essays. Translated by the REV. A. R. SHILLETO, M.A. Small post 8vo, *s.*

PROPERTIUS. Translated by REV. P. J. F. GANTILLON, M.A., and accompanied by Poetical Versions, from various sources. Small post 8vo, 3*s.* 6*d.*

PRUDENTIUS, Translations from. A Selection from his Works, with a Translation into English Verse, and an Introduction and Notes, by FRANCIS ST. JOHN THACKERAY, M.A., F.S.A., Vicar of Mapledurham, formerly Fellow of Lincoln College, Oxford, and Assistant-Master at Eton. Wide post 8vo, 7*s.* 6*d.*

QUINTILIAN: Institutes of Oratory, or, Education of an Orator. Translated by the REV. J. S. WATSON, M.A. 2 vols. small post 8vo, 5*s.* each.

SALLUST, FLORUS, and VELLEIUS PATERCULUS. Translated by J. S. WATSON, M.A. Small post 8vo, 5*s.*

SENECA: On Benefits. Translated by A. STEWART, M.A., late Fellow of Trinity College, Cambridge. Small post 8vo, 3*s.* 6*d.*

— **Minor Essays and On Clemency.** Translated by A. STEWART, M.A. Small post 8vo, 5*s.*

SOPHOCLES. Translated, with Memoir, Notes, etc., by E. P. COLERIDGE, B.A. Small post 8vo, 5*s.*

    Or the plays separately, crown 8vo, sewed, 1*s.* each.

— **The Tragedies of.** The Oxford Translation, with Notes, Arguments, and Introduction. Small post 8vo, 5*s.*

— **The Dramas of.** Rendered in English Verse, Dramatic and Lyric, by SIR GEORGE YOUNG, BART., M.A., formerly Fellow of Trinity College, Cambridge. 8vo, 12s. 6*d.*

— **The Œdipus Tyrannus.** Translated into English Prose. By PROF. B. H. KENNEDY. Crown 8vo, in paper wrapper, 1*s.*

SUETONIUS. Lives of the Twelve Caesars and Lives of the Grammarians. Thomson's revised Translation, by T. FORESTER. Small post 8vo, 5*s.*

TACITUS, The Works of. Translated, with Notes and Index. 2 vols. Small post 8vo, 5*s.* each.

    Vol. I.—The Annals.

    Vol. II.—The History, Germania, Agricola, Oratory, and Index.

TERENCE and PHAEDRUS. Translated by H. T. RILEY, B.A. Small post 8vo, 5*s.*

THEOCRITUS, BION, MOSCHUS, and TYRTAEUS. Translated by the REV. J. BANKS, M.A. Small post 8vo, 5*s.*

THEOCRITUS. Translated into English Verse by C. S. CALVERLEY, M.A., late Fellow of Christ's College, Cambridge. *New edition, revised.* Crown 8vo, 7*s.* 6*d.*

THUCYDIDES. The Peloponnesian War. Translated by the REV..H. DALE. *With Portrait.* 2 vols., 3*s.* 6*d.* each.
— **Analysis and Summary of.** By J. T. WHEELER. Small post 8vo, 5*s.*
VIRGIL. Translated by A. HAMILTON BRYCE, LL.D. With Memoir and Introduction. Small post 8vo, 3*s.* 6*d.*
 Also in 6 vols., crown 8vo, sewed, 1*s.* each.

Georgics.	Æneid IV.-VI.
Bucolics.	Æneid VII.-IX.
Æneid I.-III.	Æneid X.-XII.

XENOPHON. The Works of. In 3 vols. Small post 8vo, 5*s.* each.
 Vol. I.—The Anabasis, and Memorabilia. Translated by the REV. J. S. WATSON, M.A. With a Geographical Commentary, by W. F. AINSWORTH, F.S.A., F.R.G.S., etc.
 Vol. II.—Cyropaedia and Hellenics. Translated by the REV. J. S. WATSON, M.A., and the REV. H. DALE.
 Vol. III.—The Minor Works. Translated by the REV. J. S. WATSON, M.A.
SABRINAE COROLLA In Hortulis Regiae Scholae Salopiensis con-texuerunt tres viri floribus legendis. *4th edition, revised and re-arranged.* By the late BENJAMIN HALL KENNEDY, D.D., Regius Professor of Greek at the University of Cambridge. Large post 8vo, 10*s.* 6*d.*
SERTUM CARTHUSIANUM Floribus trium Seculorum Contextum. Cura GULIELMI HAIG BROWN, Scholae Carthusianae Archididascali. Demy 8vo, 5*s.*
TRANSLATIONS into English and Latin. By C. S. CALVERLEY, M.A., late Fellow of Christ's College, Cambridge. *3rd edition.* Crown 8vo, 7*s.* 6*d.*
TRANSLATIONS from and into the Latin, Greek and English. By R. C. JEBB, M.A., Regius Professor of Greek in the University of Cam-bridge, H. JACKSON, M.A., LITT. D., Fellows of Trinity College, Cam-bridge, and W. E. CURREY, M.A., formerly Fellow of Trinity College, Cambridge. Crown 8vo. *2nd edition. revised.* 8*s.*

GRAMMAR AND COMPOSITION.

BADDELEY. Auxilia Latina. A Series of Progressive Latin Exercises. By M. J. B. BADDELEY, M.A. Fcap. 8vo. Part I., Accidence. *5th edition.* 2*s.* Part II. *5th edition.* 2*s.* Key to Part II. 2*s.* 6*d.*
BAIRD. Greek Verbs. A Catalogue of Verbs, Irregular and Defective ; their leading formations, tenses in use, and dialectic inflexions, with a copious Appendix, containing Paradigms for conjugation, Rules for formation of tenses, &c., &c. By J. S. BAIRD, T.C.D. *New edition, re-vised.* 2*s.* 6*d.*
— Homeric Dialect. Its Leading Forms and Peculiarities. By J. S. BAIRD, T.C.D. *New edition, revised.* By the REV. W. GUNION RUTHERFORD, M.A., LL.D., Head Master at Westminster School. 1*s.*
BAKER. Latin Prose for London Students. By ARTHUR BAKER, M.A., Classical Master, Independent College, Taunton. Fcap. 8vo, 2*s.*

BARRY. Notes on Greek Accents. By the RIGHT REV. A. BARRY, D.D. *New edition, re-written.* 1s.

CHURCH. Latin Prose Lessons. By A. J. CHURCH, M.A., Professor of Latin at University College, London. *9th edition.* Fcap. 8vo, 2s. 6d.

CLAPIN. Latin Primer. By the REV. A. C. CLAPIN, M.A., Assistant Master at Sherborne School. *3rd edition.* Fcap. 8vo, 1s.

COLLINS. Latin Exercises and Grammar Papers. By T. COLLINS, M.A., Head Master of the Latin School, Newport, Salop. *7th edition.* Fcap. 8vo, 2s. 6d.

— **Unseen Papers** in Latin Prose and Verse. With Examination Questions. *6th edition.* Fcap. 8vo, 2s. 6d.

— **Unseen Papers** in Greek Prose and Verse. With Examination Questions. *3rd edition.* Fcap. 8vo, 3s.

—. **Easy Translations** from Nepos, Caesar, Cicero, Livy, &c., for Retranslation into Latin. With Notes. 2s.

COMPTON. Rudiments of Attic Construction and Idiom. An Introduction to Greek Syntax for Beginners who have acquired some knowledge of Latin. By the REV. W. COOKWORTHY COMPTON, M.A., Head Master of Dover College. Crown 8vo, 3s.

FROST. Eclogae Latinae; or, First Latin Reading Book. With Notes and Vocabulary by the late REV. P. FROST, M.A. Fcap. 8vo, 1s. 6d.

— **Analecta Graeca Minora.** With Notes and Dictionary. *New edition.* Fcap. 8vo, 2s.

— **Materials for Latin Prose Composition.** By the late REV. P. FROST, M.A. *New edition.* Fcap. 8vo. 2s. Key. 4s. net.

— **A Latin Verse Book.** *New edition.* Fcap. 8vo, 2s. Key. 5s. net.

— **Materials for Greek Prose Composition.** *New edition.* Fcap. 8vo, 2s. 6d. Key. 5s. net.

— **Greek Accidence.** *New edition.* 1s.

— **Latin Accidence.** 1s.

HARKNESS. A Latin Grammar. By ALBERT HARKNESS. Post 8vo, 6s.

KEY. A Latin Grammar. By the late T. H. KEY, M.A., F.R.S. *6th thousand.* Post 8vo, 8s.

— **A Short Latin Grammar for Schools.** *16th edition.* Post 8vo, 3s. 6d.

HOLDEN. Foliorum Silvula. Part I. Passages for Translation into Latin Elegiac and Heroic Verse. By H. A. HOLDEN, LL.D. *11th edition.* Post 8vo, 7s. 6d.

— **Foliorum Silvula.** Part II. Select Passages for Translation into Latin Lyric and Comic Iambic Verse. *3rd edition.* Post 8vo, 5s.

— **Foliorum Centuriae.** Select Passages for Translation into Latin and Greek Prose. *10th edition.* Post 8vo, 8s.

JEBB, JACKSON, and CURREY. Extracts for Translation in Greek, Latin, and English. By R. C. JEBB, LITT.D., LL.D., Regius Professor of Greek in the University of Cambridge; H. JACKSON, LITT.D., Fellow of Trinity College, Cambridge; and W. E. CURREY, M.A., late Fellow of Trinity College, Cambridge. 4s. 6d.

Latin Syntax, Principles of. 1s.

Latin Versification. 1s.

MASON. Analytical Latin Exercises By C. P. MASON, B.A. *4th edition.* Part I., 1s. 6d. Part II., 2s. 6d.

— **The Analysis of Sentences Applied to Latin.** Post 8vo, 1s. 6d.

NETTLESHIP. **Passages for Translation into Latin Prose.** Preceded by Essays on :—I. Political and Social Ideas. II. Range of Metaphorical Expression. III. Historical Development of Latin Prose Style in Antiquity. IV. Cautions as to Orthography. By H. NETTLESHIP, M.A., late Corpus Professor of Latin in the University of Oxford. Crown 8vo, 3s. A Key, 4s. 6d. net.

Notabilia Quaedam; or the Principal Tenses of most of the Irregular Greek Verbs, and Elementary Greek, Latin, and French Constructions. *New edition.* 1s.

PALEY. **Greek Particles** and their Combinations according to Attic Usage. A Short Treatise. By F. A. PALEY, M.A., LL.D. 2s. 6d.

PENROSE. **Latin Elegiac Verse,** Easy Exercises in. By the REV. J. PENROSE. *New edition.* 2s. (Key, 3s. 6d. net.)

PRESTON. **Greek Verse Composition.** By G. PRESTON, M.A. *5th edition.* Crown 8vo, 4s. 6d.

PRUEN. **Latin Examination Papers.** Comprising Lower, Middle, and Upper School Papers, and a number of the Woolwich and Sandhurst Standards. By G. G. PRUEN, M.A., Senior Classical Master in the Modern Department, Cheltenham College. Crown 8vo, 2s. 6d.

SEAGER. **Faciliora.** An Elementary Latin Book on a New Principle. By the REV. J. L. SEAGER, M.A. 2s. 6d.

STEDMAN (A. M. M.). **First Latin Lessons.** By A. M. M. STEDMAN, M.A., Wadham College, Oxford. *2nd edition, enlarged.* Crown 8vo, 2s.

— **Initia Latina.** Easy Lessons on Elementary Accidence. *2nd edition.* Fcap. 8vo, 1s.

— **First Latin Reader.** With Notes adapted to the Shorter Latin Primer and Vocabulary. Crown 8vo, 1s. 6d.

— **Easy Latin Passages** for Unseen Translation. *2nd and enlarged edition.* Fcap. 8vo, 1s. 6d.

Exempla Latina. First Exercises in Latin Accidence. With Vocabulary. Crown 8vo, 1s. 6d.

— **The Latin Compound Sentence;** Rules and Exercises. Crown 8vo, 1s. 6d. With Vocabulary, 2s.

— **Easy Latin Exercises** on the Syntax of the Shorter and Revised Latin Primers. With Vocabulary. *3rd edition.* Crown 8vo, 2s. 6d.

— **Latin Examination Papers** in Miscellaneous Grammar and Idioms. *3rd edition.* 2s. 6d. Key (for Tutors only), 6s. net.

— **Notanda Quaedam.** Miscellaneous Latin Exercises. On Common Rules and Idioms. *2nd edition.* Fcap. 8vo 1s. 6d. With Vocabulary, 2s.

— **Latin Vocabularies** for Repetition. Arranged according to Subjects. *3rd edition.* Fcap. 8vo, 1s. 6d.

— **First Greek Lessons.** [*In preparation.*

— **Easy Greek Passages** for Unseen Translation. Fcap. 8vo, 1s. 6d.

— **Easy Greek Exercises** on Elementary Syntax. [*In preparation.*

— **Greek Vocabularies** for Repetition. Fcap. 8vo, 1s. 6d.

— **Greek Testament Selections** for the Use of Schools. *2nd edition.* With Introduction, Notes, and Vocabulary. Fcap. 8vo, 2s. 6d.

— **Greek Examination Papers** in Miscellaneous Grammar and Idioms. *2nd edition.* 2s. 6d. Key (for Tutors only), 6s. net.

THACKERAY. **Anthologia Graeca.** A Selection of Greek Poetry, with Notes. By F. ST. JOHN THACKERAY. *5th edition.* 16mo, 4s. 6d.

THACKERAY, Anthologia Latina. A Selection of Latin Poetry, from Naevius to Boëthius, with Notes. By REV. F. ST. JOHN THACKERAY. *6th edition.* 16mo, 4*s.* 6*d.*
— **Hints and Cautions on Attic Greek Prose Composition.** Crown 8vo, 3*s.* 6*d.*
— **Exercises on the Irregular and Defective Greek Verbs.** 1*s.* 6*d.*
WELLS. Tales for Latin Prose Composition. With Notes and Vocabulary. By G. H. WELLS, M.A., Assistant Master at Merchant .Taylor's School. Fcap. 8vo, 2*s.*

HISTORY, GEOGRAPHY, AND REFERENCE BOOKS, ETC.

TEUFFEL'S History of Roman Literature. *5th edition,* revised by DR. SCHWABE, translated by PROFESSOR G. C. W. WARR, M.A , King's College, London. Medium 8vo. 2 vols. 30*s.* Vol. I. (The Republican Period), 15*s.* Vol. II. (The Imperial Period), 15*s.*
KEIGHTLEY'S Mythology of Ancient Greece and Italy. *4th edition,* revised by the late LEONHARD SCHMITZ, PH.D., LL.D., Classical Examiner to the University of London With 12 Plates. Small post 8vo, 5*s.*
DONALDSON'S Theatre of the Greeks. *10th edition.* Small post 8vo, 5*s.*
DICTIONARY OF LATIN AND GREEK QUOTATIONS; including Proverbs, Maxims, Mottoes, Law Terms and Phrases. With all the Quantities marked, and English Translations. With Index Verborum. Small post 8vo, 5*s.*
A GUIDE TO THE CHOICE OF CLASSICAL BOOKS. By J. B. MAYOR, M.A., Professor of Moral Philosophy at King's College, late Fellow and Tutor of St. John's College, Cambridge. *3rd edition,* with Supplementary List. Crown 8vo, 4*s.* 6*d.* Supplement separate, 1*s.* 6*d.*
PAUSANIAS' Description of Greece. Newly translated, with Notes and Index, by A. R. SHILLETO, M.A. 2 vols. Small post 8vo, 5*s.* each.
STRABO'S Geography. Translated by W. FALCONER, M.A., and H. C. HAMILTON. 3 vols. Small post 8vo, 5*s.* each.
AN ATLAS OF CLASSICAL GEOGRAPHY. By W. HUGHES and G. LONG, M.A. Containing Ten selected Maps. Imp. 8vo, 3*s.*
AN ATLAS OF CLASSICAL GEOGRAPHY. Twenty-four Maps by W. HUGHES and GEORGE LONG, M.A. With coloured outlines. Imperial 8vo, 6*s.*
ATLAS OF CLASSICAL GEOGRAPHY. 22 large Coloured Maps. With a complete Index. Imp. 8vo, chiefly engraved by the Messrs. Walker. 7*s.* 6*d.*

MATHEMATICS.

ARITHMETIC AND ALGEBRA.

BARRACLOUGH (T.). The Eclipse Mental Arithmetic. By TITUS BARRACLOUGH, Board School, Halifax. Standards I., II., and III., sewed, 6*d.* ; Standards II., III., and IV., sewed, 6*d.* net ; Book III., Part A, sewed, 4*d.* ; Book III., Part B, cloth, 1*s.* 6*d.*

BEARD (W. S.). Graduated Exercises in Addition (Simple and Compound). For Candidates for Commercial Certificates and Civil Service appointments. By W. S. BEARD, F.R.G.S., Head Master of the Modern School, Fareham. 2*nd edition.* Fcap. 4to, 1*s.*

— *See* **PENDLEBURY.**

ELSEE (C.). Arithmetic. By the REV. C. ELSEE, M.A., late Fellow of St. John's College, Cambridge, Senior Mathematical Master at Rugby School. 14*th edition.* Fcap. 8vo, 3*s.* 6*d.*
[*Camb. School and College Texts.*

— **Algebra.** By the REV. C. ELSEE, M.A. 8*th edition.* Fcap. 8vo, 4*s.*
[*Camb. S. and C. Texts.*

FILIPOWSKI (H. E.). Anti-Logarithms, A Table of. By H. E. FILIPOWSKI. 3*rd edition.* 8vo, 15*s.*

GOUDIE (W. P.). *See* **Watson.**

HATHORNTHWAITE (J. T.). Elementary Algebra for Indian Schools. By J. T. HATHORNTHWAITE, M.A., Principal and Professor of Mathematics at Elphinstone College, Bombay. Crown 8vo, 2*s.*

HUNTER (J.). Supplementary Arithmetic, with Answers. By REV. J. HUNTER, M.A. Fcap. 8vo, 3*s.*

MACMICHAEL (W. F.) and PROWDE SMITH (R.). Algebra. A Progressive Course of Examples. By the REV. W. F. MACMICHAEL, and R. PROWDE SMITH, M.A. 4*th edition.* Fcap. 8vo, 3*s.* 6*d.* With answers, 4*s.* 6*d.* [*Camb. S. and C. Texts.*

MATHEWS (G. B.). Theory of Numbers. An account of the Theories of Congruencies and of Arithmetical Forms. By G. B. MATHEWS, M.A., Professor of Mathematics in the University College of North Wales. Part I. Demy 8vo, 12*s.*

PENDLEBURY (C.). Arithmetic. With Examination Papers and 8,000 Examples. By CHARLES PENDLEBURY, M.A., F.R.A.S., Senior Mathematical Master of St. Paul's, Author of " Lenses and Systems of Lenses, treated after the manner of Gauss." 7*th edition.* Crown 8vo. Complete, with or without Answers, 4*s.* 6*d.* In Two Parts, with or without Answers, 2*s.* 6*d.* each.
Key to Part II. 7*s.* 6*d.* net. [*Camb. Math. Ser.*

— **Examples in Arithmetic.** Extracted from Pendlebury's Arithmetic. With or without Answers. 5*th edition.* Crown 8vo, 3*s.*, or in Two Parts, 1*s.* 6*d.* and 2*s.* [*Camb. Math. Ser.*

— **Examination Papers in Arithmetic.** Consisting of 140 papers, each containing 7 questions ; and a collection of 357 more difficult problems. 2*nd edition.* Crown 8vo, 2*s.* 6*d.* Key, for Tutors only, 5*s.* net.

PENDLEBURY (C.) and TAIT (T. S.). Arithmetic for Indian Schools. By C. PENDLEBURY, M.A. and T. S. TAIT, M.A., B.SC., Principal of Baroda College. Crown 8vo, 3*s*. [*Camb. Math. Ser.*

PENDLEBURY (C.) and BEARD (W. S.). Arithmetic for the Standards. By C. PENDLEBURY, M.A., F.R.A.S., and W. S. BEARD, F.R.G.S. Standards I., II , III., sewed, 2*d*. each, cloth, 3*d*. each ; IV., V., VI., sewed, 3*d*. each, cloth, 4*d*. each ; VII., sewed, 6*d*., cloth, 8*d*. Answers to I. and II., 4*d*., III.-VII., 4*d*. each.

— **Elementary Arithmetic.** 3*rd edition*. Crown 8vo, 1*s*. 6*d*.

POPE (L. J.). Lessons in Elementary Algebra. By L. J. POPE, B.A. (Lond.), Assistant Master at the Oratory School, Birmingham. First Series, up to and including Simple Equations and Problems. Crown 8vo, 1*s*. 6*d*.

PROWDE SMITH (R.). *See* Macmichael.

SHAW (S. J. D.). Arithmetic Papers. Set in the Cambridge Higher Local Examination, from June, 1869, to June, 1887, inclusive, reprinted by permission of the Syndicate. By S. J. D. SHAW, Mathematical Lecturer of Newnham College. Crown 8vo, 2*s*. 6*d*. ; Key, 4*s*. 6*d*. net.

TAIT (T. S.). *See* Pendlebury.

WATSON (J.) and GOUDIE (W. P.). Arithmetic. A Progressive Course of Examples. With Answers. By J. WATSON, M.A., Corpus Christi College, Cambridge, formerly Senior Mathematical Master of the Ordnance School, Carshalton. 7*th edition, revised and enlarged*. By W. P. GOUDIE, B.A. Lond. Fcap. 8vo, 2*s*. 6*d*. [*Camb. S. and C. Texts.*

WHITWORTH (W. A.). Algebra. Choice and Chance. An Elementary Treatise on Permutations, Combinations, and Probability, with 640 Exercises and Answers. By W. A. WHITWORTH, M.A., Fellow of St. John's College, Cambridge. 4*th edition, revised and enlarged*. Crown 8vo, 6*s*. [*Camb. Math. Ser.*

WRIGLEY (A.) Arithmetic. By A. WRIGLEY, M.A., St. John's College. Fcap. 8vo, 3*s*. 6*d*. [*Camb. S. and C. Texts.*

BOOK-KEEPING.

CRELLIN (P.). A New Manual of Book-keeping, combining the Theory and Practice, with Specimens of a set of Books. By PHILLIP CRELLIN, Chartered Accountant. Crown 8vo, 3*s*. 6*d*.

— **Book-keeping for Teachers and Pupils.** Crown 8vo, 1*s*. 6*d*. Key, 2*s*. net.

FOSTER (B. W.). Double Entry Elucidated. By B. W. FOSTER. 14*th edition*. Fcap. 4to, 3*s*. 6*d*.

MEDHURST (J. T.). Examination Papers in Book-keeping. Compiled by JOHN T. MEDHURST, A.K.C., F.S.S., Fellow of the Society of Accountants and Auditors, and Lecturer at the City of London College. 3*rd edition*. Crown 8vo, 3*s*.

THOMSON (A. W.). A Text-Book of the Principles and Practice of Book-keeping. By PROFESSOR A. W. THOMSON, B.SC., Royal Agricultural College, Cirencester. Crown 8vo, 5*s*.

GEOMETRY AND EUCLID.

BESANT (W. H.). **Geometrical Conic Sections.** By W. H. BESANT, SC.D., F.R.S., Fellow of St. John's College, Cambridge. *8th edition.* Fcap. 8vo, 4*s.* 6*d.* Enunciations, separately, sewed, 1*s.*
[*Camb. S. and C. Texts.*

BRASSE (J.). The Enunciations and Figures of Euclid, prepared for Students in Geometry. By the REV. J. BRASSE, D.D. *New edition.* Fcap. 8vo, 1*s.* Without the Figures, 6*d.*

DEIGHTON (H.). **Euclid.** Books I.-VI., and part of Book XI., newly translated from the Greek Text, with Supplementary Propositions, Chapters on Modern Geometry, and numerous Exercises. By HORACE DEIGHTON, M.A., Head Master of Harrison College, Barbados. *3rd edition.* 4*s.* 6*d.*, or Books I.-IV., 3*s.* Books V.-XI., 2*s.* 6*d.* Key, 5*s.* net.
[*Camb. Math. Ser.*
Also issued in parts :—Book I., 1*s.* ; Books I. and II., 1*s.* 6*d.* ; Books I.-III., 2*s.* 6*d.* ; Books III. and IV., 1*s.* 6*d.*

DIXON (E. T.). The Foundations of Geometry. By EDWARD T. DIXON, late Royal Artillery. Demy 8vo, 6*s.*

MASON (C. P.). **Euclid.** The First Two Books Explained to Beginners. By C. P. MASON, B.A. *2nd edition.* Fcap. 8vo, 2*s.* 6*d.*

McDOWELL (J.) **Exercises on Euclid** and in Modern Geometry, containing Applications of the Principles and Processes of Modern Pure Geometry. By the late J. McDOWELL, M.A., F.R.A.S., Pembroke College, Cambridge, and Trinity College, Dublin. *4th edition.* 6*s.*
[*Camb. Math. Ser.*

TAYLOR (C.). An Introduction to the Ancient and Modern Geometry of Conics, with Historical Notes and Prolegomena. 15*s.*
— The Elementary Geometry of Conics. By C. TAYLOR, D.D., Master of St. John's College. *7th edition, revised.* With a Chapter on the Line Infinity, and a new treatment of the Hyperbola. Crown 8vo, 4*s.* 6*d.*
[*Camb. Math. Ser.*

WEBB (R.). The Definitions of Euclid. With Explanations and Exercises, and an Appendix of Exercises on the First Book by R. WEBB, M.A. Crown 8vo, 1*s.* 6*d.*

WILLIS (H. G.). **Geometrical Conic Sections.** An Elementary Treatise. By H. G. WILLIS, M.A., Clare College, Cambridge, Assistant Master of Manchester Grammar School. Crown 8vo, 5*s.*
[*Camb. Math. Ser.*

ANALYTICAL GEOMETRY, ETC.

ALDIS (W. S.). **Solid Geometry,** An Elementary Treatise on. By W. S. ALDIS, M.A., late Professor of Mathematics in the University College, Auckland, New Zealand. *4th edition, revised.* Crown 8vo, 6*s.*
[*Camb. Math. Ser.*

BESANT (W. H.). **Notes on Roulettes and Glissettes.** By W. H. BESANT, SC.D., F.R.S. *2nd edition, enlarged.* Crown 8vo, 5*s.*
[*Camb. Math. Ser.*

CAYLEY (A.). Elliptic Functions, An Elementary Treatise on. By ARTHUR CAYLEY, Sadlerian Professor of Pure Mathematics in the University of Cambridge. Demy 8vo. *New edition in the Press.*

TURNBULL (W. P.). Analytical Plane Geometry, An Introduction to. By W. P. TURNBULL, M.A., sometime Fellow of Trinity College. 8vo, 12*s.*

VYVYAN (T. G.). Analytical Geometry for Schools. By REV. T. VYVYAN, M.A., Fellow of Gonville and Caius College, and Mathematical Master of Charterhouse. *6th edition.* 8vo, 4*s.* 6*d.*
[*Camb. S. and C. Texts.*

— Analytical Geometry for Beginners. Part I. The Straight Line and Circle. Crown 8vo, 2*s.* 6*d.* [*Camb. Math. Ser.*

WHITWORTH (W. A.). Trilinear Co-ordinates, and other methods of Modern Analytical Geometry of Two Dimensions. By W. A. WHITWORTH, M.A., late Professor of Mathematics in Queen's College, Liverpool, and Scholar of St. John's College, Cambridge. 8vo, 16*s.*

TRIGONOMETRY.

DYER (J. M.) and WHITCOMBE (R. H.). Elementary Trigonometry. By J. M. DYER, M.A. (Senior Mathematical Scholar at Oxford), and REV. R. H. WHITCOMBE, Assistant Masters at Eton College. *2nd edition.* Crown 8vo, 4*s.* 6*d.* [*Camb. Math. Ser.*

VYVYAN (T. G.). Introduction to Plane Trigonometry. By the REV. T. G. VYVYAN, M.A., formerly Fellow of Gonville and Caius College, Senior Mathematical Master of Charterhouse. *3rd edition, revised and augmented.* Crown 8vo, 3*s.* 6*d.* [*Camb. Math. Ser.*

WARD (G. H.). Examination Papers in Trigonometry. By G. H. WARD, M.A., Assistant Master at St. Paul's School. Crown 8vo, 2*s.* 6*d.* Key, 5*s.* net.

MECHANICS AND NATURAL PHILOSOPHY.

ALDIS (W. S.). Geometrical Optics, An Elementary Treatise on. By W. S. ALDIS, M.A. *4th edition.* Crown 8vo, 4*s.* [*Camb. Math. Ser.*

— An Introductory Treatise on Rigid Dynamics. Crown 8vo, 4*s.*
[*Camb. Math. Ser.*

— Fresnel's Theory of Double Refraction, A Chapter on. *2nd edition, revised.* 8vo, 2*s.*

BASSET (A. B.). A Treatise on Hydrodynamics, with numerous Examples. By A. B. BASSET, M.A., F.R.S., Trinity College, Cambridge. Demy 8vo. Vol. I., price 10*s.* 6*d.* ; Vol. II., 12*s.* 6*d.*

— An Elementary Treatise on Hydrodynamics and Sound. Demy 8vo, 7*s.* 6*d.*

— A Treatise on Physical Optics. Demy 8vo, 16*s.*

BESANT (W. H.). Elementary Hydrostatics. By W. H. BESANT, SC.D., F.R.S. *16th edition.* Crown 8vo, 4*s.* 6*d.* Solutions, 5*s.*
[*Camb. Math. Ser.*

— Hydromechanics, A Treatise on. Part I. Hydrostatics. *5th edition revised, and enlarged.* Crown 8vo, 5*s.* [*Camb. Math. Ser.*

BESANT (W. H.). **A Treatise on Dynamics.** *2nd edition.* Crown 8vo, 10s. 6d. [*Camb. Math. Ser.*

CHALLIS (PROF.). Pure and Applied Calculation. By the late REV. J. CHALLIS, M.A., F.R.S., &c. Demy 8vo, 15s.

— Physics, The Mathematical Principle of. Demy 8vo, 5s.

— Lectures on Practical Astronomy. Demy 8vo, 10s.

EVANS (J. H.) and MAIN (P. T.). Newton's Principia, The First Three Sections of, with an Appendix; and the Ninth and Eleventh Sections. By J. H. EVANS, M.A., St. John's College. The *5th edition*, edited by P. T. MAIN, M.A., Lecturer and Fellow of St. John's College. Fcap. 8vo, 4s. [*Camb. S. and C. Texts.*

GALLATLY (W.). Elementary Physics, Examples and Examination Papers in. Statics, Dynamics, Hydrostatics, Heat, Light, Chemistry, Electricity, London Matriculation, Cambridge B.A., Edinburgh, Glasgow, South Kensington, Cambridge Junior and Senior Papers, and Answers. By W. GALLATLY, M.A., Pembroke College, Cambridge, Assistant Examiner, London University. Crown 8vo, 4s. [*Camb. Math. Ser.*

GARNETT (W.). Elementary Dynamics for the use of Colleges and Schools. By WILLIAM GARNETT, M.A., D.C.L., Fellow of St. John's College, late Principal of the Durham College of Science, Newcastle-upon-Tyne. *5th edition, revised.* Crown 8vo, 6s. [*Camb. Math. Ser.*

— Heat, An Elementary Treatise on. *6th edition, revised.* Crown 8vo, 4s. 6d. [*Camb. Math. Ser.*

GOODWIN (H.). **Statics.** By H. GOODWIN, D.D., late Bishop of Carlisle. *2nd edition.* Fcap. 8vo, 3s. [*Camb. S. and C. Texts.*

HOROBIN (J. C.). Elementary Mechanics. Stage I. II. and III., 1s. 6d. each. By J. C. HOROBIN, M.A., Principal of Homerton New College, Cambridge.

— Theoretical Mechanics. Division I. Crown 8vo, 2s. 6d.

*** This book covers the ground of the Elementary Stage of Division I. of Subject VI. of the "Science Directory," and is intended for the examination of the Science and Art Department.

JESSOP (C. M.). The Elements of Applied Mathematics. Including Kinetics, Statics and Hydrostatics. By C. M. JESSOP, M.A., late Fellow of Clare College, Cambridge, Lecturer in Mathematics in the Durham College of Science, Newcastle-on-Tyne. Crown 8vo, 6s. [*Camb. Math. Ser.*

MAIN (P. T.). Plane Astronomy, An Introduction to. By P. T. MAIN, M.A., Lecturer and Fellow of St. John's College. *6th edition, revised.* Fcap. 8vo, 4s. [*Camb. S. and C. Texts.*

PARKINSON (R. M.). Structural Mechanics. By R. M. PARKINSON, ASSOC. M.I.C.E. Crown 8vo, 4s. 6d.

PENDLEBURY (C.). Lenses and Systems of Lenses, Treated after the Manner of Gauss. By CHARLES PENDLEBURY, M.A., F.R.A.S., Senior Mathematical Master of St. Paul's School, late Scholar of St. John's College, Cambridge. Demy 8vo, 5s.

STEELE (R. E.). Natural Science Examination Papers. By R. E. STEELE, M.A., F.C.S., Chief Natural Science Master, Bradford Grammar School. Crown 8vo. Part I., Inorganic Chemistry, 2s. 6d. Part II., Physics (Sound, Light, Heat, Magnetism, Electricity), 2s. 6d. [*School Exam. Series.*

WALTON (W.). Theoretical Mechanics, Problems in. By W. WAL-
TON, M.A, Fellow and Assistant Tutor of Trinity Hall, Mathematical
Lecturer at Magdalene College. *3rd edition, revised.* Demy 8vo, 16s.
— Elementary Mechanics, Problems in. *2nd edition.* Crown 8vo, 6s.
[*Camb. Math. Ser.*

DAVIS (J. F.). Army Mathematical Papers. Being Ten Years'
Woolwich and Sandhurst Preliminary Papers. Edited, with Answers, by
J. F. DAVIS, D.LIT., M.A. Lond. Crown 8vo, 2s. 6d.
DYER (J. M.) and PROWDE SMITH (R.). Mathematical Ex-
amples. A Collection of Examples in Arithmetic, Algebra, Trigono-
metry, Mensuration, Theory of Equations, Analytical Geometry, Statics,
Dynamics, with Answers, &c. For Army and Indian Civil Service
Candidates. By J. M. DYER, M.A., Assistant Master, Eton College
(Senior Mathematical Scholar at Oxford), and R. PROWDE SMITH, M.A.
Crown 8vo, 6s. [*Camb. Math. Ser.*
GOODWIN (H.). Problems and Examples, adapted to "Goodwin's
Elementary Course of Mathematics." By T. G. VYVYAN, M.A. *3rd
edition.* 8vo, 5s. ; Solutions, *3rd edition,* 8vo, 9s.
SMALLEY (G. R.). A Compendium of Facts and Formulae in
Pure Mathematics and Natural Philosophy. By G. R. SMALLEY,
F.R.A.S. *New edition, revised and enlarged.* By J. McDOWELL, M.A.,
F.R.A.S. Fcap. 8vo, 2s.
WRIGLEY (A.). Collection of Examples and Problems in Arith-
metic, Algebra, Geometry, Logarithms, Trigonometry, Conic Sections,
Mechanics, &c., with Answers and Occasional Hints. By the REV. A.
WRIGLEY. *10th edition, 20th thousand.* Demy 8vo, 8s. 6d.
    A Key. By J. C. PLATTS, M.A. and the REV. A. WRIGLEY. *2nd edition.*
Demy 8vo, 10s. 6d.

MODERN LANGUAGES.

ENGLISH.

ADAMS (E.). The Elements of the English Language. By ERNEST
ADAMS, PH.D. *26th edition.* Revised by J. F. DAVIS, D.LIT., M.A.,
(LOND.). Post 8vo, 4s. 6d.
— The Rudiments of English Grammar and Analysis. By ERNEST
ADAMS, PH.D. *19th thousand.* Fcap. 8vo, 1s.
ALFORD (DEAN). The Queen's English: A Manual of Idiom and
Usage. By the late HENRY ALFORD, D.D., Dean of Canterbury. *6th
edition.* Small post 8vo. Sewed, 1s., cloth, 1s. 6d.
ASCHAM'S Scholemaster. Edited by PROFESSOR J. E. B. MAYOR. Small
post 8vo, sewed, 1s.
BELL'S ENGLISH CLASSICS. A New Series, Edited for use in
Schools, with Introduction and Notes. Crown 8vo.
    BACON'S Essays Modernized. Edited by F. J. ROWE, M.A., Professor of
    English Literature at Presidency College, Calcutta.

BELL'S ENGLISH CLASSICS—*continued.*

BROWNING'S Strafford. Edited by R. H. HICKEY. With Introduction by S. R. GARDINER, LL.D. 2*s.* 6*d.*

BURKE'S Letters on a Regicide Peace. I. and II. Edited by H. G. KEENE, M.A., C.I.E. 3*s.*; sewed, 2*s.*

BYRON'S Childe Harold. Edited by H. G. KEENE, M.A., C.I E., Author of "A Manual of French Literature," etc. 3*s.* 6*d.* Also Cantos I. and II. separately; sewed, 1*s.* 9*d.*

— Siege of Corinth. Edited by P. HORDERN, late Director of Public Instruction in Burma. 1*s.* 6*d.*; sewed, 1*s.*

CHAUCER, SELECTIONS FROM. Edited by J. B. BILDERBECK, B.A., Professor of English Literature, Presidency College, Madras. [*Preparing.*

DE QUINCEY'S Revolt of the Tartars and The English Mail-Coach. Edited by CECIL M. BARROW, M.A., Principal of Victoria College, Palghât, and MARK HUNTER, B.A., Principal of Coimbatore College. [*In the press.*

GOLDSMITH'S Good-Natured Man and She Stoops to Conquer. Edited by K. DEIGHTON. Each, 2*s.* cloth; 1*s.* 6*d.* sewed.

IRVING'S Sketch Book. Edited by R. G. OXENHAM, M A. [*Preparing.*

JOHNSON'S Life of Addison. Edited by F. RYLAND, Author of "The Students' Handbook of Psychology," etc. 2*s.* 6*d.*

— Life of Swift. Edited by F. RYLAND, M.A. 2*s.*

— Life of Pope. Edited by F. RYLAND, M.A. 2*s.* 6*d.*

— Life of Milton. Edited by F. RYLAND, M.A. 2*s.* 6*d.*

— Life of Dryden. Edited by F. RYLAND, M.A. 2*s.* 6*d.*

LAMB'S Essays. Selected and Edited by K. DEIGHTON. 3*s.*; sewed, 2*s.*

MACAULAY'S Lays of Ancient Rome. Edited by P. HORDERN. 2*s.* 6*d.*; sewed, 1*s.* 9*d.*

— Essay on Clive. Edited by CECIL BARROW, M.A. [*Preparing.*

MASSINGER'S A New Way to Pay Old Debts. Edited by K. DEIGHTON. 3*s.*; sewed, 2*s.*

MILTON'S Paradise Lost. Books III. and IV. Edited by R. G. OXENHAM, M.A., Principal of Elphinstone College, Bombay. 2*s.*; sewed, 1*s.* 6*d.*, or separately, sewed, 10*d.* each.

— Paradise Regained. Edited by K. DEIGHTON. 2*s.* 6*d.*; sewed, 1*s.* 9*d.*

POPE, SELECTIONS FROM. Containing Essay on Criticism, Rape of the Lock, Temple of Fame, Windsor Forest. Edited by K. DEIGHTON. 2*s.* 6*d.*; sewed, 1*s.* 9*d.*

SHAKESPEARE'S Julius Caesar. Edited by T. DUFF BARNETT, B.A. (Lond.). 2*s.*

— Merchant of Venice. Edited by T. DUFF BARNETT, B.A. (Lond.). 2*s.*

— Tempest. Edited by T. DUFF BARNETT, B.A. (Lond.). 2*s.*

Others to follow.

BELL'S READING BOOKS. Post 8vo, cloth, illustrated.

Infants.
Infant's Primer. 3*d.*
Tot and the Cat. 6*d.*
The Old Boathouse. 6*d.*
The Cat and the Hen. 6*d.*

Standard I.
School Primer. 6*d.*
The Two Parrots. 6*d.*
The Three Monkeys. 6*l.*
The New-born Lamb. 6*l.*
The Blind Boy. 6*d.*

Standard II.
The Lost Pigs. 6*d.*
Story of a Cat. 6*d.*
Queen Bee and Busy Bee. 6*d.*

Gulls' Crag. 6*d.*
Great Deeds in English History. 1*s.*

Standard III.
Adventures of a Donkey. 1*s.*
Grimm's Tales. 1*s.*
Great Englishmen. 1*s.*
Andersen's Tales. 1*s.*
Life of Columbus. 1*s.*

Standard IV.
Uncle Tom's Cabin. 1*s.*
Great Englishwomen. 1*s.*
Great Scotsmen. 1*s.*
Edgeworth's Tales. 1*s.*
Gatty's Parables from Nature. 1*s.*
Scott's Talisman. 1*s.*

BELL'S READING BOOKS—*continued.*

Standard V.
Dickens' Oliver Twist. 1*s.*
Dickens' Little Nell. 1*s.*
Masterman Ready. 1*s.*
Marryat's Poor Jack. 1*s.*
Arabian Nights. 1*s.*
Gulliver's Travels. 1*s.*
Lyrical Poetry for Boys and Girls. 1*s.*
Vicar of Wakefield. 1*s.*

Standards VI. and VII.
Lamb's Tales from Shakespeare. 1*s.*
Robinson Crusoe. 1*s.*
Tales of the Coast. 1*s.*
Settlers in Canada. 1*s.*
Southey's Life of Nelson. 1*s.*
Sir Roger de Coverley. 1*s.*

BELL'S GEOGRAPHICAL READERS. By M. J. BARRINGTON-WARD, M A. (Worcester College, Oxford).

The Child's Geography. Illustrated. Stiff paper cover, 6*d.*
The Map and the Compass. (Standard I) Illustrated. Cloth, 8*d.*

The Round World. (Standard II.) Illustrated. Cloth, 10*d.*
About England. (Standard III.) With Illustrations and Coloured Map. Cloth, 1*s.* 4*d.*

EDWARDS (F.). Examples for Analysis in Verse and Prose from well-known sources, selected and arranged by F. EDWARDS. *New edition.* Fcap. 8vo, cloth, 1*s.*

GOLDSMITH. The Deserted Village. Edited, with Notes and Life, by C. P. MASON, B.A., F.C.P. *4th edition.* Crown 8vo, 1*s.*

HANDBOOKS OF ENGLISH LITERATURE. Edited by J. W. HALES, M.A., formerly Clark Lecturer in English Literature at Trinity College, Cambridge, Professor of English Literature at King's College, London. Crown 8vo, 3*s.* 6*d.* each.

    The Age of Pope. By JOHN DENNIS.   [*Ready.*

In preparation.

    The Age of Chaucer. By PROFESSOR HALES.
    The Age of Shakespeare. By PROFESSOR HALES.
    The Age of Milton. By J. BASS MULLINGER, M.A.
    The Age of Dryden. By W. GARNETT, LL.D.
    The Age of Wordsworth. By PROFESSOR C. H. HERFORD, LITT.D.

Other volumes to follow.

HAZLITT (W.). Lectures on the Literature of the Age of Elizabeth. Small post 8vo, sewed, 1*s.*

— Lectures on the English Poets. Small post 8vo, sewed, 1*s.*

— Lectures on the English Comic Writers. Small post 8vo, sewed, 1*s.*

LAMB (C.). Specimens of English Dramatic Poets of the Time of Elizabeth. With Notes, together with the Extracts from the Garrick Plays.

MASON (C. P.). Grammars by C. P. MASON, B.A., F.C.P., Fellow of University College, London.

— First Notions of Grammar for Young Learners. Fcap. 8vo. 85*th thousand.* Cloth, 1*s.*

— First Steps in English Grammar, for Junior Classes. Demy 18mo. 54*th thousand.* 1*s.*

MASON (C. P.). Outlines of English Grammar, for the Use of Junior Classes. *17th edition. 97th thousand.* Crown 8vo, 2*s.*

— **English Grammar**; including the principles of Grammatical Analysis. *35th edition, revised. 148th thousand.* Crown 8vo, green cloth, 3*s. 6d.*

— **A Shorter English Grammar**, with copious and carefully graduated Exercises, based upon the author's English Grammar. *9th edition. 49th thousand.* Crown 8vo, brown cloth, 3*s. 6d.*

— **Practice and Help in the Analysis of Sentences.** Price 2*s.* Cloth.

— **English Grammar Practice**, consisting of the Exercises of the Shorter English Grammar published in a separate form. *3rd edition.* Crown 8vo, 1*s.*

— **Remarks on the Subjunctive and the so-called Potential Mood.** *6d.,* sewn.

— **Blank Sheets** Ruled and headed for A nalysis. 1*s.* per dozen.

MILTON : Paradise Lost. Books I., II., and III. Edited, with Notes on the Analysis and Parsing, and Explanatory Remarks, by C. P. MASON, B.A., F.C.P. Crown 8vo.

    Book I. With Life. *5th edition.* 1*s.*
    Book II. With Life. *3rd edition.* 1*s.*
    Book III. With Life. *2nd edition.* 1*s.*

— **Paradise Lost.** Books V -VIII. With Notes for the Use of Schools. By C. M. LUMBY. 2*s. 6d.*.

PRICE (A. C.). Elements of Comparative Grammar and Philology. For Use in Schools. By A. C. PRICE, M.A., Assistant Master at Leeds Grammar School ; late Scholar of Pembroke College, Oxford. Crown 8vo, 2*s. 6d.*

SHAKESPEARE. Notes on Shakespeare's Plays. With Introduction, Summary, Notes (Etymological and Explanatory), Prosody, Grammatical Peculiarities, etc. By T. DUFF BARNETT, B.A. Lond., late Second Master in the Brighton Grammar School. Specially adapted for the Local and Preliminary Examinations. Crown 8vo, 1*s.* each.

    Midsummer Night's Dream.—Julius Cæsar.—The Tempest.— Macbeth.—Henry V.—Hamlet.—Merchant of Venice.— King Richard II.— King John.— King Lear.— Coriolanus — Twelfth Night.

    " The Notes are comprehensive and concise."—*Educational Times.*
    " Comprehensive, practical, and reliable."—*Schoolmaster.*

— **Hints for Shakespeare-Study.** Exemplified in an Analytical Study of Julius Cæsar. By MARY GRAFTON MOBERLY. *2nd edition.* Crown 8vo, sewed, 1*s.*

— **Coleridge's Lectures and Notes on Shakespeare and other English Poets.** Edited by T. ASHE, B.A. Small post 8vo, 3*s. 6d.*

— **Shakespeare's Dramatic Art.** The History and Character of Shakespeare's Plays. By DR. HERMANN ULRICI. Translated by L. DORA SCHMITZ. 2 vols. small post 8vo, 3*s. 6d.* each.

— **William Shakespeare.** A Literary Biography. By KARL ELZE, PH.D., LL.D. Translated by L. DORA SCHMITZ. Small post 8vo, 5*s.*

— **Hazlitt's Lectures on the Characters of Shakespeare's Plays.** Small post 8vo, 1*s.*

. See **BELL'S ENGLISH CLASSICS.**

SKEAT (W. W.). **Questions for Examinations in English Litera-ture.** With a Preface containing brief hints on the study of English. Arranged by the REV. W. W. SKEAT, LITT. D., Elrington and Bosworth Professor of Anglo-Saxon in the University of Cambridge. *3rd edition.* Crown 8vo, 2*s.* 6*d.*

SMITH (C. J.) **Synonyms and Antonyms of the English Language.** Collected and Contrasted by the VEN. C. J. SMITH, M.A. *2nd edition, revised.* Small post 8vo, 5*s.*

— **Synonyms Discriminated.** A Dictionary of Synonymous Words in the English Language. Illustrated with Quotations from Standard Writers. By the late VEN. C. J. SMITH, M.A. With the Author's latest Corrections and Additions, edited by the REV. H. PERCY SMITH, M.A., of Balliol College, Oxford, Vicar of Great Barton, Suffolk. *4th edition.* Demy 8vo, 14*s.*

TEN BRINK'S History of English Literature. Vol. I. Early English Literature (to Wiclif). Translated into English by HORACE M. KENNEDY, Professor of German Literature in the Brooklyn Collegiate Institute. Small post 8vo, 3*s.* 6*d.*

— Vol. II. (Wiclif, Chaucer, Earliest Drama, Renaissance). Translated by W. CLARKE ROBINSON, PH.D. Small post 8vo, 3*s.* 6*d.*

THOMSON : Spring. Edited by C. P. MASON, B.A., F.C.P. With Life. *2nd edition.* Crown 8vo, 1*s.*

— **Winter.** Edited by C. P. MASON, B.A., F.C.P. With Life. Crown 8vo, 1*s.*

WEBSTER'S INTERNATIONAL DICTIONARY of the English Language. Including Scientific, Technical, and Biblical Words and Terms, with their Significations, Pronunciations, Alternative Spellings, Derivations, Synonyms, and numerous illustrative Quotations, with various valuable literary Appendices, with 83 extra pages of Illustrations grouped and classified, rendering the work a COMPLETE LITERARY AND SCIENTIFIC REFERENCE-BOOK. *New edition* (1890). Thoroughly revised and en-larged under the supervision of NOAH PORTER, D.D., LL.D. 1 vol. (2,118 pages, 3,500 woodcuts), 4to, cloth, 31*s.* 6*d.* ; half calf, £2 2*s.* ; half russia, £2 5*s.* ; calf, £2 8*s.* ; or in 2 vols. cloth, £1 14*s.*

Prospectuses, with specimen pages, sent post free on application.

WEBSTER'S BRIEF INTERNATIONAL DICTIONARY. A Pronouncing Dictionary of the English Language, abridged from Webster's International Dictionary. With a Treatise on Pronunciation, List of Prefixes and Suffixes, Rules for Spelling, a Pronouncing Vocabulary of Proper Names in History, Geography, and Mythology, and Tables of English and Indian Money, Weights, and Measures. With 564 pages and 800 Illustrations. Demy 8vo, 3*s.*

WRIGHT (T.). **Dictionary of Obsolete and Provincial English.** Containing Words from the English Writers previous to the 19th century, which are no longer in use, or are not used in the same sense, and Words which are now used only in the Provincial Dialects. Compiled by THOMAS WRIGHT, M.A., F.S.A , etc. 2 vols. 5*s.* each.

FRENCH CLASS BOOKS.

BOWER (A. M.). **The Public Examination French Reader.** With a Vocabulary to every extract, suitable for all Students who are preparing for a French Examination. By A. M. BOWER, F.R.G.S., late Master in University College School, etc. Cloth, 3*s.* 6*d.*

BARBIER (PAUL). **A Graduated French Examination Course.** By PAUL BARBIER, Lecturer in the South Wales University College, etc. Crown 8vo, 3*s.*

BARRERE (A.) **Junior Graduated French Course.** Affording Materials for Translation, Grammar, and Conversation. By A. BARRÈRE, Professor R.M.A., Woolwich. 1*s.* 6*d.*
— **Elements of French Grammar and First Steps in Idioms.** With numerous Exercises and a Vocabulary. Being an Introduction to the Précis of Comparative French Grammar. Crown 8vo, 2*s.*
— **Précis of Comparative French Grammar and Idioms and Guide to Examinations.** *4th edition.* 3*s.* 6*d.*
— **Récits Militaires.** From Valmy (1792) to the Siege of Paris (1870). With English Notes and Biographical Notices. *2nd edition.* Crown 8vo, 3*s.*

CLAPIN (A. C.). **French Grammar for Public Schools.** By the REV. A. C. CLAPIN, M.A., St. John's College, Cambridge, and Bachelier-ès lettres of the University of France. Fcap. 8vo. *13th edition.* 2*s.* 6*d.* Key to the Exercises. 3*s.* 6*d.* net.
— **French Primer.** Elementary French Grammar and Exercises for Junior Forms in Public and Preparatory Schools. Fcap. 8vo. *10th edition.* 1*s.*
— **Primer of French Philology.** With Exercises for Public Schools. *6th edition.* Fcap. 8vo, 1*s.*
— **English Passages for Translation into French.** Crown 8vo, 2*s.* 6*d.* Key (for Tutors only), 4*s.* net.

DAVIS (J. F.) **Army Examination Papers in French.** Questions set at the Preliminary Examinations for Sandhurst and Woolwich, from Nov., 1876, to June, 1890, with Vocabulary. By J. F. DAVIS, D.LIT., M.A., Lond. Crown 8vo, 2*s.* 6*d.*

DAVIS (J. F.) and THOMAS (F.). **An Elementary French Reader.** Compiled, with a Vocabulary, by J. F. DAVIS, M.A., D.LIT., and FERDINAND THOMAS, Assistant Examiners in the University of London. Crown 8vo, 2*s.*

DELILLE'S GRADUATED FRENCH COURSE.

The Beginner's own French Book. 2*s.* Key, 2*s.*	Repertoire des Prosateurs. 3*s.* 6*d.*
	Modèles de Poesie. 3*s.* 6*d.*
Easy French Poetry for Beginners. 2*s.*	Manuel Etymologique. 2*s.* 6*d.*
French Grammar. 3*s.* Key, 3*s.*	Synoptical Table of French Verbs. 6*d.*

GASC (F. E. A.). **First French Book;** being a New, Practical, and Easy Method of Learning the Elements of the French Language. *Reset and thoroughly revised.* 116*th thousand.* Crown 8vo, 1*s.*
— **Second French Book;** being a Grammar and Exercise Book, on a new and practical plan, and intended as a sequel to the "First French Book." 52*nd thousand.* Fcap. 8vo, 1*s.* 6*d.*

GASC (F. E. A.). **Key** to First and Second French Books. *5th edition,* Fcap. 8vo, 3*s.* 6*d.* net.

— **French Fables,** for Beginners, in Prose, with an Index of all the Words at the end of the work. *16th thousand.* 12mo, 1*s.* 6*d.*

— **Select Fables of La Fontaine.** *19th thousand.* Fcap. 8vo, 1*s.* 6*d.*

— **Histoires Amusantes et Instructives** ; or, Selections of Complete Stories from the best French modern authors, who have written for the young. With English notes. *17th thousand.* Fcap. 8vo, 2*s.*

— **Practical Guide to Modern French Conversation,** containing :— I. The most current and useful Phrases in Everyday Talk. II. Everybody's necessary Questions and Answers in Travel-Talk. *19th edition.* Fcap. 8vo, 1*s.* 6*d.*

— **French Poetry for the Young.** With Notes, and preceded by a few plain Rules of French Prosody. *5th edition, revised.* Fcap. 8vo, 1*s.* 6*d.*

— **French Prose Composition,** Materials for. With copious footnotes, and hints for idiomatic renderings. *21st thousand.* Fcap. 8vo, 3*s.* Key. *2nd edition.* 6*s.* net.

— **Prosateurs Contemporains** ; or, Selections in Prose chiefly from contemporary French literature. With notes. *11th edition.* 12mo, 3*s.* 6*d.*

— **Le Petit Compagnon** ; a French Talk-Book for Little Children. *14th edition.* 16mo, 1*s.* 6*d.*

— **French and English Dictionary,** with upwards of Fifteen Thousand new words, senses, &c., hitherto unpublished. *5th edition, with numerous additions and corrections.* In one vol. 8vo, cloth, 10*s.* 6*d.* **In use at Harrow, Rugby, Shrewsbury, &c.**

— **Pocket Dictionary of the French and English Languages** ; for the everyday purposes of Travellers and Students. Containing more than Five Thousand modern and current words, senses, and idiomatic phrases and renderings, not found in any other dictionary of the two languages. *New edition.* 51*st thousand.* 16mo, cloth, 2*s.* 6*d.*

GOSSET (A.). **Manual of French Prosody** for the use of English Students. By ARTHUR GOSSET, M.A., Fellow of New College, Oxford. Crown 8vo, 3*s.*

"This is the very book we have been looking for. We hailed the title with delight, and were not disappointed by the perusal. The reader who has mastered the contents will know, what not one in a thousand of Englishmen who read French knows, the rules of French poetry."— *Journal of Education.*

LE NOUVEAU TRESOR ; designed to facilitate the Translation of English into French at Sight. By M. E. S. *18th edition.* Fcap. 8vo, 1*s.* 6*d.*

STEDMAN (A. M. M.). **French Examination Papers** in Miscellaneous Grammar and Idioms. Compiled by A. M. M. STEDMAN, M.A. *5th edition.* Crown 8vo, 2*s.* 6*d.*

A Key. By G. A. SCHRUMPF. For Tutors only. 6*s.* net.

— **Easy French Passages** for Unseen Translation. Fcap. 8vo, 1*s.* 6*d.*

— **Easy French Exercises** on Elementary Syntax. Crown 8vo, 2*s.* 6*d.*

— **First French Lessons.** Crown 8vo, 1*s.*

— **French Vocabularies** for Repetition. Fcap. 8vo, 1*s.*

— **Steps to French.** 12mo, 8*d.*

FRENCH ANNOTATED EDITIONS.

BALZAC. Ursule Mirouët. By HONORÉ DE BALZAC. Edited, with Introduction and Notes, by JAMES BOÏELLE, B.-ès-L., Senior French Master, Dulwich College. 3*s.*

CLARÉTIE. Pierrille. By JULES CLARÉTIE. With 27 Illustrations. Edited, with Introduction and Notes, by JAMES BOÏELLE, B.-ès-L. 2*s.* 6*d.*

DAUDET. La Belle Nivernaise. Histoire d'un vieux bateau et de son équipage. By ALPHONSE DAUDET. Edited, with Introduction and Notes, by JAMES BOÏELLE, B.-ès-L. With Six Illustrations. 2*s.*

FÉNELON. Aventures de Télémaque. Edited by C. J. DELILLE. *4th edition.* Fcap. 8vo, 2*s.* 6*d.*

GOMBERT'S FRENCH DRAMA. Re-edited, with Notes, by F. E. A. GASC. Sewed, 6*d.* each.

MOLIÈRE.

Le Misanthrope.	Les Fourberies de Scapin.
L'Avare.	Les Précieuses Ridicules.
Le Bourgeois Gentilhomme.	L'Ecole des Femmes.
Le Tartuffe.	L'Ecole des Maris.
Le Malade Imaginaire.	Le Médecin Malgré Lui.
Les Femmes Savantes.	

RACINE.

La Thébaïde, ou Les Frères Ennemis.	Britannicus.
	Phèdre.
Andromaque.	Esther.
Les Plaideurs.	Athalie.
Iphigénie.	

CORNEILLE.

Le Cid.	Cinna.
Horace.	Polyeucte.

VOLTAIRE.—Zaïre.

GREVILLE. Le Moulin Frappier. By HENRY GREVILLE. Edited, with Introduction and Notes, by JAMES BOÏELLE, B.-ès-L. 3*s.*

HUGO. Bug Jargal. Edited, with Introduction and Notes, by JAMES BOÏELLE, B.-ès-L. 3*s.*

LA FONTAINE. Select Fables. Edited by F. E. A. GASC. 19*th thousand.* Fcap. 8vo, 1*s.* 6*d.*

LAMARTINE. Le Tailleur de Pierres de Saint-Point. Edited with Notes by JAMES BOIELLE, B.-ès-L. 6*th thousand.* Fcap. 8vo, 1*s.* 6*d.*

SAINTINE. Picciola. Edited by DR. DUBUC. 16*th thousand.* Fcap. 8vo, 1*s.* 6*d.*

VOLTAIRE. Charles XII. Edited by L. DIREY. 7*th edition.* Fcap. 8vo, 1*s.* 6*d.*

GERMAN CLASS BOOKS.

BUCHHEIM (DR. C. A.). German Prose Composition. Consisting of Selections from Modern English Writers. With grammatical notes, idiomatic renderings, and general introduction. By C. A. BUCHHEIM, PH.D., Professor of the German Language and Literature in King's College, and

Examiner in German to the London University. 14*th edition, enlarged and revised.* With a list of subjects for original composition. Fcap. 8vo, 4*s.* 6*d.* A KEY to the 1st and 2nd parts. 3*rd edition.* 3*s.* net. To the 3rd and 4th parts. 4*s.* net.

BUCHHEIM (DR. C. A.). **First Book of German Prose.** Being Parts I. and II. of the above. With Vocabulary by H. R. Fcap. 8vo, 1*s.* 6*d.*

CLAPIN (A. C.). **A German Grammar for Public Schools.** By the REV. A. C. CLAPIN, and F. HOLL-MÜLLER, Assistant Master at the Bruton Grammar School. 6*th edition.* Fcap. 8vo, 2*s.* 6*d.*

— **A German Primer.** With Exercises. 2*nd edition.* Fcap. 8vo, 1*s.*

German. **The Candidate's Vade Mecum.** Five Hundred Easy Sentences and Idioms. By an Army Tutor. Cloth, 1*s.* For Army Prelim. Exam.

LANGE (F.). **A Complete German Course for Use in Public Schools.** By F. LANGE, PH.D., Professor R.M.A. Woolwich, Examiner in German to the College of Preceptors, London ; Examiner in German at the Victoria University, Manchester. Crown 8vo.

Concise German Grammar. With special reference to Phonology, Comparative Philology, English and German Equivalents and Idioms. Comprising Materials for Translation, Grammar, and Conversation. Elementary, 2*s.* ; Intermediate, 2*s.* ; Advanced, 3*s.* 6*d.*

Progressive German Examination Course. Comprising the Elements of German Grammar, an Historic Sketch of the Teutonic Languages, English and German Equivalents, Materials for Translation, Dictation, Extempore Conversation, and Complete Vocabularies. I. Elementary Course, 2*s.* II. Intermediate Course, 2*s.* III. Advanced Course. *Second revised edition.* 1*s.* 6*d.*

Elementary German Reader. A Graduated Collection of Readings in Prose and Poetry. With English Notes and a Vocabulary. 4*th edition.* 1*s.* 6*d.*

Advanced German Reader. A Graduated Collection of Readings in Prose and Poetry. With English Notes by F. LANGE, PH.D., and J. F. DAVIS, D.LIT. 2*nd edition.* 3*s.*

MORICH (R. J.). German Examination Papers in Miscellaneous Grammar and Idioms. By R. J. MORICH, Manchester Grammar School. 2*nd edition.* Crown 8vo, 2*s.* 6*d.* A Key, for Tutors only. 5*s.* net.

STOCK (DR.). **Wortfolge,** or Rules and Exercises on the order of Words in German Sentences. With a Vocabulary. By the late FREDERICK STOCK, D.LIT., M.A. Fcap. 8vo, 1*s.* 6*d.*

KLUGE'S Etymological Dictionary of the German Language. Translated by J. F. DAVIS, D.LIT. (Lond.). Crown 4to, 18*s.*

GERMAN ANNOTATED EDITIONS.

AUERBACH (B.). **Auf Wache.** Novelle von BERTHOLD AUERBACH. **Der Gefrorene Kuss.** Novelle von OTTO ROQUETTE. Edited by A. A. MACDONELL, M.A., PH.D. 2*nd edition.* Crown 8vo, 2*s.*

BENEDIX (J. R.). **Doktor Wespe.** Lustspiel in fünf Aufzügen von JULIUS RODERICH BENEDIX. Edited by PROFESSOR F. LANGE, PH.D. Crown 8vo, 2*s.* 6*d.*

EBERS (G.). Eine Frage. Idyll von GEORG EBERS. Edited by F. STORR, B.A., Chief Master of Modern Subjects in Merchant Taylors' School. Crown 8vo, 2*s.*

FREYTAG (G.). Die Journalisten. Lustspiel von GUSTAV FREYTAG. Edited by PROFESSOR F. LANGE, PH.D. *4th revised edition.* Crown 8vo, 2*s.* 6*d.*

— SOLL UND HABEN. Roman von GUSTAV FREYTAG. Edited by W. HANBY CRUMP, M.A. Crown 8vo, 2*s.* 6*d.*

GERMAN BALLADS from Uhland, Goethe, and Schiller. With Introductions, Copious and Biographical Notices. Edited by C. L. BIELEFELD. *4th edition.* Fcap. 8vo, 1*s.* 6*d.*

GERMAN EPIC TALES IN PROSE. I. Die Nibelungen, von A. F. C. VILMAR. II. Walther und Hildegund, von ALBERT RICHTER. Edited by KARL NEUHAUS, PH.D., the International College, Isleworth. Crown 8vo, 2*s.* 6*d.*

GOETHE. Hermann und Dorothea. With Introduction, Notes, and Arguments. By E. BELL, M.A., and F. WÖLFEL. *2nd edition.* Fcap. 8vo, 1*s.* 6*d.*

GOETHE FAUST. Part I. German Text with Hayward's Prose Translation and Notes. Revised, With Introduction by C. A. BUCHHEIM, PH.D., Professor of German Language and Literature at King's College, London. Small post 8vo, 5*s.*

GUTZKOW (K.). Zopf und Schwert. Lustspiel von KARL GUTZKOW. Edited by PROFESSOR F. LANGE, PH.D. Crown 8vo, 2*s.* 6*d.*

HEY'S FABELN FÜR KINDER. Illustrated by O. SPECKTER. Edited, with an Introduction, Grammatical Summary, Words, and a complete Vocabulary, by PROFESSOR F. LANGE, PH.D. Crown 8vo, 1*s.* 6*d.*

— The same. With a Phonetic Introduction, and Phonetic Transcription of the Text. By PROFESSOR F. LANGE, PH.D. Crown 8vo, 2*s.*

HEYSE (P.). Hans Lange. Schauspiel von PAUL HEYSE. Edited by A. A. MACDONELL, M.A., PH.D., Taylorian Teacher, Oxford University. Crown 8vo, 2*s.*

HOFFMANN (E. T. A.). Meister Martin, der Küfner. Erzählung von E. T. A. HOFFMANN. Edited by F. LANGE, PH.D. *2nd edition.* Crown 8vo, 1*s.* 6*d.*

MOSER (G. VON). Der Bibliothekar. Lustspiel von G. VON MOSER. Edited by F. LANGE, PH.D. *4th edition.* Crown 8vo, 2*s.*

ROQUETTE (O.). *See* Auerbach.

SCHEFFEL (V. VON). Ekkehard. Erzählung des zehnten Jahrhunderts, von VICTOR VON SCHEFFEL. Abridged edition, with Introduction and Notes by HERMAN HAGER, PH.D., Lecturer in the German Language and Literature in The Owens College, Victoria University, Manchester. Crown 8vo, 3*s.*

SCHILLER'S Wallenstein. Complete Text, comprising the Weimar Prologue, Lager, Piccolomini, and Wallenstein's Tod. Edited by DR. BUCHHEIM, Professor of German in King's College, London. *6th edition.* Fcap. 8vo, 5*s.* Or the Lager and Piccolomini, 2*s.* 6*d.* Wallenstein's Tod, 2*s.* 6*d.*

— Maid of Orleans. With English Notes by DR. WILHELM WAGNER. *3rd edition.* Fcap. 8vo, 1*s.* 6*d.*

— Maria Stuart. Edited by V. KASTNER, B.-ès-L., Lecturer on French Language and Literature at Victoria University, Manchester. *3rd edition.* Fcap. 8vo, 1*s.* 6*d.*

C

ITALIAN.

CLAPIN (A. C.). **Italian Primer.** With Exercises. By the REV. A. C.
CLAPIN, M.A., B.-ès-L. *3rd edition.* Fcap. 8vo, 1*s.*

DANTE. **The Inferno.** A Literal Prose Translation, with the Text of the
Original collated with the best editions, printed on the same page, and
Explanatory Notes. By JOHN A. CARLYLE, M.D. With Portrait. *2nd
edition.* Small post 8vo, 5*s.*

— **The Purgatorio.** A Literal Prose Translation, with the Text of Bianchi
printed on the same page, and Explanatory Notes. By W. S. DUGDALE.
Small post 8vo, 5*s.*

BELL'S MODERN TRANSLATIONS.

*A Series of Translations from Modern Languages, with Memoirs,
Introductions, etc. Crown 8vo, 1s. each.*

GOETHE. **Egmont.** Translated by ANNA SWANWICK. With Memoir.
— **Iphigenia in Tauris.** Translated by ANNA SWANWICK. With Memoir.
HAUFF. **The Caravan.** Translated by S. MENDEL. With Memoir.
— **The Inn in the Spessart.** Translated by S. MENDEL. With Memoir.
LESSING. **Laokoon.** Translated by E. C. BEASLEY. With Memoir.
— **Nathan the Wise.** Translated by R. DILLON BOYLAN. With Memoir.
— **Minna von Barnhelm.** Translated by ERNEST BELL, M.A. With
Memoir.
MOLIÈRE. **The Misanthrope.** Translated by C. HERON WALL. With
Memoir.
— **The Doctor in Spite of Himself.** (Le Médecin malgré lui). Trans-
lated by C. HERON WALL. With Memoir.
— **Tartuffe; or, The Impostor.** Translated by C. HERON WALL. With
Memoir.
— **The Miser.** (L'Avare). Translated by C. HERON WALL. With Memoir.
— **The Shopkeeper turned Gentleman.** (Le Bourgeois Gentilhomme).
Translated by C. HERON WALL. With Memoir.
RACINE. **Athalie.** Translated by R. BRUCE BOSWELL, M.A. With
Memoir.
— **Esther.** Translated by R. BRUCE BOSWELL, M.A. With Memoir.
SCHILLER. **William Tell.** Translated by SIR THEODORE MARTIN,
K.C.B., LL.D. *New edition, entirely revised.* With Memoir.
— **The Maid of Orleans.** Translated by ANNA SWANWICK. With Memoir.
— **Mary Stuart.** Translated by J. MELLISH. With Memoir.
  ⁎ For other Translations of Modern Languages, *see* the Catalogue of
Bohn's Libraries, which will be forwarded on application.

SCIENCE, TECHNOLOGY, AND ART.

CHEMISTRY.

STÖCKHARDT (J. A.). **Experimental Chemistry.** Founded on the
work of J. A. STÖCKHARDT. A Handbook for the Study of Science by
Simple Experiments. By C. W. HEATON, F.I.C., F.C.S., Lecturer in
Chemistry in the Medical School of Charing Cross Hospital, Examiner in
Chemistry to the Royal College of Physicians, etc. *Revised edition.* 5*s.*

WILLIAMS (W. M.). The Framework of Chemistry. Part I. Typical Facts and Elementary Theory. By W. M. WILLIAMS, M.A., St John's College, Oxford ; Science Master, King Henry VIII.'s School, Coventry. Crown 8vo, paper boards, 9*d.* net.

BOTANY.

EGERTON-WARBURTON (G.). Names and Synonyms of British Plants. By the REV. G. EGERTON-WARBURTON. Fcap. 8vo, 3*s.* 6*d.* (*Uniform with Hayward's Botanist's Pocket Book.*)

HAYWARD (W. R.). The Botanist's Pocket-Book. Containing in a tabulated form, the chief characteristics of British Plants, with the botanical names, soil, or situation, colour, growth, and time of flowering of every plant, arranged under its own order ; with a copious Index. By W. R. HAYWARD. 6*th edition, revised.* Fcap. 8vo, cloth limp, 4*s.* 6*d.*

MASSEE (G.). British Fungus-Flora. A Classified Text-Book of Mycology. By GEORGE MASSEE, Author of "The Plant World." With numerous Illustrations. 3 vols. post 8vo. Vols. I., II., and III. ready, 7*s.* 6*d.* each. Vol. IV. in the Press.

SOWERBY'S English Botany. Containing a Description and Life-size Drawing of every British Plant. Edited and brought up to the present standard of scientific knowledge, by T. BOSWELL (late SYME), LL.D., F.L.S., etc. 3*rd edition, entirely revised.* With Descriptions of all the Species by the Editor, assisted by N. E. BROWN. 12 vols., with 1,937 *coloured plates,* £24 3*s.* in cloth, £26 11*s.* in half-morocco, and £30 9*s.* in whole morocco. Also in 89 parts, 5*s.*, except Part 89, containing an Index to the whole work, 7*s.* 6*d.*

⁂ A Supplement, to be completed in 8 or 9 parts, is now publishing. Parts I., II., and III. ready, 5*s.* each, or bound together, making Vol. XIII. of the complete work, 17*s.*

TURNBULL (R.). Index of British Plants, according to the London Catalogue (Eighth Edition), including the Synonyms used by the principal authors, an Alphabetical List of English Names, etc. By ROBERT TURNBULL. Paper cover, 2*s.* 6*d.*, cloth, 3*s.*

GEOLOGY.

JUKES-BROWNE (A. J.). Student's Handbook of Physical Geology. By A. J. JUKES-BROWNE, B.A., F.G.S., of the Geological Survey of England and Wales. With numerous Diagrams and Illustrations. 2*nd edition, much enlarged,* 7*s.* 6*d.*

— Student's Handbook of Historical Geology. With numerous Diagrams and Illustrations. 6*s.*

"An admirably planned and well executed ' Handbook of Historical Geology.' "—*Journal of Education.*

— The Building of the British Isles. A Study in Geographical Evolution. With Maps. 2*nd edition revised.* 7*s.* 6*d.*

MEDICINE.

CARRINGTON (R. E.), and LANE (W. A.). A Manual of Dissec-tions of the Human Body. By the late R. E. CARRINGTON, M.D. (Lond.), F.R.C.P., Senior Assistant Physician, Guy's Hospital. *2nd edition.* Revised and enlarged by W. ARBUTHNOT LANE, M.S., F.R.C.S., Assistant Surgeon to Guy's Hospital, etc. Crown 8vo, 9*s.*
"As solid a piece of work as ever was put into a book ; accurate from beginning to end, and unique of its kind."—*British Medical Journal.*

HILTON'S Rest and Pain. Lectures on the Influence of Mechanical and Physiological Rest in the Treatment of Accidents and Surgical Diseases, and the Diagnostic Value of Pain. By the late JOHN HILTON, F.R.S., F.R.C.S., etc. Edited by W. H. A. JACOBSON, M.A., M.CH. (Oxon.), F.R.C.S. 5*th edition.* 9*s.*

HOBLYN'S Dictionary of Terms used in Medicine and the Collateral Sciences. 12*th edition.* Revised and enlarged by J. A. P. PRICE, B.A., M.D. (Oxon.). 10*s.* 6*d.*

LANE (W. A.). Manual of Operative Surgery. For Practitioners and Students. By W. ARBUTHNOT LANE, M.B., M.S., F.R.C.S., Assistant Surgeon to Guy's Hospital. Crown 8vo, 8*s.* 6*d.*

SHARP (W.) Therapeutics founded on Antipraxy. By WILLIAM SHARP, M.D., F.R.S. Demy 8vo, 6*s.*

BELL'S AGRICULTURAL SERIES.

In crown 8vo, Illustrated, 160 *pages, cloth,* 2*s.* 6*d. each.*

CHEAL (J.). Fruit Culture. A Treatise on Planting, Growing, Storage of Hardy Fruits for Market and Private Growers. By J. CHEAL, F.R.H.S., Member of Fruit Committee, Royal Hort. Society, etc.

FREAM (DR.). Soils and their Properties. By DR. WILLIAM FREAM, B.SC. (Lond.)., F.L.S., F.G.S., F.S.S., Associate of the Surveyor's Institu-tion, Consulting Botanist to the British Dairy Farmers' Association and the Royal Counties Agricultural Society ; Prof. of Nat. Hist. in Downton College, and formerly in the Royal Agric. Coll., Cirencester.

GRIFFITHS (DR.). Manures and their Uses. By DR. A. B. GRIFFITHS, F.R.S.E., F.C.S., late Principal of the School of Science, Lincoln ; Membre de la Société Chimique de Paris ; Author of "A Treatise on Manures," etc., etc. *In use at Downton College.*

— The Diseases of Crops and their Remedies.

MALDEN (W. J.). Tillage and Implements. By W. J. MALDEN, Prof. of Agriculture in the College, Downton.

SHELDON (PROF.). The Farm and the Dairy. By PROFESSOR J. P. SHELDON, formerly of the Royal Agricultural College, and of the Downton College of Agriculture, late Special Commissioner of the Canadian Government. *In use at Downton College.*

Specially adapted for Agricultural Classes. Crown 8vo. Illustrated. 1*s.* each.

Practical Dairy Farming. By PROFESSOR SHELDON. Reprinted from the author's larger work entitled "The Farm and the Dairy."

Practical Fruit Growing. By J. CHEAL, F.R.H.S. Reprinted from the author's larger work, entitled "Fruit Culture."

TECHNOLOGICAL HANDBOOKS.

Edited by Sir H. Trueman Wood.

Specially adapted for candidates in the examinations of the City Guilds Institute. Illustrated and uniformly printed in small post 8vo.

BEAUMONT (R.). **Woollen and Worsted Cloth Manufacture.** By ROBERTS BEAUMONT, Professor of Textile Industry, Yorkshire College, Leeds; Examiner in Cloth Weaving to the City and Guilds of London Institute. *2nd edition. 7s. 6d.*

BENEDIKT (R), and KNECHT (E.). **Coal-tar Colours,** The Chemistry of. With special reference to their application to Dyeing, etc. By DR. R. BENEDIKT, Professor of Chemistry in the University of Vienna. Translated by E. KNECHT, PH.D. of the Technical College, Bradford. *2nd and enlarged edition, 6s. 6d.*

CROOKES (W.). **Dyeing and Tissue-Printing.** By WILLIAM CROOKES, F.R.S., V.P.C.S. *5s.*

GADD (W. L.). **Soap Manufacture.** By W. LAWRENCE GADD, F.I.C., F.C.S., Registered Lecturer on Soap-Making and the Technology of Oils and Fats, also on Bleaching, Dyeing, and Calico Printing, to the City and Guilds of London Institute. *5s.*

HELLYER (S. S.). **Plumbing: Its Principles and Practice.** By S. STEVENS HELLYER. With numerous Illustrations. *5s.*

HORNBY (J.). **Gas Manufacture.** By J. HORNBY, F.I.C., Lecturer under the City and Guilds of London Institute. *[Preparing.*

HURST (G.H.). **Silk-Dyeing and Finishing.** By G. H. HURST, F.C.S., Lecturer at the Manchester Technical School, Silver Medallist, City and Guilds of London Institute. With Illustrations and numerous Coloured Patterns. *7s. 6d.*

JACOBI (C. T.). **Printing.** A Practical Treatise. By C. T. JACOBI, Manager of the Chiswick Press, Examiner in Typography to the City and Guilds of London Institute. With numerous Illustrations. *5s.*

MARSDEN (R.). **Cotton Spinning: Its Development, Principles, and Practice,** with Appendix on Steam Boilers and Engines. By R. MARSDEN, Editor of the "Textile Manufacturer." *4th edition. 6s. 6d.*

— **Cotton Weaving** With numerous Illustrations. *[In the press.*

POWELL (H.), CHANCE (H.), and HARRIS (H. G.). **Glass Manufacture.** Introductory Essay, by H. POWELL, B.A. (Whitefriars Glass Works); **Sheet Glass,** by HENRY CHANCE, M.A. (Chance Bros., Birmingham): **Plate Glass,** by H. G. HARRIS, Assoc. Memb. Inst. C.E. *3s. 6d.*

ZAEHNSDORF (J. W.) **Bookbinding.** By J. W. ZAEHNSDORF, Examiner in Bookbinding to the City and Guilds of London Institute. With 8 Coloured Plates and numerous Diagrams. *2nd edition, revised and enlarged. 5s.*

_**_* *Complete List of Technical Books on Application.*

MUSIC.

BANISTER (H. C.). **A Text Book of Music:** By H. C. BANISTER, Professor of Harmony and Composition at the R.A. of Music, at the Guild

BANISTER (H. C.)—*continued.*
hall School of Music, and at the Royal Normal Coll. and Acad. of Music for the Blind. 15*th edition.* Fcap. 8vo. 5*s.*
> This Manual contains chapters on Notation, Harmony, and Counterpoint ; Modulation, Rhythm, Canon, Fugue, Voices, and Instruments ; together with exercises on Harmony, an Appendix of Examination Papers, and a copious Index and Glossary of Musical Terms.

— **Lectures on Musical Analysis.** Embracing Sonata Form, Fugue, etc., Illustrated by the Works of the Classical Masters. 2*nd edition, revised.* Crown 8vo, 7*s.* 6*d.*
— **Musical Art and Study** : Papers for Musicians. Fcap. 8vo, 2*s.*
CHATER (THOMAS). Scientific Voice, Artistic Singing, and Effective Speaking. A Treatise on the Organs of the Voice, their Natural Functions, Scientific Development, Proper Training, and Artistic Use. By THOMAS CHATER. With Diagrams. Wide fcap. 2*s.* 6*d.*
HUNT (H. G. BONAVIA). A Concise History of Music, from the Commencement of the Christian era to the present time. For the use of Students. By REV. H. G. BONAVIA HUNT, Mus. Doc. Dublin ; Warden of Trinity College, London ; and Lecturer on Musical History in the same College. 13*th edition, revised to date* (1895). Fcap. 8vo, 3*s.* 6*d.*

ART.

BARTER (S.) Manual Instruction—Woodwork. By S. BARTER Organizer and Instructor for the London School Board, and to the Joint Committee on Manual Training of the School Board for London, the City and Guilds of London Institute, and the Worshipful Company of Drapers. With over 300 Illustrations. Fcap. 4to, cloth. 7*s.* 6*d.*
BELL (SIR CHARLES). The Anatomy and Philosophy of Expression, as connected with the Fine Arts. By SIR CHARLES BELL, K.H. 7*th edition, revised.* 5*s.*
BRYAN'S Biographical and Critical Dictionary of Painters and Engravers. With a List of Ciphers, Monograms, and Marks. A new Edition, thoroughly Revised and Enlarged. By R. E. GRAVES and WALTER ARMSTRONG. 2 volumes. Imp. 8vo, buckram, 3*l.* 3*s.*
CHEVREUL on Colour. Containing the Principles of Harmony and Contrast of Colours, and their Application to the Arts. 3*rd edition,* with Introduction. Index and several Plates. 5*s.*—With an additional series of 16 Plates in Colours, 7*s.* 6*d.*
DELAMOTTE (P. H.). The Art of Sketching from Nature. By P. H. DELAMOTTE, Professor of Drawing at King's College, London. Illustrated by Twenty-four Woodcuts and Twenty Coloured Plates, arranged progressively, from Water-colour Drawings by PROUT, E. W. COOKE, R.A., GIRTIN, VARLEY, DE WINT, and the Author. *New edition.* Imp. 4to, 21*s.*
FLAXMAN'S CLASSICAL COMPOSITIONS, reprinted in a cheap form for the use of Art Students. Oblong paper covers, 2*s.* 6*d.* each.
> The Iliad of Homer. 39 Designs.
> The Odyssey of Homer. 34 Designs.
> The Tragedies of Æschylus. 36 Designs.
> The "Works and Days" and "Theogony" of Hesiod. 37 Designs.
> Select Compositions from Dante's Divine Drama. 37 Designs.

FLAXMAN'S Lectures on Sculpture, as delivered before the President and Members of the Royal Academy. With Portrait and 53 plates. 6s.

HEATON (MRS.). A Concise History of Painting. By the late MRS. CHARLES HEATON. *New edition.* Revised by COSMO MONKHOUSE. 5s.

LELAND (C. G.). Drawing and Designing. In a series of Lessons for School use and Self Instruction. By CHARLES G. LELAND, M.A., F.R.L.S. Paper cover, 1s. ; or in cloth, 1s. 6d.

— **Leather Work:** Stamped, Moulded, and Cut, Cuir-Bouillé, Sewn, etc. With numerous Illustrations. Fcap. 4to, 5s.

— **Manual of Wood Carving.** By CHARLES G. LELAND, M.A., F.R.L.S. Revised by J. J. HOLTZAPFFEL, A.M. INST.C.E. With numerous Illustrations. Fcap. 4to, 5s.

— **Metal Work** With numerous Illustrations. Fcap. 4to, 5s.

LEONARDO DA VINCI'S Treatise on Painting. Translated from the Italian by J. F. RIGAUD, R.A. With a Life of Leonardo and an Account of his Works, by J. W. BROWN. With numerous Plates. 5s.

MOODY (F. W.). Lectures and Lessons on Art. By the late F. W. MOODY, Instructor in Decorative Art at South Kensington Museum. With Diagrams to illustrate Composition and other matters. *A new and cheaper edition.* Demy 8vo, sewed, 4s. 6d.

WHITE (GLEESON). Practical Designing: A Handbook on the Preparation of Working Drawings, showing the Technical Methods employed in preparing them for the Manufacturer and the Limits imposed on the Design by the Mechanism of Reproduction and the Materials employed. Edited by GLEESON WHITE. Freely Illustrated. *2nd edition.* Crown 8vo, 6s. net.

Contents :—Bookbinding, by H. ORRINSMITH—Carpets, by ALEXANDER MILLAR—Drawing for Reproduction, by the Editor—Pottery, by W. P. RIX—Metal Work, by R. LL. RATHBONE—Stained Glass, by SELWYN IMAGE—Tiles, by OWEN CARTER—Woven Fabrics, Printed Fabrics, and Floorcloths, by ARTHUR SILVER—Wall Papers, by G. C. HAITÉ.

MENTAL, MORAL, AND SOCIAL SCIENCES.

PSYCHOLOGY AND ETHICS.

ANTONINUS (M. Aurelius). The Thoughts of. Translated literally, with Notes, Biographical Sketch, Introductory Essay on the Philosophy, and Index, by GEORGE LONG, M.A. *Revised edition.* Small post 8vo, 3s. 6d., or new edition on Handmade paper, buckram, 6s.

BACON'S Novum Organum and Advancement of Learning. Edited, with Notes, by J. DEVEY, M.A. Small post 8vo, 5s.

EPICTETUS. The Discourses of. With the Encheiridion and Fragments. Translated with Notes, a Life of Epictetus, a View of his Philosophy, and Index, by GEORGE LONG, M.A. Small post 8vo, 5s., or new edition on Handmade paper, 2 vols., buckram, 10s. 6d.

KANT'S Critique of Pure Reason. Translated by J. M. D. MEIKLEJOHN, Professor of Education at St. Andrew's University. Small post 8vo, 5s.

— **Prolegomena and Metaphysical Foundations of Science.** With Life. Translated by E. BELFORT BAX. Small post 8vo, 5s.

LOCKE'S Philosophical Works. Edited by J. A. ST. JOHN. 2 vols. Small post 8vo, 3s. 6d. each.

RYLAND (F.). The Student's Manual of Psychology and Ethics, designed chiefly for the London B.A. and B.Sc. By F. RYLAND, M.A., late Scholar of St. John's College, Cambridge. Cloth, red edges. *5th edition, revised and enlarged.* With lists of books for Students, and Examination Papers set at London University. Crown 8vo, 3s. 6d.

— Ethics : An Introductory Manual for the use of University Students. With an Appendix containing List of Books recommended, and Examination Questions. Crown 8vo, 3s. 6d.

SCHOPENHAUER on the Fourfold Root of the Principle of Sufficient Reason, and On the Will in Nature. Translated by MADAME HILLEBRAND. Small post 8vo, 5s.

— Essays. Selected and Translated. With a Biographical Introduction and Sketch of his Philosophy, by E. BELFORT BAX. Small post 8vo, 5s.

SMITH (Adam). Theory of Moral Sentiments. With Memoir of the Author by DUGALD STEWART. Small post 8vo, 3s. 6d.

SPINOZA'S Chief Works. Translated with Introduction, by R. H. M. ELWES. 2 vols. Small post 8vo, 5s. each.
> Vol. I.—Tractatus Theologico-Politicus—Political Treatise.
> II.—Improvement of the Understanding—Ethics—Letters.

HISTORY OF PHILOSOPHY.

BAX (E. B.). Handbook of the History of Philosophy. By E. BELFORT BAX. *2nd edition, revised.* Small post 8vo, 5s.

DRAPER (J. W.). A History of the Intellectual Development of Europe. By JOHN WILLIAM DRAPER, M.D., LL.D. With Index. 2 vols. Small post 8vo, 5s. each.

HEGEL'S Lectures on the Philosophy of History. Translated by J. SIBREE, M.A. Small post 8vo, 5s.

LAW AND POLITICAL ECONOMY.

KENT'S Commentary on International Law. Edited by J. T. ABDY, LL.D., Judge of County Courts and Law Professor at Gresham College, late Regius Professor of Laws in the University of Cambridge. *2nd edition, revised and brought down to a recent date.* Crown 8vo, 10s. 6d.

LAWRENCE (T. J.). Essays on some Disputed Questions in Modern International Law. By T. J. LAWRENCE, M.A., LL.M. *2nd edition, revised and enlarged.* Crown 8vo, 6s.

— Handbook of Public International Law. *2nd edition.* Fcap. 8vo, 3s.

MONTESQUIEU'S Spirit of Laws. A New Edition, revised and corrected, with D'Alembert's Analysis, Additional Notes, and a Memoir, by J. V. PRITCHARD, A.M. 2 vols. Small post 8vo, 3s. 6d. each.

RICARDO on the Principles of Political Economy and Taxation. Edited by E. C. K. GONNER, M.A., Lecturer in University College, Liverpool. Small post 8vo, 5s.

SMITH (Adam). The Wealth of Nations. An Inquiry into the Nature and Causes of. Reprinted from the Sixth Edition, with an Introduction by ERNEST BELFORT BAX. 2 vols. Small post 8vo, 3s. 6d. each.

HISTORY.

BOWES (A.). A Practical Synopsis of English History; or, A General Summary of Dates and Events. By ARTHUR BOWES. 10*th* *edition.* Revised and brought down to the present time. Demy 8vo, 1*s.*

COXE (W.). History of the House of Austria, 1218-1792. By ARCHDN. COXE, M.A., F.R.S. Together with a Continuation from the Accession of Francis I. to the Revolution of 1848. 4 vols. Small post 8vo. 3*s. 6d.* each.

DENTON (W.). England in the Fifteenth Century. By the late REV. W. DENTON, M.A., Worcester College, Oxford. Demy 8vo, 12*s.*

DYER (Dr. T. H.). History of Modern Europe, from the Taking of Constantinople to the Establishment of the German Empire, A.D. 1453-1871. By DR. T. H. DYER. *A new edition.* In 5 vols. £2 12*s. 6d.*

GIBBON'S Decline and Fall of the Roman Empire. Complete and Unabridged, with Variorum Notes. Edited by an English Churchman. With 2 Maps. 7 vols. Small post 8vo, 3*s. 6d.* each.

GREGOROVIUS' History of the City of Rome in the Middle Ages. Translated by ANNIE HAMILTON. Vols. I. and II. Crown 8vo, 6*s.* each net.

GUIZOT'S History of the English Revolution of 1640. Translated by WILLIAM HAZLITT. Small post 8vo, 3*s. 6d.*

— History of Civilization, from the Fall of the Roman Empire to the French Revolution. Translated by WILLIAM HAZLITT. 3 vols. Small post 8vo, 3*s. 6d.* each.

HENDERSON (E. F.). Select Historical Documents of the Middle Ages. Including the most famous Charters relating to England, the Empire, the Church, etc., from the sixth to the fourteenth centuries. Translated and edited, with Introductions, by ERNEST F. HENDERSON, A.B., A.M., PH.D. Small post 8vo, 5*s.*

— A History of Germany in the Middle Ages. Post 8vo, 7*s. 6d.* net.

HOOPER (George). The Campaign of Sedan : The Downfall of the Second Empire, August-September, 1870. By GEORGE HOOPER. With General Map and Six Plans of Battle. Demy 8vo, 14*s.*

— Waterloo : The Downfall of the First Napoleon : a History of the Campaign of 1815. With Maps and Plans. Small post 8vo, 3*s. 6d.*

LAMARTINE'S History of the Girondists. Translated by H. T. RYDE. 3 vols. Small post 8vo, 3*s. 6d.* each.

— History of the Restoration of Monarchy in France (a Sequel to his History of the Girondists). 4 vols. Small post 8vo, 3*s. 6d.* each.

— History of the French Revolution of 1848. Small post 8vo, 3*s. 6d.*

LAPPENBERG'S History of England under the Anglo-Saxon Kings. Translated by the late B. THORPE, F.S.A. *New edition,* revised by E. C. OTTÉ. 2 vols. Small post 8vo, 3*s. 6d.* each.

LONG (G.). The Decline of the Roman Republic : From the Destruction of Carthage to the Death of Cæsar. By the late GEORGE LONG, M.A. Demy 8vo. In 5 vols. 5*s.* each.

MACHIAVELLI'S History of Florence, and of the Affairs of Italy from the Earliest Times to the Death of Lorenzo the Magnificent : together with the Prince, Savonarola, various Historical Tracts, and a Memoir of Machiavelli. Small post 8vo, 3*s. 6d.*

MARTINEAU (H.). History of England from 1800-15. By HARRIET MARTINEAU. Small post 8vo, 3*s. 6d.*

MARTINEAU (H.). History of the Thirty Years' Peace, 1815-46. 4 vols. Small post 8vo, 3s. 6d. each.

MAURICE (C. E.). The Revolutionary Movement of 1848-9 in Italy, Austria, Hungary, and Germany. With some Examination of the previous Thirty-three Years. By C. EDMUND MAURICE. With an engraved Frontispiece and other Illustrations. Demy 8vo, 16s.

MENZEL'S History of Germany, from the Earliest Period to 1842. 3 vols. Small post 8vo, 3s. 6d. each.

MICHELET'S History of the French Revolution from its earliest indications to the flight of the King in 1791. Small post 8vo, 3s. 6d.

MIGNET'S History of the French Revolution, from 1789 to 1814. Small post 8vo, 3s. 6d.

PARNELL (A.). The War of the Succession in Spain during the Reign of Queen Anne, 1702-1711. Based on Original Manuscripts and Contemporary Records. By COL. THE HON. ARTHUR PARNELL, R.E. Demy 8vo, 14s. With Map, etc.

RANKE (L.). History of the Latin and Teutonic Nations, 1494-1514. Translated by P. A. ASHWORTH. Small post 8vo, 3s. 6d.

— History of the Popes, their Church and State, and especially of their conflicts with Protestantism in the 16th and 17th centuries. Translated by E. FOSTER. 3 vols. Small post 8vo, 3s. 6d. each.

— History of Servia and the Servian Revolution. Translated by MRS. KERR. Small post 8vo, 3s. 6d.

SIX OLD ENGLISH CHRONICLES: viz., Asser's Life of Alfred and the Chronicles of Ethelwerd, Gildas, Nennius, Geoffrey of Monmouth, and Richard of Cirencester. Edited, with Notes and Index, by J. A. GILES, D.C.L. Small post 8vo, 5s.

STRICKLAND (Agnes). The Lives of the Queens of England; from the Norman Conquest to the Reign of Queen Anne. By AGNES STRICKLAND. 6 vols. 5s. each.

— The Lives of the Queens of England. Abridged edition for the use of Schools and Families, Post 8vo, 6s. 6d.

THIERRY'S History of the Conquest of England by the Normans; its Causes, and its Consequences in England, Scotland, Ireland, and the Continent. Translated from the 7th Paris edition by WILLIAM HAZLITT. 2 vols. Small post 8vo, 3s. 6d. each.

WRIGHT (H. F.). The Intermediate History of England, with Notes, Supplements, Glossary, and a Mnemonic System. For Army and Civil Service Candidates. By H. F. WRIGHT, M.A., LL.M. Crown 8vo, 6s.

For other Works of value to Students of History, see Catalogue of Bohn's Libraries, sent post-free on application.

DIVINITY, ETC.

ALFORD (DEAN). Greek Testament. With a Critically revised Text, a digest of Various Readings, Marginal References to verbal and idiomatic usage, Prolegomena, and a Critical and Exegetical Commentary. For the use of theological students and ministers. By the late HENRY ALFORD, D.D., Dean of Canterbury. 4 vols. 8vo. £5 2s. Sold separately.

— The New Testament for English Readers. Containing the Authorized Version, with additional Corrections of Readings and Renderings, Marginal References, and a Critical and Explanatory Commentary. In 2 vols. £2 14s. 6d. Also sold in 4 parts separately.

AUGUSTINE de Civitate Dei. Books XI. and XII. By the REV. HENRY D. GEE, B.D., F.S.A. I. Text only. 2*s*. II. Introduction and Translation. 3*s*.

BARRETT (A. C.). Companion to the Greek Testament. By the late A. C. BARRETT, M.A., Caius College, Cambridge. 5*th edition*. Fcap. 8vo, 5*s*.

BARRY (BP.). Notes on the Catechism. For the use of Schools. By the RT. REV. BISHOP BARRY, D.D. 10*th edition*. Fcap. 2*s*.

BLEEK. Introduction to the Old Testament. By FRIEDRICH BLEEK. Edited by JOHANN BLEEK and ADOLF KAMPHAUSEN. Translated from the second edition of the German by G. H. VENABLES, under the supervision of the REV. E. VENABLES, Residentiary Canon of Lincoln. 2*nd edition*, with Corrections. With Index. 2 vols. small post 8vo, 5*s*. each.

BUTLER (BP.). Analogy of Religion. With Analytical Introduction and copious Index, by the late RT. REV. DR. STEERE. Fcap. 3*s*. 6*d*.

EUSEBIUS. Ecclesiastical History of Eusebius Pamphilus, Bishop of Cæsarea. Translated from the Greek by REV. C. F. CRUSE, M.A. With Notes, a Life of Eusebius, and Chronological Table. Sm. post 8vo, 5*s*.

GREGORY (DR.). Letters on the Evidences, Doctrines, and Duties of the Christian Religion. By DR. OLINTHUS GREGORY, F.R.A.S. Small post 8vo, 3*s*. 6*d*.

HUMPHRY (W. G.). Book of Common Prayer. An Historical and Explanatory Treatise on the. By W. G. HUMPHRY, B.D., late Fellow of Trinity College, Cambridge, Prebendary of St. Paul's, and Vicar of St. Martin's-in-the-Fields, Westminster. 6*th edition*. Fcap. 8vo, 2*s*. 6*d*. Cheap Edition, for Sunday School Teachers. 1*s*.

JOSEPHUS (FLAVIUS). The Works of. WHISTON'S Translation. Revised by REV. A. R. SHILLETO, M.A. With Topographical and Geographical Notes by COLONEL SIR C. W. WILSON, K.C.B. 5 vols. 3*s*. 6*d*. each.

LUMBY (DR.). The History of the Creeds. I. Ante-Nicene. II. Nicene and Constantinopolitan. III. The Apostolic Creed. IV. The Quicunque, commonly called the Creed of St. Athanasius. By J. RAWSON LUMBY, D.D., Norrisian Professor of Divinity, Fellow of St. Catherine's College, and late Fellow of Magdalene College, Cambridge. 3*rd edition, revised*. Crown 8vo, 7*s*. 6*d*.

— **Compendium of English Church History, from 1688-1830.** With a Preface by J. RAWSON LUMBY, D.D. Crown 8vo, 6*s*.

MACMICHAEL (J. F.). The New Testament in Greek. With English Notes and Preface, Synopsis, and Chronological Tables. By the late REV. J. F. MACMICHAEL. Fcap. 8vo (730 pp.), 4*s*. 6*d*. Also the **Four Gospels**, and the Acts of the Apostles, separately. In paper wrappers, 6*d*. each.

MILLER (E). Guide to the Textual Criticism of the New Testament. By REV. E MILLER, M.A., Oxon, Rector of Bucknell, Bicester. Crown 8vo, 4*s*.

NEANDER (DR. A). History of the Christian Religion and Church. Translated by J. TORREY. 10 vols. small post 8vo, 3*s*. 6*d*. each.

— **Life of Jesus Christ.** Translated by J. MCCLINTOCK and C. BLUMENTHAL. Small post 8vo, 3*s*. 6*d*.

— **History of the Planting and Training of the Christian Church by the Apostles.** Translated by J. E. RYLAND. 2 vols. 3*s*. 6*d*. each.

— **Lectures on the History of Christian Dogmas.** Edited by DR. JACOBI. Translated by J. E. RYLAND. 2 vols. small post 8vo, 3*s*. 6*d*. each.

NEANDER (DR. A.). Memorials of Christian Life in the Early and Middle Ages. Translated by J. E. RYLAND. Small post 8vo, 3s. 6d.

PEARSON (BP.). On the Creed. Carefully printed from an Early Edition. Edited by E. WALFORD, M.A. Post 8vo, 5s.

PEROWNE (BP.). The Book of Psalms. A New Translation, with Introductions and Notes, Critical and Explanatory. By the RIGHT REV. J. J. STEWART PEROWNE, D.D., Bishop of Worcester. 8vo. Vol. I. *8th edition, revised.* 18s. Vol. II. *7th edition, revised.* 16s.

— The Book of Psalms. Abridged Edition for Schools. Crown 8vo. *7th edition.* 10s. 6d.

SADLER (M. F.). The Church Teacher's Manual of Christian Instruction. Being the Church Catechism, Expanded and Explained in Question and Answer. For the use of the Clergyman, Parent, and Teacher. By the REV. M. F. SADLER, Prebendary of Wells, and Rector of Honiton. 43rd *thousand.* 2s. 6d.

.*. A Complete List of Prebendary Sadler's Works will be sent on application.

SCRIVENER (DR.). A Plain Introduction to the Criticism of the New Testament. With Forty-four Facsimiles from Ancient Manuscripts. For the use of Biblical Students. By the late F. H. SCRIVENER, M.A., D.C.L., LL.D., Prebendary of Exeter. *4th edition,* thoroughly revised, by the REV. E. MILLER, formerly Fellow and Tutor of New College, Oxford. 2 vols. demy 8vo, 32s.

— Novum Testamentum Græce, Textus Stephanici, 1550. Accedunt variae lectiones editionum Bezae, Elzeviri, Lachmanni, Tischendorfii, Tregellesii, curante F. H. A. SCRIVENER, A.M., D.C.L., LL.D. *Revised edition.* 4s. 6d.

— Novum Testamentum Græce [Editio Major] textus Stephanici, A.D. 1556. Cum variis lectionibus editionum Bezae, Elzeviri, Lachmanni, Tischendorfii, Tregellesii, Westcott-Hortii, versionis Anglicanæ emendatorum curante F. H. A. SCRIVENER, A.M., D.C.L., LL.D., accedunt parallela s. scripturæ loca. Small post 8vo. *2nd edition.* 7s. 6d.

An Edition on writing-paper, with margin for notes. 4to, half bound, 12s.

WHEATLEY. A Rational Illustration of the Book of Common Prayer. Being the Substance of everything Liturgical in Bishop Sparrow, Mr. L'Estrange, Dr. Comber, Dr. Nicholls, and all former Ritualist Commentators upon the same subject. Small post 8vo, 3s. 6d.

WHITAKER (C.). Rufinus and His Times. With the Text of his Commentary on the Apostles' Creed and a Translation. To which is added a Condensed History of the Creeds and Councils. By the REV. CHARLES WHITAKER, B.A., Vicar of Natland, Kendal. Demy 8vo, 5s.

Or in separate Parts.—1. Latin Text, with Various Readings, 2s. 6d. 2. Summary of the History of the Creeds, 1s. 6d. 3. Charts of the Heresies of the Times preceding Rufinus, and the First Four General Councils, 6d. each.

-— St. Augustine: De Fide et Symbolo—Sermo ad Catechumenos. St. Leo ad Flavianum Epistola—Latin Text, with Literal Translation, Notes, and History of Creeds and Councils. 5s. Also separately, Literal Translation. 2s.

— Student's Help to the Prayer-Book. 3s.

SUMMARY OF SERIES.

BIBLIOTHECA CLASSICA.

AESCHYLUS. By DR. PALEY. 8s.
CICERO. By G. LONG. Vols. I. and II. 8s. each.
DEMOSTHENES. By R. WHISTON. 2 Vols. 8s. each.
EURIPIDES. By DR. PALEY. Vols. II. and III. 8s. each.
HERODOTUS. By DR. BLAKESLEY. 2 Vols. 12s.
HESIOD. By DR. PALEY. 5s.
HOMER. By DR. PALEY. 2 Vols. 14s.
HORACE. By A. G. MACLEANE. 8s.
PLATO. Phaedrus. By DR. THOMPSON. 5s.
SOPHOCLES. Vol. I. By F. H. BLAYDES. 5s.
— Vol. II. By DR. PALEY. 6s.
VIRGIL. By CONINGTON AND NETTLESHIP. 3 Vols. 10s. 6d. each.

PUBLIC SCHOOL SERIES.

ARISTOPHANES. Peace. By DR. PALEY. 4s. 6a.
— Acharnians. By DR. PALEY. 4s. 6d.
— Frogs. By DR. PALEY. 4s. 6d.
CICERO. Letters to Atticus. Book I. By A. PRETOR. 4s. 6d.
DEMOSTHENES. De Falsa Legatione. By R. SHILLETO. 6s.
— Adv. Leptinem. By B. W. BEATSON. 3s. 6d.
LIVY. Books XXI. and XXII. By L. D. DOWDALL. 3s. 6d. each.
PLATO. Apology of Socrates and Crito. By DR. W. WAGNER. 3s. 6d. and
  2s. 6d.
— Phaedo. By DR. W. WAGNER. 5s. 6d.
— Protagoras. By W. WAYTE. 4s. 6d.
— Gorgias. By DR. THOMPSON. 6s.
— Euthyphro. By G. H. WELLS. 3s.
— Euthydemus. By G. H. WELLS. 4s.
— Republic. By G. H. WELLS. 5s.
PLAUTUS. Aulularia. By DR. W. WAGNER. 4s. 6d.
— Trinummus. By DR. W. WAGNER. 4s. 6d.
— Menaechmei. By DR. W. WAGNER. 4s. 6d.
— Mostellaria. By E. A. SONNENSCHEIN. 5s.

PUBLIC SCHOOL SERIES—*continued.*

SOPHOCLES. Trachiniae. By A. PRETOR. 4s. 6d.
— Oedipus Tyrannus. By B. H. KENNEDY. 5s.
TERENCE. By DR. W. WAGNER. 7s. 6d.
THEOCRITUS. By DR. PALEY. 4s. 6d.
THUCYDIDES. Book VI. By T. W. DOUGAN. 3s. 6d.

CAMBRIDGE GREEK AND LATIN TEXTS.

AESCHYLUS. By DR. PALEY. 2s.
CAESAR. By G. LONG. 1s. 6d.
CICERO. De Senectute, de Amicitia, et Epistolae Selectae. By G. LONG. 1s. 6d.
— Orationes in Verrem. By G. LONG. 2s. 6d.
EURIPIDES. By DR. PALEY. 3 Vols. 2s. each.
HERODOTUS. By DR. BLAKESLEY. 2 Vols. 2s. 6d. each.
HOMER'S Iliad. By DR. PALEY. 1s. 6d.
HORACE. By A. J. MACLEANE. 1s. 6d.
JUVENAL AND PERSIUS. By A. J. MACLEANE. 1s. 6d.
LUCRETIUS. By H. A. J. MUNRO. 2s.
SOPHOCLES. By DR. PALEY. 2s. 6d.
TERENCE. By DR. W. WAGNER. 2s.
THUCYDIDES. By DR. DONALDSON. 2 Vols. 2s. each.
VIRGIL. By PROF. CONINGTON. 2s.
XENOPHON. By J. F. MACMICHAEL. 1s. 6d.
NOVUM TESTAMENTUM GRAECE. By DR. SCRIVENER. 4s. 6d.

CAMBRIDGE TEXTS WITH NOTES.

AESCHYLUS. By DR. PALEY. 6 Vols. 1s. 6d. each.
EURIPIDES. By DR. PALEY. 13 Vols. (Ion, 2s.) 1s. 6d. each.
HOMER'S Iliad. By DR. PALEY. 1s.
SOPHOCLES. By DR. PALEY. 5 Vols. 1s. 6d. each.
XENOPHON. Hellenica. By REV. L. D. DOWDALL. Books I. and II. 2s. each.
— Anabasis. By J. F. MACMICHAEL. 6 Vols. 1s. 6d. each.
CICERO. De Senectute, de Amicitia, et Epistolae Selectae. By G. LONG. 3 Vols. 1s. 6d. each.
OVID. Selections. By A. J. MACLEANE. 1s. 6d.
— Fasti. By DR. PALEY. 3 Vols. 2s. each.
TERENCE. By DR. W. WAGNER. 4 Vols. 1s. 6d. each.
VIRGIL. By PROF. CONINGTON. 12 Vols. 1s. 6d. each.

GRAMMAR SCHOOL CLASSICS.

CAESAR, De Bello Gallico. By G. LONG. 4s., or in 3 parts, 1s. 6d. each.
CATULLUS, TIBULLUS, and PROPERTIUS. By A. H. WRATISLAW, and F. N. SUTTON. 2s. 6d.
CORNELIUS NEPOS. By J. F. MACMICHAEL. 2s.
CICERO. De Senectute, De Amicitia, and Select Epistles. B·G. LONG. 3s.
HOMER. Iliad. By DR. PALEY. Books I.-XII. 4s. 6d., or in 2 Parts, 2s. 6d. each.
HORACE. By A. J. MACLEANE. 3s. 6d., or in 2 Parts, 2s. each.
JUVENAL. By HERMAN PRIOR. 3s. 6d.
MARTIAL. By DR. PALEY and W. H. STONE. 4s. 6d.
OVID. Fasti. By DR. PALEY. 3s. 6d., or in 3 Parts, 1s. 6d. each.
SALLUST. Catilina and Jugurtha. By G. LONG and J. G. FRAZER. 3s. 6d., or in 2 Parts, 2s. each.
TACITUS. Germania and Agricola. By P. FROST. 2s. 6d.
VIRGIL. CONINGTON's edition abridged. 2 Vols. 4s. 6d. each, or in 9 Parts, 1s. 6d. each.
— Bucolics and Georgics. CONINGTON's edition abridged. 3s.
XENOPHON. By J. F. MACMICHAEL. 3s. 6d., or in 4 Parts, 1s. 6d. each.
— Cyropaedia. By G. M. GORHAM. 3s. 6d., or in 2 Parts, 1s. 6d. each.
— Memorabilia. By PERCIVAL FROST. 3s.

PRIMARY CLASSICS.

EASY SELECTIONS FROM CAESAR. By A. M. M. STEDMAN. 1s.
EASY SELECTIONS FROM LIVY. By A. M. M. STEDMAN. 1s. 6d.
EASY SELECTIONS FROM HERODOTUS. By A. G. LIDDELL. 1s. 6d.

BELL'S CLASSICAL TRANSLATIONS.

AESCHYLUS. By WALTER HEADLAM. 6 Vols.   [*In the press.*
ARISTOPHANES. Acharnians. By W. H. COVINGTON. 1s.
CAESAR'S Gallic War. By W. A. MCDEVITTE. 2 Vols. 1s. each.
CICERO Friendship and Old Age. By G. H. WELLS. 1s.
DEMOSTHENES. On the Crown. By C. RANN KENNEDY. 1s.
EURIPIDES. 14 Vols. By E. P. COLERIDGE. 1s. each.
LIVY. Books I.-IV. By J. H. FREESE. 1s. each.
— Book V. By E. S. WEYMOUTH. 1s.
— Book IX. By F. STORR. 1s.
LUCAN : The Pharsalia. Book I. By F. CONWAY. 1s.
OVID. Fasti. 3 Vols. By H. T. RILEY. 1s. each.
— Tristia. By H. T. RILEY. 1s.
SOPHOCLES. 7 Vols. By E. P. COLERIDGE. 1s. each.
VIRGIL. 6 Vols. By A. HAMILTON BRYCE. 1s. each.
XENOPHON. Anabasis. 3 Vols. By J. S. WATSON. 1s. each.
— Hellenics. Books I. and II. BY H. DALE.

CAMBRIDGE MATHEMATICAL SERIES.

ARITHMETIC. By C. PENDLEBURY. 4s. 6d., or in 2 Parts, 2s. 6d. each.
Key to Part II. 7s. 6d. net.
EXAMPLES IN ARITHMETIC. By C. PENDLEBURY. 3s.. or in 2 Parts,
1s. 6d. and 2s.
ARITHMETIC FOR INDIAN SCHOOLS. By PENDLEBURY and TAIT. 3s.
ELEMENTARY ALGEBRA. By J. T. HATHORNTHWAITE. 2s.
CHOICE AND CHANCE. By W. A. WHITWORTH. 6s.
EUCLID. By H. DEIGHTON. 4s. 6d., or Books I.-IV., 3s. ; Books V.-XI., 2s. 6d. ;
or Book I., 1s. ; Books I. and II., 1s. 6d. ; Books I.-III., 2s. 6d. ; Books III.
and IV., 1s. 6d. KEY. 5s. net.
EXERCISES ON EUCLID, &c. By J. MCDOWELL. 6s.
ELEMENTARY TRIGONOMETRY. By DYER and WHITCOMBE. 4s. 6d.
PLANE TRIGONOMETRY. By T. G. VYVYAN. 3s. 6d.
ANALYTICAL GEOMETRY FOR BEGINNERS Part I. By T. G.
VYVYAN. 2s. 6d.
ELEMENTARY GEOMETRY OF CONICS. By DR. TAYLOR. 4s. 6d.
GEOMETRICAL CONIC SECTIONS. By H. G. WILLIS. 5s.
SOLID GEOMETRY. By W. S. ALDIS. 6s.
GEOMETRICAL OPTICS. By W. S. ALDIS. 4s.
ROULETTES AND GLISSETTES. By DR. W. H. BESANT. 5s.
ELEMENTARY HYDROSTATICS. By DR. W. H. BESANT. 4s. 6d.
Solutions. 5s.
HYDROMECHANICS. Part I. Hydrostatics. By DR. W. H. BESANT. 5s.
DYNAMICS. By DR. W. H. BESANT. 10s. 6d.
RIGID DYNAMICS. By W. S. ALDIS. 4s.
ELEMENTARY DYNAMICS. By DR. W. GARNETT. 6s.
ELEMENTARY TREATISE ON HEAT. By DR. W. GARNETT. 4s. 6d.
ELEMENTS OF APPLIED MATHEMATICS. By C. M. JESSOP. 6s.
PROBLEMS IN ELEMENTARY MECHANICS. By W. WALTON. 6s.
EXAMPLES IN ELEMENTARY PHYSICS. By W. GALLATLY. 4s.
MATHEMATICAL EXAMPLES. By DYER and PROWDE SMITH. 6s.

CAMBRIDGE SCHOOL AND COLLEGE TEXT BOOKS.

ARITHMETIC. By C. ELSEE. 3s. 6d.
By A. WRIGLEY. 3s. 6d.
EXAMPLES IN ARITHMETIC. By WATSON and GOUDIE. 2s. 6d.
ALGEBRA By C. ELSEE. 4s.
EXAMPLES IN ALGEBRA. By MACMICHAEL and PROWDE SMITH. 3s. 6d.
and 4s. 6d.
PLANE ASTRONOMY. By P. T. MAIN. 4s.
GEOMETRICAL CONIC SECTIONS. By DR. W. H. BESANT. 4s. 6d.
STATICS. By BISHOP GOODWIN. 3s.
NEWTON'S Principia. By EVANS and MAIN. 4s.
ANALYTICAL GEOMETRY. By T. G. VYVYAN. 4s. 6d.
COMPANION TO THE GREEK TESTAMENT. By A. C. BARRETT. 5s.

CAMBRIDGE SCHOOL TEXTS—*continued.*

TREATISE ON THE BOOK OF COMMON PRAYER. By W. G. HUMPHRY. 2s. 6d.
TEXT BOOK OF MUSIC. By H. C. BANISTER. 5s.
CONCISE HISTORY OF MUSIC. By DR. H. G. BONAVIA HUNT. 3s. 6d

FOREIGN CLASSICS.

FÉNELON'S Télémaque. By C. J. DELILLE. 2s. 6d.
LA FONTAINE'S Select Fables. By F. E. A. GASC. 1s. 6d.
LAMARTINE'S Le Tailleur de Pierres de Saint-Point. By J. BOÏELLE. 1s. 6d.
SAINTINE'S Picciola. By DR. DUBEC. 1s. 6d.
VOLTAIRE'S Charles XII. By L. DIREY. 1s. 6d.
GERMAN BALLADS. By C. L. BIELEFELD. 1s. 6d.
GOETHE'S Hermann und Dorothea. By E. BELL and E. WÖLFEL. 1s. 6d.
SCHILLER'S Wallenstein. By DR. BUCHHEIM. 5s., or in 2 Parts, 2s. 6d. each.
— Maid of Orleans. By DR. W. WAGNER. 1s. 6d.
— Maria Stuart. By V. KASTNER. 1s. 6d.

MODERN FRENCH AUTHORS.

BALZAC'S Ursule Mirouët. By J. BOÏELLE. 3s.
CLARÉTIE'S Pierrille. By J. BOÏELLE. 2s. 6d.
DAUDET'S La Belle Nivernaise. By J. BOÏELLE 2s.
GREVILLE'S Le Moulin Frappier. By J. BOÏELLE. 3s.
HUGO'S Bug Jargal. By J. BOÏELLE. 3s.

MODERN GERMAN AUTHORS.

HEY'S Fabeln für Kinder. By PROF. LANGE. 1s. 6d.
— — with Phonetic Transcription of Text, &c. 2s.
FREYTAG'S Soll und Haben. By W. H. CRUMP. 2s. 6d.
BENEDIX'S Doktor Wespe. By PROF. LANGE. 2s. 6d.
HOFFMANN'S Meister Martin. By PROF. LANGE. 1s. 6d.
HEYSE'S Hans Lange. By A. A. MACDONELL. 2s.
AUERBACH'S Auf Wache, and Roquette's Der Gefrorene Kuss. By A. A. MACDONELL. 2s.
MOSER'S Der Bibliothekar. By PROF. LANGE. 2s.
EBERS' Eine Frage. By F. STORR. 2s.
FREYTAG'S Die Journalisten. By PROF. LANGE. 2s. 6d.
GUTZKOW'S Zopf und Schwert. By PROF. LANGE. 2s. 6d.
GERMAN EPIC TALES. By DR. KARL NEUHAUS. 2s. 6d.
SCHEFFEL'S Ekkehard. By DR. H. HAGER. 3s.

The following Series are given in full in the body of the Catalogue.

GOMBERT'S French Drama. *See page* 31.
BELL'S Modern Translations. *See page* 34.
BELL'S English Classics. *See pp.* 24, 25.
HANDBOOKS OF ENGLISH LITERATURE. *See page* 26.
TECHNOLOGICAL HANDBOOKS *See page* 37.
BELL'S Agricultural Series. *See page* 36.
BELL'S Reading Books and Geographical Readers. *See pp.* 25, 26.